"And what he greatly thought, he nobly dared."

—Homer

View the author's website at www.arsenex.com

Visit the author's Facebook page at www.facebook.com/stephenarseneault10

Follow on Twitter @SteveArseneault

Ask a question or leave a comment at comments@arsenex.com

Cover Art by Kaare Berg at:

bergone.deviantart.com

bitdivision.no

Cover Design by Elizabeth Mackey at:

www.elizabethmackey.com

Novels written by Stephen Arseneault

SODIUM Series (six novels)

A six-book series that takes Man from his first encounter with aliens all the way to a fight for our all-out survival. Do we have what it takes to rule the galaxy?

AMP Series (eight novels)

Cast a thousand years into the future beyond SODIUM. This eight-book series chronicles the struggles of Don Grange, a simple package deliveryman, who is thrust into an unimaginable role in the fight against our enemies. Can we win peace and freedom after a thousand years of war?

OMEGA Series (eight novels)

Cast two thousand years into the future beyond AMP. The Alliance is crumbling. When corruption and politics threaten to throw the allied galaxies into chaos, Knog Beutcher gets caught in the middle. Follow along as our hero is thrust into roles that he never expected nor sought. Espionage, intrigue, political assassinations, rebellions and full-on revolutions, they are all coming to Knog Beutcher's world!

HADRON Series (eight novels)

HADRON is a modern day story unrelated to the SODIUM-AMP-OMEGA trilogy series. After scientists using the Large Hadron Collider discover dark matter, the world is plunged into chaos. Massive waves of electromagnetic interference take out all grid power and forms of communication the world over. Cities go dark, food and water supplies are quickly used up, and marauders rule the highways. Months after the mayhem begins, and after mass starvation has taken its toll, a benevolent alien species arrives from the stars. Only, are they really so benevolent? Find out in HADRON as Man faces his first real challenge to his dominance of Earth!

ARMS Series (eight novels)

ARMS is cast in one possible future, where Earth was nearing an apocalyptic event. Two competing colony ships were built, taking five million inhabitants each through a wormhole to a pair of newly discovered planets. The planets were settled and not long after the colonies looked to the surrounding star systems for ownership and expansion, which led to a centuries-long war between them. A truce was declared after the aggressor side began to lose ground.

Tawnish Freely and Harris Gruberg are genetically engineered Biomarines. Their lives have been dedicated to fighting the war. With a truce declared, they find themselves struggling to find work among a population that fears them. Work is found only by delving into the delivery of illegal arms to the outer colonies. Things go awry when they discover their illicit dealings may just be the catalyst that brings back the Great War. They are determined to prevent that from happening.

FREEDOM Series (eight novels)

After a period of domination over the lesser alien species of the galaxy, humanity finds itself enslaved for nearly five hundred generations. A highly addictive drug called Shackle has made Humans little more than drone workers. They are abused, sold, traded, and hunted, valued only in credits. But a mysterious virus is sweeping through the Human population, altering gut bacteria, making them immune to the drug that subjugates them. Humans are becoming aware of their condition. They will fight for their freedom.

Find them all at www.arsenex.com

ARMS

(Vol. 3)

Jebwa Atrocity

Chapter 1

Several days were spent kicking around ideas about Eden, but no solutions were put forth that showed promise. After another long session with Alex, Sharvie returned to the group, resting on the grass in front of the bunker.

"You all have new accounts with your prior amounts in them. I have the account codes we can enter into your stores whenever you're ready. As a backup, we're still sitting on over four hundred million credits. And my friends say the accounts and other information we collected might lead to what they believe are other well-funded Earther operations. If they determine that's true, that four hundred million might grow."

Trish said, "Fat good it does us out here. Wealthy beyond our wildest dreams and nowhere to spend it."

"That may not be entirely true," Sharvie replied. "Alex was reviewing what we've done to date. I entered what I knew into his databanks. Anyway, he thinks we should set up trade with Jebwa.

"We can trade them credits for food. The pacifists can spend those credits back on Domicile for whatever they need. And our food situation is then taken care of. Alex projects Jebwa may be producing almost double the food they need within only a few months."

Gandy added, "Maybe we could get them to buy fuel to resell to us as well. We could certainly make it worth their while."

Harris nodded. "Would solve two of our biggest problems here. Nice work, Sharvie. I say we should make a jump to Jebwa. And, you know, we might even be able to get them to purchase a shuttle to resell to us. Would save us from getting involved in any pirating mess with New Earth."

Gandy frowned. "I was looking forward to being a pirate."

Harris stood. "Sorry to burst your adventure bubble, but if we can get what we need through Jebwa, I'd rather not risk putting us in Earther territory."

"You going somewhere?" Tawn asked.

Harris pointed at the ship. "Jebwa. Might as well get out there and see what we can trade for. Lying around here might be relaxing but it doesn't accomplish anything. We've been here for days. It's time we finally started getting stuff done. Our friends are still running out of food on Eden."

The group piled into the *Bangor*'s cabin. Two hours later they were settling on the tarmac at the Haven spaceport. A Jebwa citizen came out to meet them with a transport.

"Welcome to Haven. Can I ask what business you might have with us today?"

Harris said, "You can take us to your main meeting hall. We're interested in discussing trade with your council."

The man nodded. "Very well. Have you been here before?"

Harris smiled. "We built this place. Hope things have been working out for you."

"Oh, they couldn't be better. Everyone is busy, busy, busy. This setting is idyllic compared to Eden. Our lives have changed so much for the better. We can enjoy the outdoors, nature... our whole environment is now centered around living and not survival. Survival here comes easy."

"Glad to hear you're doing well."

"Better than well. We have a waiting list of applicants who wish to move here. That hasn't happened since our colony at Dove was first made available. It's an exciting time for us all. Life couldn't get any better."

"Sounds like you've found your utopia," said Tawn. "Driving this transport your job?"

"I volunteer for this on Tildays."

"Tildays?"

"On Jebwa, the planet rotation spans nineteen standard hours, and we traverse once around the sun every two hundred days, so we created our own timebase with new names for our months and weekdays. For instance, one hundred crons makes up a bellet. There are one hundred bellets in a meg, and one hundred megs in a talla. A talla is a Jebwa day. Tilday is the fifth day in the Jebwa week, of which there are ten days."

Harris chuckled. "Sounds like a lot of work to memorize. Why not stick with the standards that everyone else uses?"

"Because this is our colony and our planet. We want our customs and traditions to be our own. The new system makes sense for this planet. What the rest of the galaxy does with regards to time is their business. Here, it's ours."

The transport pulled to a stop in front of a domed building. After walking through the doors and down a hall they entered a great chamber. Red velvet drapes adorned the walls, while the ceiling of the dome had been covered in murals and frescoes. Large beanbag style seating circled a center stage.

Harris nodded. "I like what you've done to the place."

The man replied, "All decisions are made here by the council. If you have a request, take it to the center and let those in attendance know what you desire."

Harris looked at Tawn. "You want to do this or should I?"

Tawn chuckled. "Neither of us are salesmen, but I think our ideas might just sell themselves here."

Tawn walked to the center stage, climbing the three steps to the main platform. Twenty townies were lying about in their robes and sandals.

"Ladies and gentleman of Haven, we've come here today looking for trade. We would like to purchase food and possibly other items from you. Our current needs are meager as we only have five mouths to feed, but we are willing to pay a premium."

A question came from a townie: "What are you looking to trade?"

"Standard credits. I know you might prefer to barter instead, but I also know you have to purchase goods from Domicile from time to time. We offer credits, and as I said, we are more than willing to pay a premium to ensure we have sustenance for our small colony."

Another voice said, "Why not join this one? As you can see, we are well fed, clothed, housed, and worked."

Tawn replied, "Just as you enjoy your colony, we enjoy ours."

The awkward negotiations took two additional hours before the group was directed into another building to meet with a trade minister. After repeating much of her pitch, a deal was finalized and signed.

The Jebwa colony would provide twenty-five hundred prepackaged meals per standard month for a tidy sum of sixty thousand credits per delivery. The meals would be made available for collection on the tarmac at the preapproved dates and times. The group returned to the meeting hall for a second negotiation.

Tawn gestured toward the platform. "This one's yours."

Harris winced. "I'm not the best person for negotiating the price for a ship. I can propose it, but one of these two needs to finalize it."

Trish said, "You want a shuttle like what we just had?"

Harris nodded. "I think that one worked well."

Trish shoved him as she walked past. "Get out of my way. I'll do it."

Gandy quickly followed. "Wait, let me set the stage for your tougher deal-making."

Three hours later, the group emerged from the trade minister's office. "Will be here in three weeks at most. He has the model number and where to purchase it. We offered a 25 percent premium for them to manage the effort on Domicile. As a colony purchase for Jebwa, there won't be any scrutiny. And with them being a collective, nobody back home knows their finances either."

Sharvie said, "You transferred credits to an account, right?"

Trish nodded. "A down payment."

Sharvie smiled. "Give me the account number and I can tell you exactly how much they have. That includes what's in that account and any related accounts they've moved credits to or from."

Harris held up a hand. "No need to hack their accounts. We need to keep them happy, and our business here under wraps. Unless we have further business, I suggest we get back and figure out a way to save Eden."

The trip back saw discussion about how promising the colony of Haven looked. People were walking about with smiles on their faces. Cats, the preferred pet of the pacifists, roamed about freely. Haven would likely never have a vermin problem.

More than a thousand species of birds filled the skies and the trees with songs, to the cats' delight. Other docile animals moved freely about the colony as all predator species had been wiped out by the prior colonists. By all accounts, it was a happy and friendly place. Even the attitudes of the pacifists had changed for the better. They were living in their nirvana.

Harris paced back and forth in the grass. "We should make a run to check on the colonel."

Sharvie said, "We can open a comm to him if we want."

Harris stopped. "What? When did this happen?"

Sharvie shrugged. "Has always been. Just ask Alex to open a wormhole comm to there and you can connect. No different than what the AI has been doing to gather intel on Domicile and New Earth."

Tawn rolled her eyes. "How long have we been here and we're just now thinking of that?"

Harris said, "Sharvie, go see if you can make that happen. Have it connect to us through Farker."

Sharvie nodded and headed for the bunker door.

Harris crossed his arms. "People, this is the thing we have these brainstorming sessions for, the easy answers. Now why didn't we come up with this before?"

Tawn said, "'Cause we're slow like you?"

Harris nodded. "Exactly. No... wait. Yeah, I guess that sums it up. Anyway, what other low hanging fruit have we neglected to pick?"

"If we need to talk to Mr. Morgan we could do the same," said Trish.

Tawn huffed. "Why would we talk to him? He's a DDI collaborator."

Harris said, "Because we are both still on the same side. OK, if we need anything technical for repairs or whatnot, Bannis might be our man. What else?"

The chime of a comm came through.

Harris answered. "Colonel?"

"Mr. Gruberg? Where are you?"

Harris tasked Farker with initiating his hologram display and feeding the colonel's video image to it. In the bright sunlight, a barely visible face floated just above the dog.

Harris said, "We're safe, although we're no longer welcome on Domicile. It appears our prior connections to the DDI were phony. Those agents were actually from New Earth. The real DDI showed up with some demands and we kind of messed things up and had to run. What's your status there?"

"Six days of food left. That's with rationing. Don't suppose you could get any to us?"

Harris shook his head. "Don't have any way of getting around the Earthers."

"How is it you're getting this comm here?"

"It's just a wormhole comm."

The colonel shook his head. "That means they are listening to us. Otherwise they would be jamming all comms. Especially our frequencies. Also probably means they know where you are."

The comm shut down.

Sharvie emerged from the bunker only seconds later. "They almost had us. Broke through three firewalls before I realized they were even trying. Had they made it through the fourth, I wouldn't have been able to close the comm. They could have snooped their way around every system in there, and maybe even triggered an automatic shutdown of the boson field."

Harris asked, "Is there a way we can open that comm securely? We could use the colonel's help with ideas."

"I can't do it from here, but my friends could. That would mean giving them full access to everything in there though."

"We can't risk that," said Tawn.

Harris rubbed the back of his neck. "I agree. Any way to get their help without compromising the whole place?"

Sharvie shrugged. "I'll have to ask Alex. I do know a few things I could do to help with security, but those are only on the alert end. Blocking is a whole different beast. On a high note, it looks like we have about forty seconds before they get through the third firewall. We could talk for that length of time and then disconnect before they get inside. Cracking those firewalls should take just as long a second time as it did the first."

"Set up your alerts and punch us back through to the colonel," Harris said. "I'll tell him the situation, then we'll cut the comm and do it all over again."

"Well, I did say it should take just as long. I might limit our time to half that just to be safe. I'm only a handful of years into all this cyber stuff. Would feel better if I had my people available to discuss it with."

"Then let's go back in and open a comm to Domicile. Talk to your people. If they give a green light, we comm the colonel back."

Sharvie headed into the bunker.

Tawn stood and stretched.

"I think I'll go for a run. Might clear my brain. And I could sure use the exercise."

"Enjoy yourself. I'll be stretching out here on the lawn."

Ten minutes passed before Sharvie emerged. "They said don't do it. Second time in they would blast through those firewalls.

We might have all of five seconds. For a reset of those times you would need a different system altogether."

"Can you add more layers of security?"

"Alex is exploring that right now. He's not sure when he will have an answer. As part of his investigation he's contacting Domicile to scan document libraries for modern cyber-security methods and practices. I asked him to also look for any hardware upgrades we could make to his system that he might benefit from. The stuff that system is built on is almost two thousand years old. Perfectly maintained, but ancient."

Tawn returned from her run.

Harris asked, "So what's your breakthrough?"

"What?"

"You said a run was gonna clear your mind. Anything shake out from that?"

"Other than I'm probably in the worst shape of my life... no."

Alex opened a comm to Sharvie through Farker. "I believe I have a temporary solution, although I will have to cease all other operations to maintain vigil on access firewalls. I can construct software firewalls where each must be broken through before the next will be accessed.

"Unfortunately the monitoring necessary for this approach will consume large amounts of my processing power. In turn, speech conversion over the comm may experience delays of as much as three seconds. Conversations at times may sound broken."

Sharvie asked, "How long can you maintain that connection before we have to cut away?"

"Potentially several minutes, but as few as fifteen seconds. It depends on the skill of the attackers and the speed of the New Earth technology we have to deal with. I would suggest making a list of requests so no time is spent on coming up with things to ask."

The group pushed questions back and forth for several minutes before a list of five emerged. Harris gave the go-ahead for Sharvie to initiate the comm.

Gandy said, "Hope this works and the colonel has something for us to try."

Tawn replied, "If we get a chance, we should go back and see if the Earthers are trying to rebuild the Rumford Mine."

Harris sighed as he shook his head. "We won't have a ship to follow behind this time if we do."

"No, but it's a stationary target. We can shoot at it from farther away."

Trish frowned. "Not that far away. Anything we shoot from orbit will burn up before it makes it to the ground."

"Well, maybe we follow the lead of the Earthers and push an asteroid at it," Tawn added. "Just need one big enough to make it to the surface."

Harris nodded. "Might not be a bad idea. Maybe Alex can run the numbers for us for that."

The comm chirped to life. "Colonel, Harris again. Sorry we got cut short. I have five questions to ask. With good answers we might be on our way to a solution to some of your problems."

"Not gonna happen right now, Harris. The Earthers are attacking in force on the ground. Been sniping our lookouts for a week. Managed an assault with little notice. Don't know if we'll be able to hold them off this time. We're looking at thousands of hardcore regulars. I'll have to catch you up later."

The comm closed.

Harris looked around at the others in disbelief before turning toward the *Bangor* in a run.

"We have to get out there now! Call Sharvie in! We have to get moving!"

"Tawn followed, hustling past and into the copilot's chair. "Not what I was expecting to hear."

Harris sat as the ship's systems came to life one by one. Sharvie ran from the bunker, breathing heavily as she jumped up into the cabin. Gandy closed the hatch and the *Bangor* rocketed skyward, friction flames bursting from its forward surfaces as it accelerated.

The ride to free space, followed by a jump and then the run toward Eden, would take most of ninety minutes.

Chapter 2

The *Bangor* slowed as it approached Eden.

"Stealth mode is on," Harris said.

"I count sixty Earther ships in orbit and four personnel transports on the ground," Tawn replied. "One sec for the bios... fourteen thousand troops on the ground. Why aren't they using the rail cannons?"

Harris zoomed in with a camera feed. "They are. The Earthers are threatening with the ships."

"We have to do something," said Trish. "We can't just let this happen."

Harris shook his head in disgust. "Best we could hope for is luring away a couple of those destroyers. Anything else would be suicide."

"Can't we use the boson bomb or something?"

"Wouldn't do any good. That only stops wormhole travel. What we need is better shields or a better weapon."

Tawn watched a video feed as the Earther assault force stormed one of the dome entrances. Charge after charge was repelled. The Biomarines were holding their own against a much larger force. Harris smirked to himself as he thought about how many times before he had seen that very thing.

Tawn said, "Must be something we can do for them... some way to get food down there. Wait... those Earther soldiers are pulling back. Looks like the assault failed."

Harris nodded. "Excellent."

Trish said, "What about the other mine sites? Don't we have people there?"

Harris nodded. "Two Biomarines at each."

"Why haven't the Earthers attacked them?"

"The colonel gave orders to destroy the wells if they were. My guess is the Earthers want those wells intact, so they aren't in a hurry."

Tawn said, "Maybe it's time we took that into our own hands."

Harris asked, "What do you mean?"

"I mean we go in, grab the people and blow those wells. A single shot from one of our railguns would do it. We could get in and out of there before they could catch us."

Harris frowned as he shook his head. "Why don't we hold that in reserve. Maybe those wells can be used as a future bargaining chip."

Tawn sighed. "It just burns me up to sit here and do nothing."

"Getting ourselves killed doesn't help accomplish our goals."

A return trip to Midelon had a dejected crew filing out onto the grass in front of the bunker.

Trish asked, "If Eden falls, will we be stuck here forever?"

"Hardly," said Harris. "This may be our new home base, but we aren't stuck here. When we get the new shuttle from the pacies at Haven, you three will have the freedom to travel home if you want. This fight may have gotten far bigger than we can handle, but we aren't giving up."

Gandy shook his head. "We can't go home. We know too much about this place. Even if the DDI decided to leave us alone, it wouldn't be until after they had pried every bit of info from our heads."

Trish nodded. "I agree. Don't know that we'd be accepted back there either. Several of my close friends, even some of those that helped us restore those Banshees, were very much against whoever it was that was meddling in the affairs of Eden. I had to keep my mouth shut while they discussed it, feigning to have no opinion."

"We have other ways to keep this fight going," Tawn said. "We can pirate their shipping lanes and maybe even figure out a way to attack their shipyards. Anything where we can work autonomously to do hit-and-runs."

Gandy smiled. "Pirates. I like the sound of that."

Over the next several days, the offices of Bannis Morgan were raided. No evidence of any wrongdoing was found. His powerful connections persuaded others to drop any further investigations. Several political bridges had been burned as a result, but the elderly industrialist walked free.

A trip to the Retreat was made and saw Bannis Morgan's shuttle parked on the tarmac. Trish, Gandy, and Sharvie stayed on the ship as Tawn and Harris made the hop to the colonel's home, where Bannis was staying. A small transport deposited the Biomarines on a concrete pad a short walk from the colonel's main house.

Tawn's head turned from side to side as she walked toward the grand entrance with Harris next to her. "This place is beautiful. Check out the stonework on that wall."

"The colonel built much of this himself," Harris nodded. "I mostly like the creek under the bridge up here. Makes it look like a moat."

The duo stopped in front of a four-meter-tall steel door. A welcome station sat to the left. They pressed a button and a video image of Bannis appeared.

"Thanks for coming. Come in. Take the hall to your right. I'm in the room at the end."

Several locks on the steel door clanged as it slid partly open. Harris pulled on the handle as Tawn walked in from just beside him. Digital video renderings of various warships dotted the stone-covered walls of the hall. Arched ceilings loomed five meters above.

As they walked into the colonel's study, an apparent change in gravity had them off-balance.

Harris said, "Standard grav in here?"

Bannis nodded. "It's adjustable in this room and several others. The colonel thought he might have the occasional guest from Domicile, and as a result the need to have a room where they would be comfortable. It's set just above standard."

Tawn nodded. "Does feel like Domicile. Eden was a little on the light side. Impressive home he has here."

Bannis Morgan stood beside a bookshelf. "His collection of written works is outstanding. I've been a collector for years and don't have anything like this."

Harris said, "We saw your shuttle at the tarmac. Sorry we caused you such a mess back home. You out here on the lam?"

Bannis waved his hand as he responded. "No, no. You aren't to blame for any of that. We are where we are because of the Earthers. I'm here because the colonel wanted me to look over his gravity system."

"That the only reason you're here? Seems that could have been discussed over a comm."

"I'm also here deciding whether or not to build a dome. We have all the materials, and given the imminent collapse of our dome building company, I'll be able to scoop up much of what we have for a small percentage of the value. Investors will be thrilled to get at least a portion of their credits back."

Bannis gestured for the others to have a seat as he sat at the colonel's desk. "The colonel asked me out here to have a look at his gravity enhanced rooms. And to try to persuade me we could do this to an entire dome. It would be a game changer. And not only here.

"There are three worlds in our space that have no inhabitants because of the gravity situation on each. Trophe VI, for instance, has a high quality atmosphere, plenty of water, and an otherwise very livable environment. But with gravity at 18 percent over standard, that leaves it barren of regulars."

Tawn nodded. "Interesting. So you would build domed cities with their own gravity?"

Bannis smiled. "Humans are able to tolerate about 6 percent over without major issue. We build a dome and run it at plus 6 percent and suddenly it's not such a leap for inhabitants to go out into the high gravity. Much like standard gravity to going outside here. Tolerable, just not livable. You Bios have the advantage of denser bones and muscles that allow you to adapt. For geezers like me, that adaptation will never happen."

"So you'd use this place as your model for building domes on high gravity worlds?" Harris asked.

"Exactly. The plants out here don't care. The water doesn't care. Even the native animals don't care. Not that we're advocating moving regulars out here to live among you Bios, but with this technology we could do just that."

"Interesting," Harris said.

Bannis leaned forward. "Now, imagine a planet with plus 20 percent gravity. We build a few domes and defend them like we did those on Eden. What human force would be able to land and effectively fight in that sort of environment? The Eden scenario wouldn't happen."

"So why not build on one of those planets to start with?" Tawn asked. "Why build here?"

"We built here to protect you Biomarines. Having to fight in this gravity would be overwhelming for any regular Human in only a few hours' time. If they came here, camped, and had time to prepare their bodies, they might be ready to fight in six months."

Harris said, "Why come here and camp? Couldn't they just turn up the gravity on their transport ship for six months?"

"Hadn't considered that." Bannis sat back. "I suppose it is possible. Anyway, our main reason for building a dome here is for the protection of your citizens. I would be providing the materials. The Bios would supply the labor."

"How will you protect the dome?"

"We plan on building a number of those rail cannons we had on Eden."

Tawn winced. "Won't the DDF and the politicians be all over you for that? Those are major weapons. Much more powerful than a repeating plasma rifle. Won't they shut you down?"

"I'll ask you not to repeat this," said Bannis, "but the colonel plans to eventually secede from the Union of Planets."

"Can he do that?"

"It's possible under the Domicile constitution. If a planet can show that it's self-sustaining, and that 95 percent of its inhabitants want to strike out on their own, they can do so, *if* they are not considered a physical threat to the union or her other colonies."

"Didn't know it was even possible."

"The inhabitants of Bella III have been pushing for that since the Great War came to a stop. Best they've been able to accomplish is a 78 percent vote. The bar is set intentionally high."

Harris chuckled. "Aren't we kind of missing the whole self-sustaining part? We don't grow enough food here to feed everyone."

Bannis nodded. "At the moment that is true. We can't. But we're working on it. This planet has five large bodies of water. Those waters are inhabited by native species. We're setting up teams to investigate the fishing prospects. We'll also be bringing several small herds of boglers here. They're adaptable creatures. This planet has ample grassy plains for them to feed and grow strong on.

"And in the interim we plan on inking a deal with the pacifists at Haven. They will have a surplus of food in only a few short months."

"That will all take money," said Tawn. "We were generous with the credits we gave the foundation, but that hardly seems enough for something like this."

Bannis crossed his arms. "I plan to contribute, but you're right. It isn't enough. I'll be hitting up my friends and associates to provide whatever assistance they can."

Harris raised a finger. "We might be able to help."

"We don't have that kind of money." Tawn shook her head.

Harris smiled. "We do in fact. We have the funds confiscated from the Earthers."

Bannis tilted his head to one side. "What Earthers?"

Harris took in a long breath. "Turns out our handlers weren't from the DDI. They were Earthers posing as the DDI. You know the real DDI. Our people were fakes."

"So what happened? You rob a bank or something?"

Harris grinned. "Actually? Yes. We hacked their accounts and stripped out their credits. We have a good stockpile available if we need it. This sounds like it might be a worthy cause."

Morgan sat forward. "I heard about this. My people said there was a roundup of more than two hundred Earther agents and sympathizers. Very hush-hush. How were you able to pull that off?"

"You have to have friends. And please don't divulge this to anyone, even to your most trusted associates, that it was us. I'd like to protect those responsible."

Bannis stood and then sat on the front of the colonel's desk. "I have it on good authority the DDI and DDF are pressuring the politicians to reverse their stance on Eden. They want it to go back to being neutral. And they are trying to use the unwrapping of this network of spies against the Earthers for just that purpose. I'd call it a long-shot, but we might get the mines on Eden shuttered for both parties if that were to happen."

"Won't happen," said Harris. "The Earthers will threaten immediate war and the pacifists will cave. Just a hint of that threat is why they abandoned us."

Bannis asked, "What kind of funding do you have available?"

Harris shrugged. "Would a hundred million credits help?"

"It would more than help. It would fund the entire project."

Tawn said, "We can't promise those credits are available. Best we can do is say that we'll try to make it happen."

Harris stood and began to pace the room. "I have a few other things to ask. Right now we are being hunted by the DDI over the little mix-up we had at the warehouse. Any chance of getting all charges dropped? Would make our efforts easier if we were allowed to return home."

"I'll check into it," said Bannis. "Given the fact the Earther network was uncovered, I would say makes it difficult. You had a connection to those people which would keep you high on their lists. However, if it were known that it was you who uncovered them, that might go a long way toward clearing your names."

Harris shook his head. "Can't reveal that for a couple reasons. First is we promised to protect those who helped us. Second is we would lose the funds we potentially have available to us. Our freedom on Domicile isn't worth either of those."

After the conversation had passed an hour of discussion, Bannis asked, "How long were you on-planet before getting here?"

Tawn replied, "Five minutes. We basically came straight over. Why?"

"I don't think we have any spies among the slugs and stumps here at the Retreat, but it's possible. If someone were to hop a ship up to free space and open a comm wormhole to Domicile, the DDI could have a ship here in about ninety minutes. You've been over an hour. Might be time to go. I'll ask the colonel's second to keep watch for any incoming ships after you leave. That should tell us if we have spies among us."

Tawn stood. "Let's get going, honcho."

"Honcho? What's that supposed mean?"

Tawn shrugged. "Dunno. Heard it in a movie once. I think it was an old Earth word. Don't have any other reference to it. Just sounds funny to say."

Harris returned a curious look. "I definitely think some of you slugs were mis-wired at the factory."

Tawn chuckled. "Yeah, I'll take that with a grain of salt since it's coming from such a titan of comedy."

A short ride, followed by a wormhole jump, had the team back at Midelon. When the hatch opened, Farker raced out the door, disappearing into the bunker.

Chapter 3

Sharvie walked toward the bunker door. "If anyone needs me, I'll be inside."

Trish and Gandy followed.

Harris asked, "Where you going?"

Gandy looked over his shoulder. "Gonna answer some questions to see if we can move up a level."

Harris turned to Tawn with a half-hearted frown. "Guess it wouldn't hurt us to join them."

Tawn shook her head. "I think that's too big a crowd. Besides, shouldn't we be checking on our shuttle at Haven? If it's not there, it should be on its way."

Harris smirked. "The dog's inside the bunker. We aren't going anywhere."

"We should ask Alex what happens if we just up and head out from here. From the outside they can't get in. Will it let us out?"

Harris gestured toward the bunker door. "Uh, I believe he already said we can leave at sub-light speed. Just can't come back without Farker."

The team was soon standing in front of the table in the main room. Harris stood to the side as Gandy and Tawn looked over Trish's shoulder.

Gandy said, "Can we communicate with Sharvie through you while she is in there?"

Alex replied, "I am allowed to relay an important message. Any other contact is not allowed."

Gandy turned. "We need to figure out how to get in there."

Harris chuckled. "I've given up on trying to force it. If it happens it happens."

"Alex, are there any group questions you could ask that would improve our positions?" Tawn asked.

"Yes."

Harris laughed. "Well, can you ask us then?"

"This will be a series of hypothetical questions," Alex said. "Just answer honestly. Harris, I'll start with you."

"Shoot."

"Tawn believes there are ten individuals being held hostage. The hostage takers have threatened to kill all ten unless she first kills Trish and Gandy Boleman. What do you do?"

"What do you mean what do I do?"

"It would seem that you have a choice. You could prevent Tawn from killing the Bolemans, or take the chance that the hostage takers are bluffing. Do you stop Tawn or do you allow her to act?"

Harris rubbed the back of his neck. "You mean stop as in I kill Tawn?"

"Perhaps."

Harris pursed his lips. "If I believed she would do it, then yes, I suppose I would have to take her out. Seems like an impossible situation either way. The hostage takers could still kill the ten, regardless of Tawn being successful or not. At least in this way there is guaranteed to be only a single death. And I believe Tawn would want me to do that so she wasn't left with that decision."

Tawn nodded. "I would. And I'd do the same for him if he was in that situation."

Harris scowled. "I knew it. I was just kidding, but now I know you'd shoot me first chance you got."

"What? No. What are you talking about?"

Harris chuckled. "Just having some fun. As I said, I'd take her out with the hope of limiting the damage."

The image of Alex nodded. "It would appear that you are prepared to sacrifice your friend if it meant saving other friends. What if Tawn had been asked to kill two complete strangers?"

"No difference to me. Still a one for two deal. My friend doesn't deserve to live any more than two other innocent people."

Alex looked directly at the Boleman twins. "Gandy? Same question to you. Would you be prepared to sacrifice Trish to save two strangers?"

Gandy winced. "That's tough. She's my sister. Any way I could just knock her out or tie her up instead?"

Alex nodded. "Prevention of any guaranteed death is an admirable goal. Suppose you didn't have those choices."

Gandy fidgeted for several seconds. "I guess I'd have to, then. Just as Mr. Gruberg said. And I'd hope she'd do the same for me."

Trish nodded with a smile. "I would."

Gandy crossed his arms. "Well, you don't have to look happy about it."

The clang of a door lock could be heard from behind them. Farker emerged. Instead of joining the others he sat beside the still-open door.

Tawn said, "That look like an invitation to you?"

"Each of you has been granted access to level two," said Alex.

"Finally, we can talk to Sharvie about it," said Gandy.

The image of Alex shook its head. "Discussion of the levels beyond this point is prohibited. The journey for each of you should not be influenced by that of the others. If it is determined information was passed from one of you to another, both parties will be removed from the structure and any reentry barred. Is that statement clear?"

"Understood," said Gandy.

Trish and Tawn nodded.

Harris stood with his hand grasping his chin as if in thought.

"Harris? Is there a problem? Do you require further explanation?"

Harris shook his head. "Nope. I understand. Was just going for dramatic effect."

"Would removal of your level two access have a dramatic effect?"

Harris slowly rocked his head back and forth. "I suppose it would."

"I see."

The image of Alex was silent for several seconds.

Harris asked, "Are you just being snide with me, Alex?"

"Perhaps."

Tawn sighed. "Can we just go through before the dog has to recharge again, or whatever he does."

The hallway on the other side of the door contained several doors of its own. Gandy tried the first and was rewarded with it opening. A video image of Alex showed on a display beside the door.

"Only one person per room. Gandy, please enter. Instructions will follow."

Harris glanced into the room before the door closed. "Hmm. A lounge chair, a helmet, and gloves. Looks about like our training simulators from back in the service."

"Precisely," said the image of Alex. "Please proceed to your rooms. Instructions will follow."

Harris opened a door and walked in. The chair was a full-body-length recliner, covered in thick but soft leather.

Harris settled back as he reached for the helmet and gloves hanging on a hook to the side. "This doesn't feel half bad. How is it you kept it in this shape for two thousand years?"

"When unoccupied, the room air is evacuated and replaced with nitrogen. The normal decay because of chemical interaction with oxygen doesn't happen. An oil rub applied every twenty standard years or so allows the material to last indefinitely."

"I assume I'm supposed to put this helmet on?"

"Yes. The gloves first please. The helmet will provide stimulus for sight, hearing, and smell. The gloves will add feedback for touch. Taste will not be simulated in this environment."

Harris sighed. "Great. Now I'm hungry."

"Place the helmet on your head, cinch in the strap to secure. The simulations will begin once those steps are complete."

Harris pulled the helmet over his head. "Kind of a tight fit."

"The helmet was designed to accommodate a large head. If smaller, padding inside will inflate to keep it snug. It seems you are just at or over the maximum. Is it uncomfortable?"

Harris shook his head as he fastened the strap under his chin. "No. Just tight."

"Excellent. Let's begin. You will be taken through a variety of simulations where your responses will be evaluated. Should those responses be determined to be wholly unacceptable at any time during the evaluation, you will be asked to leave and all further access will be terminated."

Harris chuckled. "So no pressure, huh?"

The interior of the helmet illuminated. Harris Gruberg was standing on a sidewalk from a two thousand year old Human city. Wheeled vehicles moved up and down the street beside him. Pedestrians walked as if having somewhere they intended to go. A vendor standing several meters away wore a full body sign with pockets containing paper fliers.

The vendor held out an ad. "Hey, buddy, need any dry-cleaning done?"

Harris shook his head. "Dry-cleaning? Not even sure what that is."

The man gave an irritated look. "You know, for suits and dresses. Business or evening wear. Like for those slacks you're wearing. You need those cleaned? Murray's has the means."

Harris looked down. His feet were adorned with striped socks covered by a pair of polished brown loafers. His brown and white plaid slacks were held up with a wide belt and oversized buckle. A bolo-style tie and cowboy-ish shirt were capped off with a light brown, felt Stetson.

Harris chuckled. "What kind of nightmare scenario did you drop me into, Alex?"

No reply was returned.

The vendor pushed the flier. "You want this or not, pal?"

Harris looked intently at the text on the paper in front of him. "Welby Street? Where is that?"

The vendor pointed. "Two blocks down. Turn right. You can't miss it."

The irritated man again pushed the paper. "Take this flier and you get 5 percent off. You here in town for the big rodeo?"

Harris reached up, adjusting his hat. "Rodeo?"

"Yeah, in the arena."

"Where would that be?"

The man sighed. "Three blocks east. Turn south. Let's see... four... no, five blocks from there. Just past restaurant row."

"Restaurant row?"

The vendor shook his head. "Never been to New Denver, have you? Look, cross over here. Walk the three blocks. Turn right on Alabaster. Keep walking from there. You can't miss the arena. And if you don't already have tickets you'll want to get moving. First rides are in about an hour."

Harris turned, stepping out into the street. A horn from a passing vehicle blared, followed by a verbal insult to his intelligence. A quick jog across had him moving down a side street.

As restaurant row was reached, the olfactory mechanism of the helmet kicked out the smell of the many foods. A scowling Harris Gruberg, with no means to actually sample the foodstuffs for sale, hurried past. A block later he was standing in front of the arena, and approached a ticket window.

"How many?"

Harris replied, "What?"

"Tickets. How many? And do you have a preferred section?"

Harris glanced at his empty wrist before lifting his hat and rubbing his head. "I don't seem to have a credit store."

"A what?"

"You know. A credit store."

The man at the ticket counter scowled. "Look, you want in, pull out your wallet and give me the eighteen dollars, like it says here on the sign. You cowboys normally keep them in your coat pocket, right?"

"Keep what?"

The ticket-seller shook his head. "You just fall off your horse and hit your head? Reach in your coat, retrieve your wallet, and give me a twenty."

Harris reached in, finding a leather billfold just as the man had advised. Inside was a paper bill with the number twenty printed in each corner.

Harris handed it to the man and received a single ticket and change in return. He stood reading the print.

The man said, "Rides are starting. You might want to go in."

After a short walk through the wickets, Harris handed the ticket to another man. He continued down a hall and through an aisle entry to a view of the open field of the rodeo. Announcements were made over a loudspeaker as he walked the steps down to the location as marked on his ticket. The seat number, 4A, had him sitting by a large woman. She eyed him intently as she feasted on a corn dog.

"Want one?" The half-eaten, breaded delight was held up in front of his face.

Harris took a whiff; his nostrils flared. "Sure."

"You'll have to go back up to concession. You ain't gettin' one of mine."

A cackly laugh filled the Biomarine's ears.

"Alex, why are you torturing me with the food?"

Again the question went unanswered.

As the rodeo began, a large Earth bull was paraded around the dirt-covered floor of the arena. A cowgirl, sitting high on a horse, was at the ready inside a pen.

The woman sitting beside him reached out, grabbing the right sleeve of his shirt with her mustard-covered fingers. "This is it. That's Bobbi Holmes. She's the best roper on the planet."

As Harris glanced down at his stained sleeve in disgust, a series of excited screams came from the crowd. A young boy had fallen over the rail, dropping to the arena floor. The bull, startled by the noise of the concerned patrons, turned toward the terrified boy.

Harris scanned the crowd, wincing at the lack of any action for a rescue. With two long steps and a leap, the hundred and fourteen kilogram Biomarine was over the rail and on the arena floor. He yelled to grab the attention of the bull as he sprinted for the boy. A half dozen long steps saw the boy's only protector slamming into the side of the charging and irritated beast.

As the bull rammed into the rail beside the boy, Harris grabbed the boy's arm, swinging him up and over the rail to safety. The angry bull charged, catching the Bio with its horns and slinging him into the air. After crashing hard to the ground, Harris was up and sprinting across the arena floor, kicking dust and dirt into the air. A jump up and over the rail on the other side had the Biomarine sprawled out on the steps as the bull slid to a stop.

The large woman in the seat beside his own held out a complete corn dog. "Here, you earned it."

As Harris reached out, the simulation came to an end.

A scowl covered his face. "Now why'd you stop it? You heard her. I earned that corn dog."

Alex replied, "While you would experience the touch and even the smell of your prize, you would not have been able to consume it."

"So are these simulations a test to see how much you can piss me off?"

"The simulations are intended to record psychological responses to a series of stimuli. Your reaction to the boy falling into the arena will be analyzed and evaluated against a number of criteria."

"That mean I passed?"

"There are no passing or failing criteria for the individual scenarios. Only reactional weightings."

Harris chuckled. "OK. Well, I'm guessing that saving the boy was a win. What else you got?"

The simulated situations continued for several hours. Each time, Harris Gruberg's actions brought an out-of-control situation back to a manageable footing. Lives were saved, wrongs righted.

Harris removed his helmet.

Alex asked, "Where are you going?"

"I'm going for a break. I want to eat and I want to rest. How many more of those do I have to sit through?"

"As many as it takes."

Harris huffed. "Well, I guess I'll be back after I stuff my face. Anyone else outside or they all still in the simulations?"

"Tawn Freely and Sharvie Withrow are both outside."

Harris nodded. "Good."

"And, Harris, remember, activities within the simulations cannot be discussed."

"I got it."

A short trek had the Biomarine standing in the doorway to the supply hut. Tawn and Sharvie were seated at a table, working over a set of MREs.

Harris grabbed a package and joined them. "Without saying what you did or didn't do, what do you think of level two?"

Tawn replied, "Already finished and moved on."

"What?"

"Yeah. Don't know why it took Sharvie so long."

Harris asked, "You finished too?"

Sharvie gave a reluctant reply. "I have, and I've been told that from this point on I can no longer comment on what level I've achieved."

Harris shook his head. "I nailed every scenario. How is it you got moved up so quick?"

Sharvie stood with her meal. "We shouldn't be discussing this. I'm going outside."

Chapter 4

Tawn looked at Harris. "She's right. Not supposed to discuss."

Gandy plodded in the door, his shirt soaked with sweat.

Harris chuckled. "What happened to you?"

Gandy shook his head. "Can't talk about it other than to say I don't imagine I'll ever make it through."

Harris pointed with his thumb. "Free Ride over here has already moved to level three."

"How is that possible?"

Tawn sighed. "It's not. I just wanted to see his reaction. And I think Sharvie is right. We shouldn't be talking about this."

Harris looked on in disgust. "I knew you couldn't have made it through already. I kicked ass and I'm not through."

Tawn held up a hand. "Don't get too big a head over whatever you did. You won't be able to fit in that helmet when you go back."

Harris ripped open a package, revealing the heavily salted and sweetened meal within. "I have to guess you had issues with your helmet as well."

Tawn nodded. "Almost ripped my ears off trying to pull it on."

Gandy snickered. "You two do both have enormous heads."

Harris laughed. "That's to hold our enormous brains."

Tawn sniped: "I'm guessing that pinhead you're sporting was rattling around inside your helmet?"

Gandy smiled. "Nope. Snug and secure."

Trish joined the group. "You all flunk out?"

"No," said Harris. "Just making fun of your brother's tiny head. Without breaking the rules by asking what you saw or did, how was your experience?"

Trish slowly nodded. "Interesting, just as Sharv said. I'm almost anxious to get back in there, but my brain said I needed a break."

Tawn said, "What I find interesting is that we all came out within a few minutes of each other after being in there for hours. Oh, and the fact that Sharvie has moved on to level three. So maybe there's hope for us to keep moving up."

Harris finished his meal, tossing the packaging into a recycler. "I think we need to make a run out to Eden. I still think there has to be a way we can get food down to the colonel."

Gandy shook his head. "We've been over this. We've got nothing. And you laughed at my last idea."

Harris chuckled. "Disguise a freighter as an asteroid and send it in? First off, that's not happening in the next two days. Aside from that, it was just plain dumb."

Tawn sighed. "Dumb is that we can't come up with anything. They will just have to surrender."

Harris motioned toward the door. "I'm heading over there to assess the situation. You can all stay here or go with me. Your choice."

The two Biomarines and three regulars, followed by Farker, boarded the *Bangor*. A short flight and a wormhole jump had the team checking the sensor display of the surrounding Eden space.

Harris scowled. "They're leaving. Those are transports down there. The colonel must have given up."

"Not like he had a choice," said Tawn.

Harris zoomed in on a video image of the first dome and its surroundings. "Wait... that look like they are loading equipment?"

Tawn nodded. "And we have a ship almost to free space. Let's see where they jump to."

A wormhole opened with the transport moving calmly through.

"That's the Retreat. That ship just went through to the Retreat."

Harris turned the control stick while pushing the throttle to full.

Tawn asked, "Where we going?"

"The Retreat. Somebody there can tell us what's happening."

"Why not just open a comm wormhole?"

Harris stared at Tawn for several seconds. "I'm claiming brain fatigue from being in the simulations too long. What's your excuse?"

Tawn shook her head. "Don't need one. I came up with the idea."

"OK. Get technical about it."

A wormhole comm request was sent and accepted. "This is Lieutenant Barrows. What can I help you with, Mr. Gruberg?"

"What happened? What's going on?"

"The colonel negotiated a surrender. We get to leave peacefully along with all our gear. Everything can go except the first dome and the wellhead for it."

"The diggers?"

"Being loaded as we speak. We even managed the railguns, the housing, and all the electrical, plumbing and processing gear. The Earthers get to keep the one dome."

"What's happening with the others?" asked Tawn.

"We have the transports prepping to move them to the Retreat. We'll also be stripping the titanium plating from the first dome. They want titanium, they have to dig their own."

"How'd the colonel manage all that?"

The lieutenant shook his head. "He let the word out that we had another four months of food. The spies got that word back to the Earthers and they took the bait. They caved on everything but the one dome. Colonel thought it wise to take the deal. Each of us had five rationed meals left."

Harris turned toward the others. "This changes everything for us. Figuring out how to destroy a single dome will be a lot easier than protecting and feeding six or eight thousand. And we now have at least a few months to figure out how. Will take them that long to outfit that mine and bring it online."

"Maybe we go back to Midelon and ask Alex what we might do," said Gandy.

Sharvie hummed. "Have we taken hacking their systems off the table?"

"Not at all," Harris said. "We just don't know how we do that effectively. You talking stealing ships?"

"Actually, this time I was thinking about ground equipment. Whatever systems they put in that dome and whatever they use on their mining vehicles will be far less secure than those warships. If we can hack the ground operations we might be able to delay any production they could bring online."

Harris nodded. "I hereby place you in charge of all hacking. Do whatever you can to stall or slow their progress. All I ask is that you tell us what you have planned before you implement it. That lets us coordinate our efforts."

Sharvie smiled. "I can do that."

"When we get back to Midelon, work with Alex to open a comm to Eden. So long as he can keep up a good firewall you should have time to get into their ground systems."

"What about the rest of us?" asked Trish.

"The rest of us will be working on a plan to attack and destroy that dome."

They returned to Midelon and Sharvie, Trish, and Gandy disappeared into the bunker. Harris and Tawn stayed in the *Bangor*, bringing up a projection of Alex Gaerten above Farker.

Harris crossed his arms. "I just passed the design plans of the dome to your comm. What we need is a way to destroy it. There are a dozen or more Earther warships guarding it. We're looking for suggestions."

"I am sorry, Harris. My programming does not allow the evaluation of physically destructive questions. I could offer suggestions for design improvements if that would help."

Tawn shook her head. "We're looking for ways to prevent the Earthers from mining titanium ore. If we destroy that dome they'll have to build something else. That buys us time."

Harris said, "Could you make a simulation of the dome, the surrounding landscape, and Earther warships that might be there?"

"I could."

Tawn asked, "What are you thinking?"

"I'm thinking with a simulation I could try attacks using the *Bangor* until I find a weakness. Maybe a certain approach or an egress even. Some way for us to get close and not get killed."

"What we need is a big bomb. Stealth maybe. Something we could launch from space while running full speed. By the time they spot it, it would be too late to react."

Harris looked at the hovering hologram. "Alex, you think you could design us a bomb that would do that?"

"Again, my programming does not allow weapons designs or suggestions. The best I can offer is enhancements to an existing system."

"Maybe we're still looking at this wrong," Tawn said. "Alex, any further progress on suggestions for improving our shielding or our speed? You said that boson negator is closely tied to the dampener fields we use on these ships. Any way to disrupt a dampener field?"

"I will have to investigate that possibility, Tawn. Temporarily disabling a field is not destructive."

Harris shook his head. "You make something that will take out a dampener field, it will affect us too."

Tawn nodded. "I realize that. And it might just be what we're looking to do. Imagine us jetting along about two hundred meters above the surface of Eden. We set up a device and detonate it. All we have to do then is maintain course until we are out of the field's reach."

"And how does that solve any problem?"

Tawn chuckled. "We still fire the railguns as we're passing the dome, doofus. Alex, can we disable all dampener fields in an area?"

"I will have to investigate. Would you like to make that a priority?"

Tawn nodded. "I think so."

Harris said, "Alex, can you open a comm portal to Domicile? I'd like to contact Bannis Morgan."

"You think he might be able to help?" Tawn asked.

"Maybe. He's in the defense industry. He might be the one we ask about a bomb."

Bannis answered. "I assume you've heard the news about Eden."

Harris nodded. "Found out earlier today. Had to be a blow to your consortium."

"I've lost a few friends. Although perhaps friends isn't the correct term. They seem to be more interested in their credits than the security of our world. They aren't willing to believe the one is useless without the other. I'm currently in the process of unwinding those relationships. What is it you need of me today?"

Harris took a deep breath. "We're now looking for ways to destroy the remaining dome. You wouldn't happen to know of a stealth bomb we could use, would you? Something we could launch from space and have drop through the atmosphere toward the dome before being detected and destroyed."

Bannis scratched the side of his head. "We have stealth abilities built into some of our craft. Problem with it is the amount of power required to run the equipment. By the time you outfit a bomb with shielding and any other tech needed to keep it hidden, it winds up being about two thirds the size of the *Bangor*. You can only hide that just so much."

"But it can be done?"

"I suppose. I hesitate to approve going that route because we've never had success with bombing ground targets from space. And that's with trying it for centuries. Both sides have countermeasures that are good at defeating such weapons, so no one uses them."

Alex said, "Harris, I have a simulation ready for you should you want to practice raids against the dome."

"Thanks, Alex. I'll give that a shot when we're done here. Mr. Morgan, I'm sure you know a few higher-ups in the military. You think you could ask around about how one might attack a ground target from space? And I don't have ten thousand soldiers to dump on the ground either, so it needs to be some type of hit and run."

"I do count a number of generals and admirals among my close associates, Mr. Gruberg. I'll attempt to have a chat with a few. Comm me back in two or three days."

Bannis Morgan continued: "By the way, I am offering the colonel all the assistance I can with moving the other domes out to the Retreat. The first of those should be in place in about a week. A site has been selected for that particular dome and the foundation is already being poured."

"Good news, Mr. Morgan. And thanks again for all you've done and are doing."

Bannis nodded as the comm closed. In the days that followed, several trips were made to Eden. On the fourth day, the last personnel transport was loaded and lifted off toward the heavens. A lone dome sat empty as the superheated air of Eden wafted through its open doors.

Harris turned the *Bangor* toward Midelon as the first Earther ship began to drop through the atmosphere.

"There we have it. Eden is now fully controlled by New Earth."

"We knew it was coming," said Tawn.

Harris scowled. "See the signature of that third ship? Baxter. She's finally got her dream."

"Well, maybe she can be there when we destroy it."

Harris chuckled as he shook his head. "I have to think she would somehow survive. Still not sure what game she's playing or who she's playing for."

Tawn scowled. "You're not serious, are you? She does nothing but lie. You can't trust anything she says. You don't believe she is responsible for keeping us alive through all this, do you?"

Harris sighed. "I'll agree we can't trust her, but she's taken actions that don't make any sense if she's really working for the Earthers."

"That's because she's working for herself. Whether it's on New Earth or Domicile, her goal is self enrichment. Now see what you've done? You've got me all riled up. Just take us back to Midelon before I turn this ship around for an attack."

Harris laughed. "Well at least I know what your hot button is now. Guess all that psych training was for nothing."

"Forget that training. She doesn't impair my judgment. If anything, thinking about her makes me more focused."

"If you say so."

A short while later, the *Bangor* settled on the grass outside the bunker. Trish and Gandy emerged from the complex.

Gandy hopped up into the cabin first. "We made it to level three."

"That fast?"

"I think it was just judging your reactions," said Trish. "Just did what felt right and it let me through."

Tawn said, "Speaking of simulations, how have your scenarios against the dome gone."

"I'm not supposed to talk about it."

Tawn looked at Farker. "Connect us to Alex."

A hologram of the doctor appeared. "Hello, Tawn."

"The simulations Harris is running in the complex, does he have to keep quiet about them? I'm only referring to those concerning the dome on Eden."

"Harris can talk of his experiences concerning the dome. He should, however, refrain from speaking about equipment or any other aspects of that level, even if the rest of you have moved beyond."

"I haven't made it yet," said Tawn.

Alex smiled. "That determination was made this morning. You are being moved up with Trish and Gandy."

Harris tilted his head back as he looked down at the holo-image. "What about me?"

"I am sorry, Harris. You have not completed the minimum required simulations."

An eye-roll followed. "Great. So I'm the one who gets left behind."

Tawn asked, "What happened with the dome scenarios?"

Harris returned a half scowl. "I got my butt kicked about a hundred times is what happened. I approached from almost every possible angle. Never got close enough to take a shot. Even dropped their number of ships down to three and couldn't get in. With two Earther ships guarding it I managed to get a couple shots off from a distance. Neither was a direct hit, and I got wasted right after."

"Did you try against a single vessel?"

Harris smirked. "Like we'll ever see that. No. Didn't bother. They'll keep that place locked up tight. If we're getting in close enough to shoot a few pellets, it will have to be by some other mechanism."

Tawn said, "That's all, Alex. Thanks."

Tawn turned. "You checked in with Bannis in the last day or two?"

"Farker, open a comm to Domicile."

Seconds later, Bannis Morgan replied, "Been waiting for your comm."

"What do you have for us?"

Bannis pulled up an image of one of the APCs he had donated to the effort. "You'll recognize this. It comes with a stealth package. Will let an operator drive it within a half kilometer before it's detected by any sensors. I can get you the gear for that through back channels if you're interested."

"So what option does that give us?" asked Tawn. "A raid? On foot for the last half kilometer? Sounds like a one-way ticket for anyone involved."

Bannis held up a hand. "Not suggesting that. Only telling you what we have available. One option might be to remotely drive it as close as possible and use it as a missile platform. From that distance they would only have a few seconds to react. An automated defense system would of course defeat it, but they would have to have one up and running."

"How big a missile could we transport?"

Bannis sighed. "That's the second issue. We could do multiple small warheads or a single large one. I heard estimates of a dozen holes five meters wide punched into that dome, up to a hundred meters if you managed to take out a support beam. Damage within the dome would be limited to anything in close proximity to the explosions."

Tawn frowned. "So we'd basically be letting all the cool air out for a day while they worked repairs. Doesn't sound like much of a plan. We only have one of those APCs that's still operational."

"We could build more. Give me three months and I could have another twenty ready for use. But that brings us to problem number three."

"Which is?"

"Which is the fact that we don't have access to any missiles. Those are kept under strict control. My friends were even paranoid about suggesting their use. They use technologies we don't want the Earthers to have."

Harris winced. "So we're left with a ground force. Twenty trucks that carry a dozen each... two hundred forty Bios. We could take the dome with that. Problem is we couldn't hold it. Would just be a death sentence."

Bannis said, "Sorry I don't have better news. And I don't have the finances to build those vehicles. I'm stretched a bit at the moment."

Tawn asked, "How much you need?"

Bannis thought for a moment. "Tooling, materials, labor, and I would still have to get my hands on the stealth gear. A quick guess would be in the neighborhood of ten million credits."

Tawn nodded. "Enable your store. We'll send them over. Harris, pass him five and I'll do the same."

"We're buying some trucks?"

"We're buying some trucks. Mr. Morgan, if you need more let us know. We can get it. Our pool isn't unlimited, but it's substantial. If those trucks can get us within a half kilometer, maybe we can harass them as they try to bring production online. A blown wellhead, sniping their equipment operators, there are a variety of lesser options available to us. Get started on those trucks and we'll see what options we can come up with for using them."

The comm closed.

Tawn let out a deep breath. "Not much, but it's something."

Chapter 5

A jump was made to Jebwa and the waiting shuttle collected. In addition, the *Bangor* and the shuttle were stuffed with the first supply of packaged meals. Accounts were settled and the team returned to Midelon to unload.

Harris carried a crate as he walked behind Tawn. "I know we're set for fuel at the moment, but we should make arrangements with the colonel should the need for more arise."

"Sounds reasonable."

Tawn set her crate down, glancing back out the supply hut door. "I'm glad we found the three of them, but I have to wonder if we didn't drag them away from having normal lives. They could each be back on Domicile right now, enjoying themselves in ignorant bliss of all we have going on. We're trained to survive and thrive under this kind of stress, they aren't."

Harris chuckled. "Frankly, sometimes I think they handle it better than us. This has been a huge adventure for them. Back on Domicile their lives would have consisted of the daily grind. Trish would still be an apprentice and Gandy would be a junior salesman. Sharvie? I don't even think she was employed. And from what Mr. Morgan says, the economy is not picking up pace."

"So you think we did them a favor?"

Harris shook his head. "Nope. I'm just saying we won't know the outcome, good or bad, until the story has been told. At the moment we're right in the middle of it. I'd prefer not to second guess everything when there's so much still to be done."

Gandy set down a crate. "What are you talking about?"

Harris patted him on the shoulder. "The struggles of being a woman in today's world. You have an opinion?"

Gandy winced as he turned back for another crate. "Not today."

"See how easy his interest was diverted? His mind is not burdened with stress. He's fine."

Trish set down a crate. "Who's fine?"

Harris said, "We were talking about your brother's interest in Sharvie."

"He's had the hots for her since he first saw her. But don't worry, he's too chicken to act."

"What do you think she thinks of me?" Harris said.

Trish stopped for a second. "Eww. You're old. I don't even want to think about that." Trish hurried away.

Tawn laughed. "I'd say her mind isn't overburdened either. And you disgust her. Now that's funny."

Harris shrugged. "Win some, lose some."

The team moved back into the bunker when the last of the food crates had been unloaded. Five hours later, Harris emerged from the simulators to find the others having lunch.

"Well, thanks for calling me."

Trish smirked. "Not like you were going hungry in there. How's it going?"

Harris grabbed an MRE, tearing open the sealed bag. "Finished the second level. When I go back in I guess I'll find out what you four already know."

"Yeah, well, we can't comment on it, so you'll have to wait."

Harris turned. "Farker, open a comm to the Retreat for me."

Several seconds later a response was made: "Mr. Gruberg. Was waiting to hear from you," the colonel said.

"How are things going with the domes?"

"The first set of supports are in place. We expect to be adding the crown in three days."

"That's fast."

The colonel nodded. "We've done this before. The teams are practiced. Much friendlier environment to be working in here, even with the additional gravity.

"There is something else I need to talk to the two of you about though. I had to confiscate your properties. Your land was the ideal location for this first dome. We'll have to work on restitution at some future time."

"Happy to give it up for the cause, Colonel. How are the other Bios doing?"

"They're glad to be back and to have work. I'm expecting this first dome to be complete—that includes plumbing, electrical, and housing—in about four weeks. We already have slugs and stumps waiting for it. We'll be breaking ground for dome two in a couple days. I've given up my ranch for it."

Tawn winced. "That beautiful home and those gardens?"

The colonel nodded. "It's the end of the valley and a good strategic location. Dome three will be going in at the southern end. Give us six months and the Retreat will be a heavily fortified colony. We've already begun mapping out sets of underground tunnels to connect them together."

"Mr. Morgan working on rail cannons for you?"

"He is. We're having a funding squeeze at the moment, but we'll get through it. If we all have to go off-world to work to pay for those rail cannons, we will."

Tawn sighed. "We have the credits if you need them. Do you have an estimate from Mr. Morgan as to the cost?"

"He says they cost a half million credits each. We'll be wanting at least eight per dome."

Harris smiled. "We've got you covered. Open your credit store and I'll send you more than enough to cover it. Send them on to Mr. Morgan as needed."

"That's six million credits minimum. I know the two of you have significant funds, but I would rather not send you to the poorhouse over this."

Tawn shook her head. "Don't worry. We have the funds available. I'm sending you ten million so you can keep progress moving out there. If the Earthers do as we expect, we're gonna be needing more than a few forts. And we'll be wanting to keep our Biomarine force safe and healthy. I get the feeling that when this war returns it's not gonna be played by the civilized rules of the past."

Harris said, "It's not back yet. Colonel, you have any intel from Eden?"

"We've had a steady stream of shuttles jumping out there to take a peek. The most recent was captured and warned to not return. The truce worlds are still free space. We won't be complying with that demand.

"The latest report is they are pouring a mass of resources and labor into it. The well is operational, the power and cooling equipment are in, and the dome has been sealed. They must have five thousand laborers on the ground already. There's been a near continuous line of ships landing with equipment.

"How long do you think we have before they start mining?"

"We were kicking around a couple months minimum. But from the looks of their operation, we're now thinking as few as three weeks. Once done, mining will probably ramp up to full-rate production a few weeks after."

Tawn asked, "So we aren't far from them producing a ship a day with the titanium from that mine?"

"Worse. They have camps started at all four major mining sites. Our two-year estimate for them to build up their fleet to equal ours is now at under a year."

"What? How's that possible?"

"They have a united empire. All of their resources can be dedicated to this one task. And the reports we're getting from New Earth say their people are motivated. The Earther war machine is coming to life with a vengeance."

Harris shook his head. "Meanwhile our politicians are shutting down our ability to fight."

Tawn said, "That just makes our mission on Eden all the more important. That production will have to be stopped, Colonel."

"I have a dozen snipers who are willing to be dropped in there if necessary. We pick off a machine operator or two each day and that might at least slow things down."

Harris set a Haven-produced granola bar down on the table in front of him.

"Mr. Morgan is building a number of those APCs for us. They should have the latest stealth capabilities. Each one might be a good mission house for a pair of snipers or more. That's if we can get them on the ground without being seen."

The colonel nodded. "We can get on the ground—at the moment anyway. Scouts have reported the only activity by the Earthers is directly over the mines. If we approach from the other side of that planet we can go all the way down to the surface. Huge oversight on their part as they could prevent that with a single ship."

"They don't perceive any threats at the moment. They know our military isn't planning anything, and when it comes to our team here I'm sure we would just be considered a minor nuisance."

Gandy said, "I thought you told us the other day they had to be within half a kilometer to detect the *Bangor*?"

"That's if she's sitting still on the ground with her systems mostly powered off. If you're moving, you become much more visible, unless you're coming directly at the target. That's how we managed to hit that flagship cruiser. Came straight at them at a constant speed. Even with that, as you saw, we were lucky to survive."

Tawn cut in: "If we're putting sniper teams on the ground there, I'd like to sign up for that."

Harris nodded. "I think we both go in that instance. You'll need a spotter and a pack-mule. I can manage those. Trish and Gandy can fly in the *Bangor* if needed."

Trish returned a half frown. "I wouldn't want both of you down there. I mean, I can fly the ship, but I don't want to be in charge of making decisions."

"Relax," said Harris. "All of this is speculative at the moment. If we decide to explore this course of action, I'm sure we'll be using a single team first. I'm also sure the colonel would insist on that team not being us."

"That would be a correct assumption," replied the colonel. "We would have no shortage of qualified volunteers for that duty. A trial run with a single team would be the way to go."

The conversation ended with the team of five returning to the bunker and further evaluation by the AI. Harris sat in a room by himself.

"Harris, you must complete this level before you can move on."

"The questions you're hitting me with are above my pay grade."

"You only need to answer them to the best of your ability. Please answer the next question."

"OK. I pick C."

"Book is to reading as fork is to bogler steak? Is that your final answer?"

"Yep."

"Please give me a moment to reset the remaining analogous questions to remove any references to food related items. I believe they are skewing the results."

"I thought you said to answer to the best of my ability?"

"That is the goal," replied the AI. "However, you appear to be distracted by each mention of items related to eating."

"Can't help it. I get hungry. Can we just move on?"

"Please answer the next question on your display."

"OK, F, all of the above," Harris said.

"How is it you feel a cat is a two legged animal?"

"It has four legs. Two is a subset of four. Which reminds me of a joke. This farmer had a pig he'd raised from birth. He entered it into a contest in his town and won first prize. Three months later, a neighbor came to visit and noticed the pig outside in its pen. It only had three legs. The concerned neighbor asked the farmer what had happened to his prize winning pig. The farmer replied that when you have a pig that good you don't eat it all at once."

Harris grinned.

"I see. And you find that humorous?"

"Come on! That one's a classic. Do you not understand it?"

"I fully understand the significance of the farmer's statement at the end. I'm still evaluating as to whether or not it is humorous."

Harris chuckled. "You've been trapped in this building by yourself for too long. You should really try to get out more."

"I'll take that response as an attempt to be facetious. Now, shall we continue?"

"OK. Which of the following can be used to spell a five-letter word? I'd have to go with answer B, BOFOT."

"And what word or words would that spell?"

Harris chuckled. "None. I just liked the sound of saying it. BOFOT. Not sound funny to you?"

"Do you have a more serious answer?"

"You know, for an AI you aren't very entertaining. OK, I'll go with A. STEAK. Thought you were taking out all the food words. Now I'm hungry again."

Alex replied, "A mistake on my part, and a correct answer. Please continue."

The quizzing continued for another three hours before Harris raised his hand in defeat. "I think I'm done for the day. I need to get up and walk around for a bit."

Alex replied, "This room will be available when you are ready to continue."

"You sure this all has some meaning? You aren't getting your jollies by jerking us around, are you?"

"If you are inferring that I am deriving pleasure from putting you through this process then my answer would be yes. As of now, I am deriving some pleasure from it."

Harris pointed. "Sarcasm. At least that's something I recognize. Maybe we can make a Human out of you yet."

Harris left the bunker. Sharvie was sitting out on the grass.

"Had enough of Alex?"

Sharvie replied, "Was just wanting a break. I actually enjoy our conversations."

"You like talking with the AI?"

"It has a wicked sense of humor when it wants."

Harris laughed. "You must be talking to a different machine than I am. It does give the occasional smartass remark, but mostly it's just flat and boring."

"I believe it responds to each of us differently. I get a behavior in there that I don't get when you're talking to it out here."

"I get nothing but pushback. It has called me numbskull, flake, barbarian, and any number of other intentional slights. Funny though, those are what I respond most to. I've had years of training in how to be patient, but that thing knows how to push my buttons. Will be glad when this is all over."

Harris sat beside her. Sharvie scooted to the right to what she considered a safe distance.

Harris asked, "What's going on?"

"Trish said you liked me."

Harris chuckled. "Relax, I was just trying to get a rise out of her. I said it, but only in the context of trying to get her to react. Now don't take that the wrong way. I'm sure you're a wonderful girl, but you and I? I wouldn't have the heart to put you through something like that."

Sharvie sighed. "Good. I was worried."

"I know. Worried that you couldn't keep your hands off the old man. That's OK. It happens to most of the ladies who are around me for any length of time. Nothing to be ashamed of."

Harris winked.

Sharvie slowly nodded her head. "Right then. Are the others coming out soon?"

Harris laughed. "Getting close to dinner time. They'll be out soon enough."

Chapter 6

Over the month that followed, the first dome at the Retreat was assembled, sealed, powered, and acclimatized. Crews worked in a continuous series of shifts to build out the housing section. Areas for administration, entertainment, and storage were next on the agenda. Bannis Morgan had delivered the first of dozens of rail cannons that would be used for her protection. The second and third domes were under construction.

On Domicile, the new budget had been pushed through the congress and signed into law. The military would see a 38 percent cut in expenditures that included another 32 percent reduction in force. Of the seven hundred eighty-six warships in her fleet, three hundred fifty would be mothballed, bringing the active number in line with that of the Earthers. Further budget unwindings would follow.

Military research and development would see a whopping 76 percent cut, with all new acquisitions halted and updates to existing equipment cut by two thirds. The defense industrial complex, a large employer for many centuries, was already beginning to lay-off workers. The Hosh-Morgan corporation would see a third of its revenues cut over the coming two years. Remaining incomes would be squeezed due to increased competition for the same credits.

On Eden, the Earthers were nearing completion of the dome refurbishment. Five thousand workers would be moving from makeshift housing on a number of parked transports into beds in the dome. Modular housing for another five thousand was in the beginning throes. New mining equipment was being brought in daily with the first grounds having already been tested and analyzed.

Harris emerged from a long session in the bunker, making his way to the supply hut. "How is it possible to ask that many questions. I'm on the verge of giving up. Enough is enough."

Tawn laughed. "Giving up? Maybe that's what he's testing you for."

Harris asked, "You make the next level?"

"You know I can't answer that, and you aren't supposed to ask. The journey for each of us is our own."

Harris glanced at the bunker as he rubbed his lower back. "Yeah, well, something better break soon or I'm likely to lose it and go on a rampage."

"Good thing the Earthers didn't just start asking you questions on Helm. You might have surrendered."

Harris chuckled. "I'd have been tempted. The others still in there?"

"Yes. I expect them to come out at any time though. You think Mr. Morgan has any of our APCs ready? Today is supposedly the day."

Harris sat. "One thing we haven't talked about is how do we transport them to Eden. We'll need a freighter of some sort."

"Shouldn't be hard to find. With all the defense contractors losing business, they'll be wanting to sell assets. Mr. Morgan might even have a few to spare."

Trish, followed by Gandy and then Sharvie, made her way into the supply hut.

"Any news from anywhere?" Trish asked.

"About to give Mr. Morgan a comm," replied Harris.

"Aren't we due for a run to Jebwa?"

"We are. And I think we need to cut our food order by half until we've worked through the older of our MREs."

Gandy said, "Anyone else getting antsy for some action? The Earthers are closing in on producing titanium. Isn't there something we should be doing to stop them?"

Tawn gestured toward the *Bangor*. "If Mr. Morgan has an APC ready, we'll be overseeing putting it on the ground on Eden. When that happens we'll be transporting a sniper and their spotter out to it in the *Bangor*. That's about the limit of the action we have planned."

Sharvie said, "We have this stealth ship. Should we be out there trying to hack the Earther systems? Since we decided it would be too risky to try from here, I feel like we should be doing something. Give me an isolated system and let me see what I can do."

"I thought you said you needed the help of your friends to make any further progress?"

"I do. Guess I would need two isolated systems, then, as you don't trust us with those of the *Bangor*."

Harris said, "It's my understanding that sometimes hackers get hacked. We let anyone else into our systems and we run the risk of losing everything. When I comm with Mr. Morgan I'll see if he can provide us with what you want. We have the credits to buy whatever you require."

Sharvie nodded. "Speaking about credits, I checked our accounts. They are growing. Our friends have emptied the accounts of another Earther spy network. Two hundred twenty million this time. They said it was centered around industrial espionage. A complete list of names and connections have been anonymously sent to the DDI and several other agencies. And they have leads now on what they believe to be three other rings."

Harris winced. "Sad to think our security there can't get a handle on such large scale operations. I wonder how many they have planted in the ranks of our politicians."

Sharvie frowned. "I think the politicians are one of the three networks they're on to."

Harris shook his head. "A sad state of affairs. Let's hope they're able to chop the legs out from under that one. Probably the most dangerous of them all."

After a meal was had, Harris relayed a comm to Bannis Morgan.

"Mr. Gruberg, the first two APCs are ready for use."

"We're gonna need transportation."

"Already taken care of. I just need the coordinates of where you want the ship to jump to. From there, you can coordinate getting those vehicles on the ground."

"Any last minute updates you were able to squeeze in?"

"Actually, yes. I was going to save it as a surprise. We've added a mini railgun to a turret on the roof. Not as powerful as what you have on the *Bangor*. Would deliver enough energy to take out a small fighter or a drone. Good against other vehicles too. I'm told the Earthers have tanks there on Eden now. Anyway, our teams will have that at their disposal should they need it."

Coordinates for a jump point were sent. A quick trip to the Retreat had the first team of sniper volunteers aboard. A second jump had the *Bangor* awaiting the arrival of a freighter from Domicile.

Harris turned to face the two-slug team, Sergeant Jenkins and Private Tiana. "You ladies ready to cause some havoc?"

Jenkins replied, "More than ready. Tiana here was a senior level three back in the war."

Harris raised an eyebrow. "And now a private?"

"She had a few run-ins with command just before the truce was signed. Busted rank."

Gandy said, "Miss Freely was a level four."

The sergeant turned to face her. "That was you?"

Tawn humbly replied, "Just happened to be good at it for some reason. Was in the sixth division. How about you?"

"Fourteenth. We had a level four with us as well, a regular."

Harris said, "I know you've been briefed on the mission here. Spout it back to me just for grins and giggles. What have you been told to do?"

"Disrupt production in any way we can while not putting ourselves at undue risk. Machine operators and lookouts are the primary targets. The colonel thought one target every other day for the first week would give us a good idea if this will work."

Harris nodded. "Sounds like a good strategy. Have you been briefed on the APCs?"

"Not fully."

"Then we have a surprise for you. They now have a railgun on top. Will be good for defense against other vehicles or small aircraft. They've been outfitted with a couple bunks, a potty, a sonic shower, and sixty days of MREs. You'll also get the benefit of insulation and a cooling system that will give you your own little paradise when you're inside."

Jenkins grinned. "Sounds like a dream compared to some of our prior deployments."

Trish said, "We have a freighter coming through. Looks like this is it."

The trip to the surface of Eden took two hours. There was no indication the Earthers had discovered the interlopers. Four thousand kilometers were flown across the desert landscape to a site just over the horizon from Earther detection. Harris assisted with the deployment of the APCs as Tawn sat at the ready behind the *Bangor*'s controls.

Trish said, "Gah. How much longer do we have to have that hatch open? That is boiling out there."

"Until he's back inside," Tawn replied.

Harris hopped out of the second APC as the freighter began to lift from the ground. "Park this second one at five kilometers from your base camp as a backup. Make sure to leave the active skin turned on so it blends in with wherever you park it. Other than that, good luck out there. I know you ladies will do us proud."

Jenkins nodded. "Take care, Mr. Gruberg. See you in a week."

The hatch closed behind the stump as the ship lifted into the intensely hot Eden air. The two APCs and their drivers would have an eighteen hundred kilometer, seven-day trek to reach the Fireburg mine. A pathway had been mapped out using the scan data the *Bangor* crew had originally collected. A dozen comm relays would be stretched along that path, enabling silent communications to the point of origin. The *Bangor* would be back in seven standard days to evaluate the mission.

As the ship made it to free space, Tawn said, "I'm heading to Jebwa. Might as well grab our supplies while we're out."

Harris replied, "I wouldn't mind taking a little time for a walk-around. Would like to know they have everything they need."

Tawn chuckled. "Sounds like you actually like those people."

Harris shrugged. "Other than being buttheads about the Earthers, I guess they're OK. Not my choice for living, but at least they leave everyone else alone."

After landing, Trish, Gandy, and Sharvie let out on their own to explore. Tawn talked Harris into jogging from the spaceport into town. The first stop was the meeting hall of the government offices. The normal several dozen pacies were lying about on the beanbag chairs in their usual robes and sandals. No one was speaking.

Harris asked the first person they encountered: "No pressing matters going on today?"

"Hasn't been for a week now," the man replied. "Everyone is busy... and busy is happy. Even have fifty new residents that just came in from Domicile. They were welcomed with a small celebration and are already out in the fields working."

Tawn said, "Seems like everyone is content."

"Why wouldn't we be? The sun is shining, the weather is beautiful, and the air is fresh."

The pacie drew in a deep breath.

Harris asked, "Have you had any contact with any Earthers?"

The pacie shook his head. "None. They have no interest in this planet, so they're leaving us alone. I sure would like to thank whoever came up with this alternative."

Harris smiled. "Well, that would be me. You can thank me."

Tawn rolled her eyes.

A pacie raced into the hall. "A herd of feral cats just attacked and killed a horse before running back into the woods!"

The pacies in the room rose and hurried toward the door. Harris and Tawn followed behind as they walked a kilometer to the edge of town.

Tawn looked around as they walked. "You know, something's been missing since we got here and I just now nailed it. Birds. What happened to all the birds?

Harris glanced around, eyeing several roaming cats. "I think we know what happened to the birds. And if cats are attacking horses... they must be getting hungry."

Harris tapped the closest pacie on the shoulder. "How many cats you have around here?"

The woman replied, "We don't know. There has just been this cat explosion since just after we came here. Some of them have been getting aggressive in the last few weeks. This is the second animal attack in that time. First one was a goat that had been ripped to shreds and then stripped to the bone. When we found it, there were a hundred cats feeding on it and circling around what was left."

They don't have any predators to fear. If they're out of food, namely birds, I could see some of them falling back to their more primal instincts."

Harris whispered, "I bet within a month you'll have your first Human attacked. Probably one of these younger pacies that have been running around here."

Tawn shook her head with a chuckle. "Cats. Could be the downfall of them all. If they don't take the steps needed to control this, they'll be overrun."

The group stopped as it encountered a larger group of onlookers. Thirty meters away, in a fenced in field, more than a thousand cats were circling the dead horse as several dozen tore at its flesh.

Harris laughed. "That's messed up. Would never have pictured that coming from domestic pets."

He pushed his way to the front of the crowd. "Anyone gonna stop this?"

The pacies surrounding him remained silent as the small carnivores devoured their prey.

Harris hopped over the fence, walking toward the feral mass as Tawn and the others watched. "OK, furballs, time to give up the horse and move on."

A fourteen pound Abyssinian hopped down from the back of the horse, moving directly toward the Biomarine, hissing. Several dozen of the surrounding cats followed its lead, bringing Harris to a stop.

"Whoa."

Tawn said, "You might want to come back from there."

Harris pulled his compressed helmet up from a hook on his back.

"What are you doing?" asked Tawn. "Are you nuts?"

Harris turned with a slight grin. "Oh, come on, they can't hurt me through this biosuit."

Tawn gestured toward the carcass. "I bet that horse thought the same thing."

Harris turned back to face his herd of adversaries. "Always wanted to be a cat wrestler. Looks like I finally get my chance."

His lunge forward was met with a defiant attack by the Abyssinian. Within seconds the genetically engineered Biomarine was engulfed and covered with claws and fur. The sound of a thousand hisses filled the air. The pacie onlookers took several steps backward.

Harris yelled through his comm as he attempted to sling off the wild animals. "A lot heavier than I thought!"

Cats flew, landing on their feet several meters away before leaping back into the fray. Less than a minute into the spectacle, the Human beast was taken off balance and brought down.

"This is crazy! They are way stronger than I thought!"

Tawn shook her head. "I think you should move away from that horse. They're defending their kill. Try to come back to us."

Harris began to slowly crawl toward the fence with a pile of fur mounted upon his back, clawing and biting at anything they could.

At five meters from the fence, Harris looked up. "Ow. Crap. One of them just got a claw through one of the seams. Ow! There's another!"

Tawn said, "Looks like they're prying up one of the panels on your back. That's mostly cloth and insulation if they get under there."

Harris yelled. "Gah! One of them just dug into my back!"

The hundred and fifteen kilogram Human began to fling his arms before going into a roll. As attached cats lost their grips, Harris was able to stand and take another step. Tawn flipped on her helmet and cinched it shut.

"Get your ass over here and I'll start knocking them off!"

Harris flipped around, violently kicking and flailing at the screaming herd, as a dozen animals continued with their attempt to bring him down. Two hard fought steps brought him close to the fence, where Tawn got to work stripping cats from his torso, tossing them back into the agitated herd.

A heavily breathing Biomarine pulled himself over the fence as the last of the felines was snatched from the bloodied opening on the back of his suit. The herd of cats moved toward the fence in force, hissing and screeching in anger. The pacies turned and fled as Harris taunted the aggressors with his fist.

Tawn pulled him backward. "Come on, we need to get you sewn up and disinfected. Your back is a mess."

Harris growled at his nemesis as the Abyssinian stood its ground. As it turned away, several dozen ferals stood guard as their leader returned to the feast.

Tawn shook her head. "You are a dumbass. Why'd you feel the need to do that?"

Harris grimaced as he tried to reach his stinging back. "Looked like fun. And it was until they broke through. That's just crazy they were able to do that. Didn't think they had the strength or smarts."

Tawn pulled a med-pack from a thigh pocket. "Was only one dumb animal out there today. Two, I guess, if you count the poor horse, but I'm betting it wasn't looking for trouble."

"So what are we gonna do about this?"

Tawn laughed. "We aren't doing anything. This is a problem for the pacies. They'll have to decide what they want to do."

Harris glanced over his shoulder. "That herd is only gonna grow. And these people won't be willing to take it on."

"Sounds like a perfect opportunity to sell them some coyotes."

"I thought those were almost extinct? Only in zoos?"

Tawn shrugged. "Might be time for a breeding program and for them to be reintroduced. That would be a natural remedy, which is what these people are all about."

"And then how do you control the booming coyote population?"

"Easy enough. Before you release any, you make them sterile. Problem solves itself naturally."

"Doesn't sound all that natural to me."

"We could take this on in exchange for the food we're purchasing. Would save us a few credits. Not that we need them, but just the same."

Trish and the others were contacted and told to return to the ship. Thirty days of packed meals were waiting to be loaded.

Harris turned toward the crates only to be told to get aboard and sit. Fifteen minutes later the *Bangor* was on her way back to Midelon.

"What happened to your back?" asked Trish.

"Herd of cats attacked him when he tried to take their food," Tawn said.

Trish laughed. "We just ate not long ago. You got hungry for cat food?"

"The cats attacked a horse, killed it, and were eating it. It was a herd that was probably a thousand strong of feral cats.

Mr. brilliant here thought it might be fun to mess around with them. They attacked and ripped open his suit. Chewed up a spot on his back pretty good."

Trish shook her head. "You two are a riot sometimes. What really happened?"

Chapter 7

Harris spent most of a week sitting forward in his chair as the AI of Dr. Alexander Gaerten continued with its relentless stream of questions.

"A man is confronted with a thousand feral cats eating a dead horse. Should he A) Run. B) Negotiate with the cat's leader. Or C) Antagonize the herd into an assault."

"Har, har. Aren't you the funny set of computer chips. Please just ask me something that will move me to the next level from this endless quiz."

"I have a surprise for you, Harris. Congratulations, you have moved up to level four with the others."

"Huh. Finally. Can you at least tell me what level four is about before I get up? My lower back is killing me from having to sit forward."

An image of Alex came up on the display. "Very well. I believe you will enjoy the next level. It is educational and more of a listen and ask questions type of scenario rather than being forced to answer questions. The topic is about Earth. And you may discuss it with the other members of your group, but not with anyone else. That goes for all that you have experienced thus far. Members at your level only and no others."

"Earth. Got it. Forgive me if I go take a break and lie down on my belly for a bit. This wound with all that cat-scratch bacteria is not healing well."

"When you come back you may proceed through the door at the end of the hall."

Harris walked into the supply hut, where Tawn and Trish were sitting. "Out of the way. I need that bench."

Tawn stood over him as he laid down. "Let me have look at that. Should be getting better by now."

She pulled the bandage back, revealing a pus-filled infected wound.

"Eww. That looks nasty. The antibiotics we have here aren't working."

Harris chuckled in pain. "So that's it, then. Faced down a thousand Earthers... taken out by a thousand cats. I want that as the epitaph on my grave marker by the way."

"Yeah, I think we're gonna have to take you to the Retreat. The doctors there can clear this up. Will give us a chance to poke around and look at the dome setup. We need to order you a new biosuit anyway."

"The Retreat? Really?"

Tawn smirked. "Scared your little cat incident will get out to the others? Well, don't worry about it. I commed the colonel yesterday while you were in the bunker. He already knows. And I asked him to spread the story around as it would probably be good for morale purposes. You know how we like to laugh at each other."

Harris glanced up. "Gee. Thanks."

"I help where I can."

"Oh, by the way, I made it to level four. What have you been told about Earth that's interesting?"

"We know where it is. We just don't have a way to get there."

Trish added, "We found out they have a complete ancestral database that goes back to the migration out here. My ancestors were from a place called England. That's where the city of Post London got its name. London was a city back on Earth. Tawn? Were you able to trace yours?"

Tawn returned a half-hearted frown. "Not really. We're made up of DNA from about a hundred fifty people, I'm told. The name Freely was given to me because there was supposedly a Freely among my donors. There were eighteen Freelys on the boat coming out here. I could be from any one of those. As to their origins, it seems we were spread around, although there were a couple from a place called Ireland, which was beside England."

Harris looked up. "So I'll probably find the same or similar with Gruberg?"

Tawn replied, "Well, I took the liberty of looking it up. There were no Grubergs listed on our ship. Had they been, they would likely have come from a country called Germany. I did find a few others, but you won't like the sound of it."

"Hit me with what you got."

"There were six Grubergs on the Earther ship. In the early years of the two colonies, before the Great War, there was some movement of families between the two systems. Not much, but some."

Harris pushed himself up while showing a scowl. "Wait. You trying to tell me I'm an Earther?"

Tawn shrugged. "Kind of looks that way."

Harris sat up fully. "That's... just not right. My people are Domers through and through."

Tawn again shrugged. "Sorry, I'm just going by what's in the records. No Grubergs on our ship."

Gandy came into the room. "What we talking about?"

Trish nodded toward Harris. "Mr. Gruberg's an Earther."

"What?"

"Tawn looked up the Grubergs in our Earth ship manifest. There were none, but there were six on the New Earth ship. Seems our leader is an Earther. You know, I always thought his eyes looked a little shifty."

Gandy sighed. "Don't listen to them, Mr. Gruberg. They're lying. I was just looking at the registry. A husband and wife Gruberg were on the *Enterprise*."

"*Enterprise*?"

"That was the name of the Earth ship that came to Domicile. Didn't they teach you that in history class?"

"Tawn? If he's telling the truth, you're in for a good beat-down when I'm back on my feet. Making me think I'm an Earther, that's just low."

Tawn chuckled. "Please, you would have done the same had you gotten there first and thought of it. And, Trish, thanks for piling on. That made it all the more believable."

Trish smirked at Harris. "I do what I can."

Harris growled. "That's it, then. You're fired as my first mate."

Trish laughed. "I think that title went away quite a while back. We're a team now. A team of equals."

Harris nodded. "Good. That means I don't have to pay you anymore."

Trish smiled. "Fine. But don't expect to get back the three and a half million credits of yours that I'm holding. There's no way I'm giving those back to an Earther."

The group erupted in chuckles and laughter as Sharvie walked through the door.

"What'd I miss."

Harris rolled his eyes. "They're making fun of the wounded."

"I'll fill you in later," said Trish. "Just having some fun at his expense."

Tawn stood. "Now that we're all here, what say we take a jump to the Retreat? His back is all infected. Looks pretty bad."

Two hours later, the *Bangor* was settling on a tarmac beside the great dome.

Two med-techs were waiting for Harris as the hatch opened. "We were told someone was suffering from cat-scratch fever?"

Harris looked up at Tawn as she stood in the doorway. "That beat-down is coming. You can count on it."

"I'll take that as a challenge then. Pistols at dawn?"

"What?"

Tawn shook her head. "We have to get you back so you can read up on some of our history. It used to be the chivalrous thing at one time to have a duel to defend one's honor. They would do this at dawn for whatever reason, with crude pistols."

Harris winced as the med-techs assisted him in stepping down from the hatch. "Pistols at dawn it is, then."

The colonel came out to greet them. "I have a surprise for you regulars. Inside the dome we have a gravity field running. You'll find it runs about 2 percent over standard gravity in there. Should be comfortable for you."

Trish stepped down. "I could actually live in something like that. This is oppressive though."

The group moved inside as Harris was escorted away for medical care.

A stump corporal joined the group. "Jess Montigue. I'll be giving you a tour this morning."

The colonel nodded. "Show them everything. I have work to tend to. We can all talk later."

As the colonel moved away, the corporal gestured toward a hallway. "We can start down here."

Trish said, "You look younger than the others."

Jess smiled. "I was the last series to come out of the lab before it was destroyed. I'm eight years younger than Miss Freely. Also have a couple extra genetic tweaks."

Trish nodded. "You look about twenty-five kilos lighter."

"Thanks for pointing that out," said Tawn.

Jess replied, "On average we were about twelve kilograms lighter than the first Biomarines. It has just as many drawbacks as it has advantages."

Jess stopped and pointed. "As you can see, the dome is completely open on the inside. This set of buildings to our left is housing. Housing covers a third of our floor space in here. This dome can house up to twenty-eight hundred Bios in its current configuration. And other than food it's completely sustainable.

"Waste products are recycled and reused or sold off for trade. Three fusion reactors provide energy. Any one of those can power this place by itself, at a reduced rate of course. Our water supply is from a well that sits atop a vast aquifer, and which is located right here inside the dome itself. We also have a much smaller backup well should anything happen to the main.

Jess continued to walk as he talked. "This section is all of the utilities I was just referring to. Power, water, recycling... they are all done here. And this next section is hydroponics and fish farms. We can grow enough to keep about a quarter of us fed for a year. I realize that leaves a lot to be desired, but we're working on improvements.

"Next we have our fabrication shops. We can manufacture just about everything we need right here. That's mechanical items by the way. All electronics, power systems, and items like the gravity generators have to come from Domicile. We're setting up supply warehouses to hold as many spares as we can."

Gandy said, "Sounds like you're preparing for war."

Jess stopped. "We have no doubt the Earthers will again wage war once they have their fleet replenished. We're just trying to prepare as best we can for that eventuality. This system is remote. Could be one of the first attacked once they've rolled through the truce worlds."

"So you really think the war is coming?"

"We're planning for it. If it doesn't happen, we'll still be prepared for normal living. Up here on the left we have our medical facilities. If you follow me we might even be able to see Mr. Gruberg. Lesser operations such as his are available for viewing."

After moving through a door in a white, sterilized-looking hall, the group was led to a viewing room. A dozen slugs and stumps were standing in front of a glass wall, swigging from beverages they had brought from the cafeteria.

"Hey! They're bringing him in!" a slug stated as she banged on the transparent wall with her fist. "Cat-man-do! Hahaha!"

Gandy shook his head as he whispered. "You Bios are brutal. He's in real pain in there."

Tawn chuckled. "That's not pain. He's been through pain before. This is an annoyance. Kind of like an itchy bug bite."

Harris was placed on a table and the wound area cleaned. A polymer spray was applied and heated to dry. A scalpel was run gently around the edge of the wound.

Trish winced. "They didn't give him any painkillers?"

Jess replied, "That would have happened when he first came in the door. The few minutes we've been walking has them in effect. I doubt he's feeling much of anything right now."

The edge of the cutout was grabbed with tweezers and the patch of infected skin pulled back.

Sharvie looked away as a stream of bodily fluids and pus ran down onto the small of his back. The surgeon brought over an irrigation and suction device. The wound area was thoroughly cleaned and vacuumed, followed by the use of a pressure injection system to push antibiotics into the entirety of the area. After looking over the wound to inspect his work, the doctor pulled a patch of synthetic skin from a tray, laid it atop the wound, and bonded it with an ultraviolet light.

Jess turned. "That's all. If you'll follow me we'll have a look at the cafeteria, followed by the entertainment area. We can grab a few beverages there if you like."

Trish said, "That's it? He's done?"

Jess nodded as he pulled up his shirt, pointing to several patches of his own. "The synth-skin works like a charm if the wound is cleaned properly. See these three discolored patches on my left rib cage? That's what it will look like in about five years. These used to be much larger. The natural skin will eventually grow in to replace it."

Trish frowned. "Those white patches are synth?"

Jess chuckled. "Most of us had at least one or two applied during the Great War. Some cover the facial grafts with makeup. Most don't care."

Jess poked at several of others. "Works great. No pain. And very durable."

The group proceeded to the cafeteria, followed by a short walk to the entertainment area.

Jess pointed: "We have a wide variety of beverages at the bar. Snacks are available over here. We have electronic, board, and card games over here. The far wall has a number of fully immersive simulators. And this section has a variety of video stations along with a very up-to-date and full library. For physical games we also have a gymnasium."

"There's hardly anyone in here," said Gandy.

Jess nodded. "Bios aren't normally big on entertainment during the normal daytime hours. The bar will fill up after hours. We're busy trying to build this place out. Once goals are met and this colony secured, you'll see this place come alive."

Tawn asked, "The layout of the other domes gonna be the same?"

"Mostly. One difference between here and dome two is the gymnasium will be swapped out for a combat training range."

Gandy tilted his head. "You can safely do that indoors?"

"Sure. You just dial the plasma output of your weapons down to a minimum and you can fight all day."

"No damage?"

"No damage, but don't mistake that for no pain. You take a hit and you definitely feel it. It's mostly set up for close quarters training, where we're clearing the deck of a ship or the street in a colony town. Suggestions have already been made to make it reconfigurable so we can practice an endless number of scenarios. Currently the options for that are limited."

"You have a control center for this place?" Sharvie asked.

Jess turned and nodded. "Follow me. That's back in the utilities section."

Tawn looked around as they walked. "You must have some areas dedicated to defense. I haven't seen any of those."

Jess stopped at the entrance to the utility area. "I'm apprehensive to show those to the regulars you have here with you. Please don't be offended. It's just that there are Earther spies who are regulars. There are no Earther spies who are Bios, that we know of."

Trish replied, "You don't have to worry about offending us. We've been around Miss Freely and Mr. Gruberg enough to know to ignore it."

Jess returned a half smile. "Good to know we can at times be tolerated. Now if you'll follow me up these steps... and out here onto the catwalk... looking down you can see our operations center. Virtually everything is controlled from here. As a redundancy we have another control room, although somewhat smaller, on the opposite side of the dome. If this center fails or is being overrun, we can still monitor and control everything from there."

A walk across the catwalk, down another set of stairs, and past two armed guards, had the group standing in the military command center. "As you can see, this area is still under construction. Over here will be your monitors for every type of sensor we have available.

"This section will be flight control and coordination should we have any aerial battles to be taken care of. This section will be for ground defense. This central area is for planning and ongoing operations. And over here communications."

Tawn said, "Looks like a well-thought-out center."

Jess nodded. "We *have* had some experience in these areas. Our officers had a lot to do with the final design and layout."

Jess pointed toward the door. "Now, if you don't mind, I've been instructed to leave you at the entertainment complex while you wait for Mr. Gruberg. He should be joining you within the hour."

Gandy pulled his head back. "He just had that procedure done."

Jess smiled as he walked. "The synth skin was a game changer when it was first introduced. Oh, and it only works on Bios. You regulars, your immune system has a high rejection rate. Has something to do with the synthetic DNA of the material nearly matching our own. He'll be tender in that spot for the duration of the normal underlying-tissue healing time, but he'll be ready to fight within the hour."

The four guests took a seat at the forty-meter-long bar. After perusing a drink menu for several minutes, beverage orders were placed.

"What'd each of you get?" asked Tawn.

Gandy said, "I'm trying the orange shrimp ale."

Sharvie returned a distorted face. "That sounds disgusting."

"Well, what are you having?"

"Frolic in the Park. It's one-third Mindian wine, which I like."

Trish said, "I thought for sure you'd get the Neuron Temple."

"That's non-alcoholic. Had it before. It's good. It's been a while though, so I thought I could use a little nip. How about you."

"Head Banger."

"Aren't those kind of strong?"

Trish nodded. "That way I only need one. Miss Freely?"

"Wretched Injection."

Trish laughed. "You planning to start a brawl? Didn't you say that was what you and your slug friends were doing before going to the brig that time?"

"We were. Don't think it will be an issue this time though. You three aren't as bad an influence as my friends were. Here's to new friends." A beverage was held up.

It was almost to the hour when Harris walked into the bar and the minor festivities came to an abrupt end.

"Colonel has feedback from the snipers. He sent in another team without telling us. I'm heading over to talk to him now."

Chapter 8

"Colonel? Did we do something wrong?"

"Not at all. You were unavailable and a decision was made before you came out here. You have the ability to contact us, but we can't contact you."

"What's happened?"

"I sent in a second team. We had the vehicles and personnel available. I wanted feedback. When they arrived, contact was made. After evaluating the situation, our snipers changed plans. Instead of targeting machine drivers, they took aim at the machines themselves. Their reasoning was that people could be quickly replaced. The machines require a run to New Earth for parts."

"Sounds like a better plan."

"It is. And it's being applied to all targets. Vehicles, mechanicals, basically anything that can be destroyed with a plasma round from a rifle is now on the priority list. They report it's a target-rich environment. Scans by the Earthers have yet to reveal their location. When the second team arrived, because of that feedback I gave the command for them to deploy. They had an accident though and are returning. We have two additional teams heading out tomorrow."

Harris said, "I'd like Tawn and me to be one of those teams."

"What are we supposed to do in the meantime?" asked Trish.

Harris shrugged. "Hang out at the bunker. See if you can advance."

"We could park there as a backup. You get spotted, we swoop in for a rescue."

Tawn shook her head. "We get spotted and there won't be a rescue. We have the gear to keep us from sight. It will be on us to use it correctly."

Gandy said, "That's means you'll be leaving Farker with us."

The stump looked down at his mechanical pet. "I guess it does. Hadn't considered that. But he'll be in good hands."

Harris turned back to face the colonel. "We'll be back here tomorrow at this time. Think you can hold the freighter until we get here?"

"If you're dead-set on doing this, it can be held."

Harris glanced at Tawn and received a nod. "We'll be here."

A return flight was made to Midelon. Seven hours after reentering the bunker complex, Harris emerged. The others were seated in the supply hut.

Tawn said, "Was wondering if you were gonna come out."

"That's some fascinating stuff. Looks like our people were warring with each other long before we came out here. So much for enlightenment."

"How far have you come on the timeline?"

"Through the Egyptian pharaohs. Just starting the Zhou Dynasty. Interesting. Who here is the farthest along?

Sharvie raised her hand. "I guess that would be me. I'm hitting the timeline at about 400 A.D. The Roman Empire is getting weak in the west and the Jin Dynasty was coming to an end in the east. I find it strange how history continues to repeat itself. It's almost like each new generation forgets the mistakes of the old."

Harris nodded. "I think that's what we're seeing here. We were winning the Great War, but the people were tired of fighting. Instead of pushing ahead and bringing it to an end, we pulled back, which puts us right where we are now."

Tawn chuckled. "Just shows that you have to finish the job if you want it to actually be done. And speaking of finishing... now that you're here we can eat."

"You waited for me? I kind of feel special now."

Tawn pointed. "Good. Get your special self over there and hand us some meals. After this, you and I need some serious rest before heading out to Eden. I plan on sleeping and lazying about all the way up until you're ready to leave."

Trish cleared her throat as she raised a hand. "Excuse me, but don't you think you need to give us some instructions as to what we should be doing when you're gone?"

Harris replied, "I thought we went over this. Just keep yourselves busy with going through Earth's history. Maybe you'll find something in there we can make use of."

"And if you don't come back?"

"Then head back and check with the colonel. If he's got nothing for you, then I suggest you go and try to live your lives as best you can. You have the credits to do so."

The following morning, Tawn and Harris were ready for the trip to Eden.

Harris said, "Farker is staying here with you. If you travel away, don't leave him anywhere or let anyone else take him. Are we clear on that?"

Trish nodded. "We won't let him out of our sight."

"Good. So here's the plan: twice a day you open a comm to the colonel to check in. Every three days you'll make a jump to Eden space. You'll come in just close enough to open a comm to our planet base. If we're available, we'll respond back through the ground relay system we have in place. If not, just leave a recording of any pertinent information. We'll do the same."

"No supplies?" said Trish. "No bringing anything down to you?"

Harris shook his head. "No contact except by comm. We have supplies for a couple months. Just keep yourselves safe and unseen."

The *Bangor* jumped to the Retreat before following the freighter to Eden. Again a trip was made to the planet's surface. A flight just above the ground had two new APCs and teams delivered to the forward base.

The freighter quickly departed after unloading its cargo. The *Bangor* settled into a ravine a half kilometer away. The active skin was switched to resemble the surroundings. After securing all systems, Tawn and Harris made their way to the APCs.

The other sniper team, also a slug and a spotter-stump, were waiting by their assigned vehicle.

Harris said, "We'll try to stay about two kilometers behind you on the way in. When we reach point Delta we'll be branching off. None of us knows where the others are posted. Just follow the instructions as given by the colonel and begin your mission."

"I worked with you once before, Mr. Gruberg. I believe it was on Landau II. You don't have to worry about us. We'll keep tight with the rules."

Harris looked intently at the slug. "Gennis?"

"Yes, sir."

"Glad to be back in the same outfit with you. Take care out there, and good hunting."

Tawn sat in the driver's seat of the APC. "Never did get behind the wheel of ours at Fireburg. It's been about six years since I drove one of these."

Harris smirked. "Eighteen hundred kilometers. You're gonna be sick of driving by the time we get there."

"Don't think so. You might be sick of my driving, but not me."

Harris shook his head. "Doubt it. I'll be back there strapped in and sleeping. Once I'm down I'm dead to the world. You could roll us over and I would probably never know."

Tawn put the vehicle in reverse and stomped on the gas. The tires spun, kicking up sand and dust. Seconds later, she threw the lever into "Drive." Again the big tires flipped sand in the air as the armored APC lurched forward. "I'll do my best to keep you from getting down, then."

The active suspension of the Morgan-made carrier translated an otherwise rough surface into a fairly smooth ride. An "honest" distance was maintained from the vehicle ahead. A bar dragging chains behind the vehicles left a track that would be difficult to detect from the air. Sensors told of empty skies above.

An hour into the journey, Tawn broke the silence. "You have any other good stories from the Corps?"

Harris took in a deep breath. "Something that you haven't heard? Give me a minute to think. If you have something in mind, spit it out."

Tawn scratched her forehead with a free hand. "Gennis back there mentioned Landau II. I was there about twelve years ago. Bloody mess that one was. We dropped in fifty Bios along with close to two thousand regulars. We were told to stop the twenty-eight hundred Earthers from crossing the Whichiachi River."

"The what?"

"Wichiachi. There was a two kilometer stretch that could be forded or easily used to construct a pontoon bridge. Ten clicks back from our side of the river was a supply depot with an artesian well. The Earthers wanted it. We weren't giving it up.

"The Earthers had the superior side of the river. We were better dug in."

Harris chuckled. "Foxholes?"

Tawn nodded. "With ion shields sitting up front. On most of them anyway. I was in a double with a stump. Ricker. He was hilarious, by the way. Made for a decent deployment on the days we weren't getting shot at. He could throw a fist-sized rock like nobody's business. Twice I saw him take out some unfortunate sap on the other side. The guy had a cannon for an arm."

"Narrow river?"

"About seventy-five meters directly in front of us. Anyway, we had several assaults where the Earthers made it to within meters of us. We repelled them all, but they kept trying. By the time they left we had cut their numbers by over half. We were down 40 percent ourselves."

"They just gave up?"

Tawn nodded. "Their CO called ours and asked if we'd allow transports to come get them. We did and they left."

Harris winced. "There were a lot of battles like that during that war. Our Earth history back there at the bunker points to some of the same."

Tawn was quiet.

"That was it?"

"Yep. You got anything?"

Harris rubbed the back of his neck. "Was on patrol once and was almost stampeded by a herd of boglers. My squad was cutting across this field with a small herd occupying a hill to our left. We didn't see the lone cow down to our right. When we cut between, the rest of them charged. Sandoval, he was our chief at the time, got caught out in the open.

"This seven hundred kilo bull charged right for him. I was just about to turn that bull into steaks when the chief swung his rifle out at it. The bull swerved, going just around him."

Tawn said, "You know, they say those boglers are on almost every inhabited planet now?"

Harris nodded. "All they do is eat and breed. They came from New Earth. At least that's what I was told. The Earthers killed off all their natural predators before shipping them off to other colonies. That massive herd on Farmingdale was from Earthers."

Tawn said, "I know where this is gonna lead, but have you ever had Earth beef? They have cattle farms on Domicile that specialize in raising them. Much more docile than boglers. Taste better too."

Harris shook his head. "Haven't had the pleasure. You thinking the beef or fish pack for lunch?" He stood and walked to the back of the cabin.

"Get me a fish. I've had about enough of the beef from the pacies food deliveries. Just doesn't taste right."

Harris chuckled. "Nobody told you?"

"What?"

"That's not beef. It's some veggie cram seasoned up to taste something like beef."

"Huh. That explains why I never feel full after eating one of their packs. Tell me we have standard issue MREs in here."

"We do. Bannis had his people pack them before the colonel picked them up."

"Finally, something I can sink my teeth into."

Harris checked the meals. "We have bogler steak, bogler ribs, bogler burgers, even a couple bogler brains."

"I never understood why you stumps liked that so much."

Harris shook his head. "Not me. Too spongy. We have sea biscuits, king buttel, cambrello, and squamish..."

"Cambrello. Those others leave you with fish-breath for most of the day."

"One cambrello meal and one bogler ribs, coming up."

A hundred kilometers turned into five hundred, and then to a thousand. Harris slept strapped to his bunk as Tawn entertained herself with Earth music she had loaded into her data store from the bunker archives. After jamming on the brakes the APC slid to a stop.

Tawn walked back, shaking Harris awake. "We got a problem."

Harris rubbed his eyes. "My turn already?"

"Nope. I think we lost Gennis and her spotter."

Harris unfastened four straps that had held him in place. "How?"

The truck was leaning hard forward. "Are we in a ditch?"

Tawn nodded. "About three meters in front of us is a crevasse. Runs out as far as the sensors can detect to either side and drops about five hundred meters straight down in front. Maybe thirty meters across."

"And you think Gennis and Jeld went into it?"

Tawn half scowled. "Should have sent out their blip about fifteen minutes ago. We got nothing."

Harris sat up. "How'd team one get across?"

Tawn shrugged. "They went well north of here. It must end at some point in that direction."

"So just turn us around and take us north."

"Might not be that easy."

"What's the issue?"

"We're on a 38 degree slope, three meters from the edge. We start backing up and we might just slide forward."

"Nothing to hook onto with the winch?"

Tawn shook her head. "We're on a sloped rock that's partially covered with dust and sand. I put on the brakes forty meters back as soon as I topped that crest. Skidded all the way to here. The winch has about thirty meters of cable on it."

Harris hopped down to the floor as he pulled on his helmet. The APC slid forward half a meter.

"Might want to keep any movement slow and deliberate."

Harris gently walked toward the back.

"Where you going?"

Harris nodded toward the rear hatch. "Out that door. If you wanna stay in here while we try to figure this out, you're more than welcome to. I'll be standing out there." Harris reached for the door.

Tawn said, "Before you hop out, you'll want to keep an eye on your footing. A slip could send you sliding down over that edge."

The hatch was opened. Harris carefully stepped out onto the sand-covered rock. "Not bad, but kind of eerie."

Tawn gently followed him out onto the steeply inclined ground. "Let's get back up top and have a look at the situation."

With Harris' first step he slipped and caught his balance. "OK ... gotta move slow."

The forty-meter trek up the hill took five minutes of careful climbing.

"How'd you even manage to get us stopped?" Harris asked.

"Luck. I hit the brakes just as we topped this rise. I guess the tires caught just enough. So how do we get her back up here?"

Harris surveyed the situation. "We need a spike. Set a spike in that rock and attach the winch to it."

Tawn waved her hand toward the APC. "You do know that beast weighs about six tons."

"And?"

"We have forty meters to pull it. This rock is not hard. Gonna need a long spike."

"We don't have to pull six tons. The truck will be doing that while the winch is running."

Tawn glanced down at the precariously positioned vehicle with an uneasy look. "That means one of us has to be driving it."

Harris nodded. "And who's the best driver here?"

"That would be me, but I'm not all too eager to get behind the wheel this time."

"You were supposed to say it was me. Give me that one little credit before I volunteer."

"Ah. OK. You're the best."

"Thank you. Now let's find us a spike."

Tawn placed her hands on her hips. "Gonna take two moves to get us back up here. That cable isn't gonna reach all the way."

Harris began the walk back down. "See that flat-ish spot about ten meters up? I say we put our first spike just above that and pull the APC up to there. After that we bring the spike up here."

Tawn nodded. "Sounds like a plan."

A steel support beam inside the APC was unbolted and carried to the first position. Harris held the beam at its base as Tawn pulled her Fox-40.

"Hold that steady down there. This may be rough until we get it started."

Harris glanced up. "Just don't miss. I'd rather not have my hand smashed."

Tawn half smiled. "Better you than me."

Tawn aimed the Fox down at the top of the beam and pulled trigger. A loud zap saw the metal beam dig a centimeter into the rock.

Harris nodded. "Good sign. Keep them coming."

With repeated low power plasma pulses, the steel spike was driven a full meter into the soft rock.

Harris stood. "That's gonna have to do it. We don't have anything longer without tearing that truck apart."

Tawn pointed. "Hop in while I hook us up."

Harris chuckled. "How about you hook us up and then I'll hop in."

"Guess that works too."

"Works much better for me. Let me know when you're ready."

Harris slipped twice as he carefully moved to the driver's side door, both times barely regaining his footing before continuing on.

Tawn called from around back. "Hooked up and tight."

Harris climbed in the cab, powering up the drive and putting the big machine in reverse.

Tawn said, "Take it slow and easy."

Harris looked over his shoulder. "Who's the best driver?"

Tawn nodded. "You are. At least from here to the top of the hill."

The first ten meters of climb passed without incident. A move of the spike to the top of the hill saw a repeat of the first section put into play.

Tawn worked the winch as she said, "These last dozen meters are the steepest. Just keep doing what you're doing and we should be golden."

With five meters to go, the tires of the APC spun when a thin piece of rock came loose from the hillside. The APC jerked and began to slide.

Tawn yelled, "Spike is coming out!"

"Well, get it back in!"

The APC began to slide down the hill, this time picking up speed, the tail end beginning to slide to the side. Harris turned the wheel, stomping on the accelerator. All four tires spun violently, spraying out sand and small bits of soft stone. The downward trajectory of the APC stopped. Slowly momentum reversed. Forty seconds later the armored truck sat on top of the hill.

Harris stepped out, taking in a deep breath. "Whoa. Can't say that was fun."

Tawn chuckled as she disconnected the loose beam and retracted the winch. "You are the best driver. And I'll let you be the best driver whenever you want."

Harris walked to the back to assist with the beam. "Let's just get this together and get back on the trail. This is gonna put us back half a day. And it's boiling out here."

Tawn nodded.

Chapter 9

A trek to the north saw the duo back on the path to their destination. Four further days of driving had them parking between two outcroppings. The skin coloring of the APC was set, gear packed, and the sniper and her spotter began a fifty kilometer hike toward Fireburg.

Harris said, "What do you think it's gonna look like?"

"A dome."

"I know that. I'm talking the rest of their operation."

"Vehicles moving dirt around? I don't know. The spot we chose has a free view of most of the mine pits. I'm sure there are plenty of targets."

Harris sighed. "Wish we could have talked to the other team."

"The relays are set. They have to be in their APC. We can check for a message when we get back. In the meantime we have some Earther equipment to destroy. You brought the blind cover, right?"

Harris nodded. "Three of them. We'll have a choice of color patterns depending on exactly how you want to position us."

"You bring the matching spray?"

"One can."

Tawn scowled. "Should have brought at least two. I told you two."

"I improvised with the other blind covers."

"Nice thought, but we only needed that base desert blind. The matching spray would let us change it if we need to. Next time bring exactly what I say."

Harris chuckled. "Didn't know I'd be working for such a hardass."

Tawn stopped. "It's called being a professional. You should try it sometime."

The hike ended as they came to a rise. Tawn dropped to her knees, crawling the last five meters to the top.

Harris asked, "Where you want it?"

Tawn pulled a scope from her pack. "Hang on while I check my angles. I want to set this up once. Especially since we only have one can of matching spray. Kind of keeps us in one spot."

"You aren't gonna let that go, are you?"

Tawn smirked. "You gave it to me. I'm just gonna keep giving it back. Hmm. See that spot about fifty meters to our left? Where that rock ledge drops off by a meter?"

"Yeah?"

"I think we set up right in that crease. Why don't you slither back down and head over. Wait at the base for me. Team one said 'target rich' and I think they were right."

Harris followed the order. Tawn joined him several minutes later. A short climb and then a crawl placed them at the selected spot.

Tawn opened Harris' pack, removing the standard desert-color blind and the can of matching spray. "I'll have this up in about five minutes. Stay down here. We're at our most vulnerable during this next few minutes."

Harris nodded and sat as the level four sniper ascended the final meters of the hill. The blind was unfolded and dragged behind her as she moved up the crease in the rock. Plastic posts gave it structure. Most of the can of matching spray had it blending in nicely with the surrounding rock. Tawn crawled back to Harris on her belly.

"We're set. Follow my path exactly. When I get you in the blind I'll be coming out to hide our tracks. You can sit tight until I come back. After that, we observe for a bit and then select our first target."

Harris followed as Tawn crawled up toward the blind. The spotter was delivered and the veteran sniper returned to clean up. Several minutes later, she slid up under the blind. "We're set."

A flap was opened and two scopes were raised.

Tawn said, "Just observe. Watch for habits and patterns. If you happen on equipment, try to determine what might be a weak point. We can discuss before selecting it as a target."

"You sure are cut and dried on this stuff."

"This is business. We follow the rules. We have to be patient. Success will come if we do those two things. Now, tell me what you see."

"I count a dozen diggers in that pit to the left. Center has eight. And the one to the right has two."

"Good. I concur. Give me your best truck count."

"I see three, four, and two, and five backed up at that hopper, so fourteen?"

"Right. Now list off any equipment or other targetable items they have out there. Ignore the hopper and the processing gear for the moment."

Harris panned the pits and the surrounding area. "I count five generator stations, three water stations, two tented areas that appear to be for personnel, and all the way to the right looks like a maintenance station."

"What about the eight watch towers? And that pool of parked vehicles. Then move up on the dome. Six watchtowers that we can see on this side. And down just by that north bay. That look like the nose of a fighter?"

Harris zoomed in. "Yeah. Guess I misunderstood what would be considered primary targets."

"We don't yet have primaries. This exercise will give us our complete target list. From there we'll divide them into four camps. Must haves—we keep that list to no more than four—primary, secondary, and finally the rest. We'll also be presented with targets of opportunity that aren't visible at the moment."

Harris said, "OK, hang on. I'll record these to my data store. We can reference that when we're ready to categorize."

Tawn shook her head. "Bad idea. If we get captured we don't want to have anything that will tell them which targets to best protect. From here on this is a memory game. We look. We discuss."

Harris nodded. "Got it."

Over the several hours that followed a list was developed and prioritized. A conveyor motor that powered a belt pulling ore from the giant hopper would be first. Next would be a fusion reactor powering a maintenance tent. Following that, taking out the nose spike on the fighter that sat parked in the north bay would require a trick shot by Tawn. The spike was integral to the fighter's sensor set, making it less useful during a search for the snipers.

Tawn opened the flap.

Harris asked, "Would any of these be better at night?"

Tawn shook her head. "Not unless you want them coming right for us. These rifles are good at suppressing the beam that usually points back to where they were fired from. That effect is really good during the day, not nearly so at night. With the right equipment they could pinpoint our location."

"During Helm, the snipers were shooting at night."

"And you knew right where the fire was coming from. Is that concept too hard for your pea-brain to fathom?"

Harris chuckled. "OK. Point taken."

"Dream of day, dead of night. Used to be our saying."

Harris checked his wrist. "We have two hours of daylight. Want to scratch off those four ultimate targets?"

Tawn sighed. "We do one. After that, we give things an hour to settle. If all looks good, we'll take on target two at that time."

Harris nodded as he looked through his scope. "Conveyor motor... we have a truck interrupting your line of sight about every forty seconds. Various personnel walking around, but they don't look to be in the way."

Tawn said, "See that control box? I'll hit that first and follow up with the motor casing. With luck we'll get it to crack where we can damage the windings with a follow-on shot."

"Wouldn't it be better to hit it while it's running? If it cracks under load I would expect more damage."

Tawn shook her head. "Not while powered. Our plasma round will have about a third less impact with the EM field surrounding that motor while its running. At stop is better."

"They teach you that in sniper training?"

"Actually they did. It's not just about hitting the target. It's about hitting it at the moment when you can effect maximum damage."

"Won't you have the same issue with that control box?"

"Those control circuits don't have much of an EM field. That big spinning motor does. And yes, those are things we were taught in sniper school."

Harris got the rhythm of the trucks as they passed. "Coming up... and clear. You have the box sighted?"

"In the hairs. Next opening is a go."

Harris nodded. "OK. Fifteen seconds... ten... five... truck is passing. Clear."

A plasma round left the sniper rifle with a whump. A puff of dust was kicked up in front of the blind. Twelve hundred forty-two meters away, a motor control box exploded, shattering into hundreds of pieces. The conveyor slowed to a stop, sending Earther workers scrambling to figure out what had happened.

Three successive shots saw the motor casing split, with a final hit sending wires from the winding out into the open Eden air.

Tawn smiled. "Scratch one conveyor."

"So we're done for an hour?"

Tawn gave a short laugh. "Hardly. See all that scramble down there? This is where we look for our targets of opportunity. If we can get them to reveal any equipment that is vital for a repair we take it out as well."

Harris scanned the field. "Wait... one of the diggers just went down. I see smoke coming from a fuel tank. We have flame and... whoa. Scratch one digger. That thing is a fireball."

"Good. Now bring your focus back here. I'm thinking that pull cart with what looks like welding gear might be just what we're looking for."

Harris nodded. "Got it. Nothing but personnel around it. No vehicles moving."

A pair of whumps saw an equipment cart explode and then burst into flames.

Harris grinned. "Beautiful work. What's next?"

"Now we sit back and wait for things to settle."

Harris winced. "You're kidding, right? The place is in chaos. Strike when it's hot."

Tawn shook her head. "Nope. At the moment that could be equipment failures."

"Nobody is buying that. Motors don't just explode."

"Not true. These are extreme conditions out here. Now it's true they are not likely to buy it, but we need it to be a possibility. Otherwise their efforts to find and stop us will go full bore. Look at each of those watchtowers. Tell me what you see the occupants doing."

Harris looked through his scope. "They're looking out at the hills."

"Precisely. How about any guards on the ground?"

"Uh... they're watching the chaos."

Tawn reached up, pulling the flap of the blind closed. "Once they're certain it's snipers they'll have patrols walking all of these hills. At the moment their priority will be searching for spies. We're hidden pretty good out here, but not if they walk up to us."

"So when they send out patrols we leave?"

"Only if they appear to be mobilizing a large part of their force for that. You have to keep in mind we aren't all that stealthy when we're in the open. With what we just did they'll send out a few patrols. If we kept going they'd send out everyone."

"Won't they eventually do that anyway?"

"Probably."

Then I would say we open up on everything we can and then leave. We'll go hide out in the APC for a couple days and then come back."

Harris opened the flap.

"What are you looking for?" Tawn asked.

"That fighter. Sure wish we had an angle looking into that bay. The fighter hasn't moved, by the way. If it was me down there, I'd have it in the air."

"You see any patrols forming up down there?"

"Let's see... one—no, two."

Tawn reached up, flipping the flap shut. "Good. Then we wait. Remember I told you this sniper game is about being patient. Well, this is where the patience comes in. Relax. I have an alert set for us in an hour."

"What are we supposed to do in the meantime?"

Tawn shook her head. "Can you not self entertain for an hour? What are you, five years old?"

Harris frowned. "Last time you said I was twelve. So I'm slipping back now?"

"Are you planning to be a chatterbug this entire deployment?"

Harris chuckled. "Does that irritate you?"

Tawn sighed. "I'm not gonna answer that. Just keep yourself busy for a while. Count your fingers and toes or something."

The hour passed without further conversation.

Harris sat up as the alert sounded. "Thank goodness. Thought I was gonna die of boredom."

"This is what being a sniper is. Very short periods of extreme stimuli followed by long periods of reflection. You should be happy with our current schedule. If things get too active out there, we might just have to sit out for a day."

Harris scoffed. "Can I at least observe during our downtime?"

"No. That flap is closed for a purpose. When open it defines a dark spot to a lookout or a scout, which draws attention."

Harris rolled his eyes. "Glad I was never a great shot then. Had they sent me to sniper school I'd have had to shoot off my foot or something to get out."

"Other than the hike in and out, you don't need your foot. That wouldn't disqualify you."

"Well, fine then. I'd shoot off my trigger hand. No way I could do this full time."

As the sun got low in the sky, Tawn reached up and opened the flap. "I'd say things are settling down. The conveyor is down, but there's a crew there working it over. Looks like they got another motor. Doesn't look the same though. Must be improvising."

Harris added, "That digger has been pulled out of the pit. There's another already in its place."

"They have a new maintenance cart out there as well."

"Next on the target list is the fusion reactor by the maintenance tent. After that we have the sensor on the nose of that fighter."

Tawn looked over the maintenance cart as Harris eyed the fusion reactor. "How we looking with that next target?"

"Not good. They have a truck parked right in our line-of-sight. Let's move on the fighter. We're clear on the fighter."

Tawn nodded. "Good. Give me a minute to set up this cart. Let me know if anything changes with the fighter."

Harris reached out, grabbing Tawn by the shoulder. "Wait. Bax just walked out of the dome."

"How do you know it's her?"

"Who else has a red, vanity, environmental suit? That has to be her."

Tawn sighed. "Doesn't matter. She's not a priority."

"How you figure?"

"We're not targeting people, for one. Other than that, we still don't know who she works for. If it is the DDI, we are killing off one of our best agents."

Harris rolled his eyes. "Just can't get rid of her, can we."

Tawn looked back through her scope. "Let's focus on the task at hand, shall we?"

The maintenance cart was targeted. A *whump* was followed by a small explosion as the power source was compromised by an invisible plasma round. Next was the fighter. In an instant the protruding nose sensor fractured and fell to the ground in pieces. Tawn reached up and closed the flap.

"I thought we were supposed to observe the aftermath?"

Tawn nodded. "We will. Give it five for them to get it in gear."

"I'd like to see what Red does down there."

"You'll see in five minutes."

Harris sat back. "Definitely wasn't cut out to be a sniper."

Tawn laughed. "You're such a baby. I thought stumps were tough, thought they could take it. You're whining like a little puppy who has to pee."

"Wish Farker were here. He's at least pleasant to talk to, even if all he does is grin at you."

The five minutes ticked by slowly.

Tawn reached up, flipping open the flap. "Let's see what we have. Activity around the strike sites. No sign of patrols forming up. I think we're good."

"Bax went back inside."

The next two days saw the targeting slow to every fourth hour. On the third day, supplies pointed toward a visit to the APC. The blind was taken down. They made the fifty kilometer trek under the added cover of darkness.

Chapter 10

Harris was the first into the back of the armored carrier. "Home at last."

Tawn followed, sealing the hatch before adjusting the temperature to a more tolerable level.

Harris removed his helmet. "Ah. Feels good to breath the natural air. Never liked the forced air in those suits."

"Keep that helmet handy. If we get visitors, you'll want to snap that on in a hurry."

Harris chuckled. "I've done this before you know."

"Just saying. We all need that reminder at times."

Harris sat in the driver's seat, powering up the comm console. "We have a message from the other team."

"Play it."

"This is Alpha. Welcome back to Eden. Since your arrival we've dropped our targeting to two per day. Would suggest you do the same. I've also recommended to the colonel that no more teams are necessary. We had their production down 80 percent in our first week. Since that time we have knocked off another 10. Your addition got a shot at that conveyor that we didn't have. Nice options by the way.

"So we've been in contact with the base. Sorry to hear about the loss of gamma. I've put in a recommendation to the colonel that we rotate teams in and out every two weeks. That will keep us fresh and well supplied at all times.

"We noticed you took a shot at the fighter sensor. Just so you know, the four fighters in that bay are all out of commission. Those were our first priority. They keep their ships up in the destroyer bays above now. Haven't sent anyone out after us either.

"On that note, we believe they are searching their ranks for spies. They've sent repeated patrols out to twelve hundred meters. If you're within that distance, I would suggest moving out to at least fifteen hundred. Might take an extra shot on a target, but not a show stopper. Anyway, this message was delivered at fourteen hundred standard time. We'll be heading out at sixteen hundred. If you catch us before then, give us a comm."

Harris checked for the time. "Uh. Just missed them by forty minutes."

"Looks like you get an early release gift. Only two weeks and you're out."

Harris nodded as he stood. "Good. Forgot how much I despised this furnace of a planet. Now, if you'll excuse me I'll be changing out my undergarments and getting a shower."

Tawn nodded. "Have at it. I'll post up our response message and file a report back to base. We'll be heading out in four hours, so enjoy being clean while you've got it."

Harris scowled as he removed the breastplate of the suit. "Ugh. I smell the stench already. You never feel uncomfortable in these things until you start to take them off."

Tawn waved her hand. "Just hurry up and get it in that sanitation box. The filtration system on this rig is good, but not that good."

Twenty minutes later, Harris emerged. "That felt great. I feel Human again."

Tawn shook her head. "Well, act like a Human and put some clothes on."

Harris pulled a fresh set of undergarments from his locker. He then stretched out on his bunk.

Tawn stood, walking back to the small shower, pulling a curtain across for privacy.

Harris said, "Had some good times camping in these APCs. Nothing like sleeping in a bunk with a military mattress. Especially when you've been dumped on some empty planet with about two dozen others. Kind of gives you that feeling of home."

Tawn shook her head as she stepped into the shower. "You're an odd bird sometimes. Entertaining, but odd."

The sound of a door closing brought the familiar hum of a sonic shower. Ten minutes later, Tawn emerged, dressed, and put on her environmental suit.

Harris chuckled. "How can you stand to put that right back on?"

"I'm clean. And I like to be prepared. If an Earther comes knocking at that door I don't want to be running around in my skivvies. I'll be pulling this Fox and taking the heat to them outside. Now, what will you have? We need to eat before we head back out."

"How many bogler ribs do we have left?"

"Two."

Harris scowled. "And we have eleven days left? This is turning out to be a harsh deployment."

Tawn laughed. "Harsh, yeah. As you lay back on your mattress in your underwear. Now, which one you want?"

Harris sighed. "Give me the bogler burger. I know I have to eat at least a few of them before we get relieved, so it might as well be now."

The meals were had, rest was taken, and a final report sent back to the main base. Two hours later, Harris suited up, stuffed his pack with supplies, and followed Tawn out into the heat. The fifty kilometer trek took nine hours.

Tawn stretched out her arm as they approached the previous hideaway. "Hold up. We have company. Over behind that dune."

A short jog had the sniper team out of sight.

Harris said, "Don't like the fact they found that place. Thought we cleaned it up pretty good."

"We did. Not sure why they've stopped there."

"If I was them I'd have laid out a line-of-sight to every hilltop surrounding this place. Forget checking ravines. Focus on where you can be seen from."

Tawn nodded. "Might be just what they're doing. They were on our hill, but not at our spot. Might just be a patrol."

"Time to head back to the fifteen hundred meter mark like team one suggested?"

"I think so. While you were napping I pegged two such spots. One looked perfect. High angle. Wide view. Good incline to come up and down from the backside."

"Sounds good. Let's go."

Tawn shook her head. "Not going that way. I don't like perfect. That's gonna be one of the first places a patrol squad will be sent should they decide to go out that far. We're taking position two."

Harris gestured with his arm. "Lead the way."

A forty minute walk had the team coming up on the new location.

Tawn crawled to the top of the ridge first. "Hmm. That's not good."

"What?"

Tawn nodded her head toward the previous hill. "That look like they're setting up camp?"

Harris peered through his spotter scope. "It does. Looks like we made the move at the right time."

Tawn scanned the other hilltops. "We've got more company. There's a squad straight out. And one to the left. Correct that, three to the left. Looks like every half kilometer at the thousand meter mark. We may not be able to make team one's quota of two targets per day. This just got a lot more dangerous for us."

"We could just pick them off from here. Heck, I could even hit some of those."

Tawn shook her head. "No personnel. They would flood these hills. Probably why they haven't already done so."

"Where we putting the blind?"

Tawn glanced to either side. "This as good a spot as any. Kind of on a mild divot. We put it up and fill in sand around it and she'll flatten out nicely."

Harris reached back for his pack.

"Stop!"

"What happened?"

"You happened, you moron. Bring your arm back around slowly, slide back over that hill edge. Then you can empty your pack. Always do the minimum when you're in direct line-of-sight."

"Got it. Won't happen again."

The blind was pieced together and moved into place. Scoops of sand were pushed into place with a makeshift shovel. A full can of matching spray saw a blind that appeared to be nothing more than a sand hump.

Harris said, "Can hardly see it from two meters away. You know your blinds."

Tawn nodded. "Yeah. Now shut up and get inside. Time for some observation."

Harris again pulled his scope. "View from the other hill was better."

"We only need two targets a day now."

"The conveyor is running again."

Tawn nodded. "Looks like you just found our first."

A voice came from behind the blind. "Hey... idiots. You in there?"

Tawn's eyes grew wide. "Bax?"

"Yeah. Slide back out here. We need to talk."

Tawn emerged with her Fox-40 aimed at her former boss.

Bax waved. "Here, back over the hill."

Harris followed on his belly.

Tawn asked, "How'd you know we were here?"

"Didn't know exactly. Just the area. only a dozen hilltops out this far can see that operation. You're on the second one I visited. Got your coordinates from the colonel. He was reluctant, but my CO talked him into it."

Harris shook his head. "What's going on? Who are you with?"

Bax nodded toward the bottom of the hill. I have two friends with me, but don't worry. They're on our side."

Harris scoffed. "And what side is our side?"

"Domicile, you idiot. I risked coming out here to tell you there's a big sweep coming tomorrow. Every hilltop within five clicks of that mine will be poked, prodded, and photographed. After the sweep, hi-res images will be taken from the top of the dome on a daily basis. If any spot shows more than a two or three centimeter change, they'll be sending out a patrol to check it."

Tawn winced. "Five kilometers. Won't be able to hit jack from there."

Bax nodded. "You'll have to make your blind collapsible. Pop it up to take your shots and keep it down for the remainder. Not ideal, but it should buy you more time. You know where the motorpool tent is?"

"Near the south dome entrance?" replied Harris.

"Yes. Wait about ten minutes after you take a shot. If you see a squad forming up by that tent, you better haul ass. They're coming this way."

"Why are you doing this?" Harris asked.

Bax laughed as she pulled him in for an awkward hug. "Because I'm on your side, dingbat. You destroying my mine gave me the opportunity to get in tight with the general running this operation. I've had him chasing spies for weeks now. They've executed sixteen of their own people. I'm starting to run out of easy targets. My team is the best at planting evidence."

Harris pushed back. "Please don't do that again."

Tawn said, "You're telling us this sniping has been a success because you're misleading the Earthers?"

Bax smiled. "I seem to be an expert at manipulating people, but I guess you two already knew that. Anyway, I'm making a small fortune off those conveyor motors. Feel free to take out as many of those as you like."

"Tawn had you in her sights the other day," said Harris. "Could have taken you out, but I talked her out of it."

"You did no such thing. I told you popping personnel was outside our mission scope. You grumbled."

Harris looked at Bax. "See what a sensitive person I have to put up with? Some people just don't have the temperament to be snipers. Not sure how she made it."

Tawn sighed. "Are you done living up to the stereotype she's already pegged us with?"

Bax said, "You two can sort this out on your own. Remember, tomorrow morning comes a big sweep. You best be far away by then."

Tawn asked, "Hey, you know what time of day they'll be snapping their pics?"

"Wish I did. They've held that close. Might even be planning to do it every hour for all I know. They said once a day, but that could be misinformation. Take care of yourselves out here and maybe I'll buy you both a drink sometime when we're back home."

Bax scurried down the hill to her waiting associates. The three spies hurried off into the dunes.

Tawn turned back toward the blind. "Come on, we've gotta move quick."

"Where we going?"

Tawn slithered into the blind, opened the flap, and held up her rifle. "First I'm taking out that motor. Next we're packing up and hustling back to the APC. We have team one's last broadcast and their coordinates. We'll have to get there before tomorrow to warn them."

Tawn took her shot. Harris slid out the back of the blind before collapsing it and pulling it from its sand base. Once over the edge of the hill, he began to break it down as he walked toward the bottom. Tawn cleaned up their tracks.

"Hurry it up. We need to be running."

"Doesn't that increase our visibility from above?"

"It does, but we'll have to live with it."

Harris slid the folded-up blind into his pack, slung it over his shoulder and cinched it tight. "Good to go."

The fifty kilometers was covered in eight hours. The APC was powered up before the duo sped off toward the northern coordinates. A twelve hour run placed the vehicle at team one's base camp.

Tawn jumped out. "Meathead, get a move on. We've got a lot of ground to cover."

Harris stepped out onto the sun bleached sand. "You lead, I'll follow. Just keep in mind we have to make the same trip coming back."

Tawn shook her head. "We only need to get past the five kilometer mark going out. We make that and we can slow our pace the rest of the way."

Progress over the dunes and sand covered rocks went as fast as could be expected. The Eden sun was just above the horizon and rising when the target coordinates were reached.

Tawn crawled to the top of the most likely peak, turning back to whisper to Harris. "Don't see them."

Harris replied in a hushed voice: "Why are we whispering?"

Tawn chuckled before responding with her normal voice: "OK. I guess we don't have to."

Harris yelled out: "Tanger! Costa!"

Three meters in front of Tawn, the ground moved. "Make a move and you get blasted."

Tawn said, "Relax, it's team beta. We're coming to pull you out. We have news."

"Awful lot of activity down there today."

"They're coming to look for us. You need to pull back your blind and clean your area. We need to go. They have plans to scour every square meter out to five kilometers. All that activity is coming this way. Nice blind, by the way."

Connie Tanger was the first to slither out. Emma Costa collapsed the blind and pulled it behind herself as she raked over any semblance of tracks.

"Where'd you get this info?"

"One of our spies down there in the complex. They're planning a sweep of all the high points surrounding the dome."

Connie pulled her scope and turned. "I'm not seeing anything that looks remotely like that. The activity I mentioned is mining related. They have twice the personnel out there as usual. I'm assuming that was you who took out the conveyor motor yesterday. Have a look. It's already back up and running."

Tawn held the scope up to her eye as she looked just over the top of the ridge. "She did it again, Harris. Have a look."

"No scout patrols. And ore is moving through that plant."

Tawn shook her head. "All she did was scare us off that ridge."

Harris removed his pack and dug inside each of the outer pockets, pulling out a tracking bug. "She worked us. And now she knows where you are too. Must have slipped it in with that weird hug."

Tawn let out a long sigh. "And she knows where our base camps are. Come on. We have to get back."

Harris asked, "What do we do with this thing?"

Tawn took it from his hand and dropped it on the ground. She pulled her Fox-40, aimed, and vaporized the tiny tracker.

"Let's go."

The two sniper teams moved at the fastest pace possible. The trek back took six hours.

As the teams moved within three kilometers, they came to an abrupt halt. There, hovering a hundred meters above their two APCs, was a large Earther ship.

Tawn gestured for the others behind her. "Get down!"

Harris crawled up beside her as she peered over the crest of a dune. "Bax?"

Tawn shook her head. "Don't know. They're just sitting there."

Harris turned, scanning the horizon. "Wait... I show another of those at forty kilos. And another back this way at the same distance."

Emma Costa moved up beside them. "I've seen one of those before. It's a transport. Carries about fifteen hundred soldiers. Was a new ship just as the war ended."

Harris nodded. "This is the sweep Bax was talking about. I'll bet anyone a hundred credits those ships all converge on that five kilometer mark. They plan on surrounding that mine and then working their way in."

Emma replied, "I would go with that. Anyone attempting to run would be driven back toward the mine."

Each of the ships began to move at once. The two sniper teams watched intently as the ring of Earther transports moved in, encircling Fireburg.

Chapter 11

Harris was the first to arrive at the APCs. "They look intact. I think that hover was just a staging point."

Tawn replied, "You know what this means... Bax was telling us the truth."

"And yet she slipped that tracker on us. It was that awkward hug she threw on me. She stuffed it into my pack."

Tawn sighed as she stepped up into the APC. "She had to know we'd find it."

"Yeah, but not before revealing our base camp. And we led her right to team one." Harris pulled the hatch shut.

Tawn walked to the front of the cabin. "We have an incoming message from the main base camp. It's live. This is team beta..."

"Major Hughes here. Was sorry to hear about gamma. The location of that crevasse has been updated on our maps. I have two new units heading your way. Do you have any strategic updates for us?"

"We do," said Tawn. "Alpha has been able to halt production on their own. Our addition along with these other two teams will be more than enough personnel to accomplish our goals here. At the moment the Earthers are flooding the perimeter of that mine out to about five kilometers. When their search is complete we plan to return.

"All teams should also be advised that the Earthers will be taking hi-res photos of the area and will be doing daily comparisons for any differences. Blinds should be flat to the terrain unless under immediate use. Patrols will be sent out to investigate any anomalies."

The major nodded. "Good to know. Is anyone in need of supplies?"

"Alpha mentioned they are starting to run low. I would suggest they stay a few hours with the new teams before allowing them to deploy. Following that, alpha should return home."

"I see. I welcome that kind of feedback, Miss Freely, but I can't promise that will happen."

"As I just reported, two teams can more than handle the mission here. Any additional personnel increase the risk of us being discovered. I would recommend two teams max."

"Consider your request taken under advisement. What is your current deployment schedule?"

"With the commotion today, we're staying away. Tonight we'll redeploy. Probably on a two day rotation with four to six hours at the vehicle. We have several targets we can hit that stop all production. Our inside source says they're pinning most of the damage on Earthers who are subsequently being executed for it. They want to suspect snipers, but so far have no evidence."

The major nodded. "I'll pass all this back to the colonel. In the meantime, keep your heads down and do exactly what you're doing. Expect a message with further instructions by the time the new units arrive."

Harris stood. "I'm heading next door to check on supplies. We have food for another five weeks."

Tawn followed. A knock on the rear hatch had the alpha APC open.

Harris asked, "What supplies are you in need of?"

"Matching spray. And maybe a few days food. That will give us another week before we have to head back."

Harris replied, "I can give you three cans of match and a week's rations."

"Fair enough. Any suggestions for a new deployment location?"

"Can you pull up a map?"

Emma complied. "Anywhere but over here. Dome blocks too many of the critical targets."

Tawn stood looking over her shoulder. "How about this hill? One of us here and the other down at this one. It's a twelve hour drive around to this location. Sixteen to this one."

Emma nodded. "This far one looks good. Will give us a new set of targets as compared to being up north."

"That hill sits low. You may not have an angle on the diggers in these two pits."

"Sounds like something you'll have to cover then."

Harris asked, "You ever see an unusual figure walking around down there with red boots?"

"Yes. Was wondering the significance of those."

"That's our spy. Try not to shoot her."

"We'll do our best."

Tawn moved back toward the hatch. "I guess that's it, then. Will meet you back here in a week. Could be your time to head home."

Emma shook her head. "Not needed. New supplies will keep us going for as long as it takes."

Harris said, "A swap to back home means you get to train new teams, as well as consult on strategies."

Emma laughed. "Big whoop. Would rather be out here in this scalding heat where the action is."

Tawn smiled. "Hard to give up, isn't it?"

"It's what we know. Back home we struggle to just be normal. Even at the Retreat. Give us a fight and we're as happy as one could be."

Goodbyes were exchanged and the two armored vehicles parted ways.

As Tawn drove she made conversation. "Those two aren't much different from us."

"How you figure?"

"Would rather be out here fighting for the cause than back home building a life."

Harris chuckled. "I'll tell you where I'd rather be: in a bath at the hotel on Chicago Port with a room service attendant bringing me plates from the Emporium Buffet."

"I could have guessed that exact scenario. Had I left you to your vices back there you'd probably tip the scales at three hundred kilos by now. You'd probably be sitting in that tub you just mentioned, licking the rib sauce off your fingers."

Harris stood.

"What'cha doing?"

"Getting one of my last rib meals. Was hoping to save them for something special, like another conveyor motor kill or something. But you've got me all hungry now."

After heating, Harris attempted to eat his ribs as Tawn drove. While taking his first chomp, a hard swerve of the APC striped sauce across the outside of his cheek.

"Was that necessary?"

Tawn chuckled. "I call it a morale booster. Good to keep the troops entertained when they're performing menial tasks."

"Well, please stop. You're wasting vital sauce."

Tawn laughed. "Vital?"

"Yes. Vital to my enjoyment of this meal. And unless you want me to be a miserable sod and a bother for the next week I'd suggest you let me eat without purposeful incident."

Tawn sighed. "Very well. Have at your precious ribs."

Harris' eyes rolled back in his head as he took a chunk of meat off the bone in his hand. "Mmm, that's a taste I don't think I'll ever tire of."

Tawn shook her head. "You're a strange bird, Harris."

"Just how I was built, that's all. My DNA donors must have been rib people."

"Not sure that's something that gets passed on with DNA."

Harris took another chew. "How else would you explain it, then?"

Tawn frowned. "Fine, you can have it as an inherited trait if you want. Don't think anyone has interest in disputing that."

The APC rolled up on banks, climbed dunes and overcame rocks before pulling to a stop after a twelve and a half hour run. "Looks like a good spot."

Harris checked the external camera views. "I'd say so."

They packed their gear and set out on their fifty kilometer trek toward Fireburg again. As the duo reached the five kilometer mark, Tawn scrambled up a dune to high ground.

"What are we looking for?"

"Anything that moves or looks Human. Looks clean—wait. Check that... at three o'clock. Meter-high post beside that rock."

"Got it. What do you think it is?"

"Some kind of sensor. I wonder if these hills are full of them now. Get out your scanner."

"What are we looking for?"

"Any type of transmission signal. If that's a sensor it's probably reporting information back to the dome."

Harris pulled the scan device from his pack. "How do we get around it?"

"Not sure we can. You get anything off it?"

"Yeah. Earther comm channel."

Tawn zoomed in with her scope. "Definitely a camera. I'd say line-of-sight limited."

"If I had Farker here we could crack into that comm and see what they're sending."

Tawn looked over her shoulder. "See that bluff back there about a kilometer?"

"The dark rock?"

"Yep. We need to get up there. We're gonna have to spend some time identifying every camera they placed out here. We do that and we might be able to pick a path in closer and find us a hill to shoot from. I have to believe there's blind spots out there."

Harris returned the scope to his pack. "Lead the way."

A twenty minute jog, followed by a precarious climb up the far side of the ridge, saw the two Biomarines sliding on their bellies up to the edge.

"I just thought of something," said Tawn.

"You couldn't go before we left the truck?"

"No, you idiot. Pull out that scanner. You should be able to identify every camera out there. They would all be broadcasting."

Harris nodded. "Good thinking. Let's see... wow. On wide-field I count forty-two comm broadcasts within five kilometers of every direction. Just about every kilometer. Almost in a grid pattern except they're all on hilltops."

"Anything look like a dead zone?"

"Give me a sec. I'll see if I can add line-of-sight to the mappings."

Harris programmed the scanner while Tawn looked over the landscape with her scope. "No activity, just those cameras. Patrols must have finished their searches."

"Hmm. Got it. That was easier than I thought. Areas in red are covered by a camera. The green are hilltops with a view of the mines."

"Let me see." Tawn studied the map. "Crap. One spot. Four hundred fifty meters from the mines. That's cutting it way close."

Harris asked, "We have a way in?"

Tawn sighed. "Straight up through here."

"If you're not comfortable, we can move further down and do this exercise again."

"It's not that," Tawn replied. "We still have to deal with them snapping pics every day. We get spotted in that close and they'll be all over us before we can run."

"Simple then. We don't get caught. I brought three cans of matching spray this time. You should be able to blend our blind right in."

Tawn nodded. "Let's go then. Before I talk myself out of it."

Harris followed the slug down the steep terrain of the back of the ridge. The map from the scanner was used to navigate their way forward.

"Four hundred fifty meters... this is gonna be a picnic for you."

Tawn half smiled. "Let's hope so. Should have a clean shot at that conveyor motor. It's been running for two days now."

As they crawled up the back side of the close hill, a ship began to descend from above them.

"Crap. Pull that blind over us."

Harris reached into his pack, retrieving the blind and unfolding it.

Tawn said, "Just pull it over us. We don't have time to spray it."

The immense ship came down to hover just above the crown of the dome. A dozen winch cables were dropped from the ship down through an opened door in the crown.

Tawn shook her head. "That's an ore pick-up."

Harris pulled his scope and zoomed in. "How good a shot are you?"

"What are you proposing?"

"We're just under five hundred meters to the mine edge. Another five hundred across to the dome, and then a kilometer to the crown. You think you can hit a cable from almost two kilometers?"

Tawn thought for a moment. "Hmm. I'll take that as a challenge."

"You wait until they have whatever container they're picking up almost up to that ship and then pop that cable. Could cause a real mess down below."

"I like the sound of that."

"You have a shot from right where we're at?"

Tawn stared through her scope. "I believe I do."

Harris chuckled. "Wish I could see inside that dome. That would be an entertaining vid to send back to the Retreat."

"Check the grounds for me. Make sure there won't be any surprises when I'm ready for the shot."

"OK, but wait for me to finish. I want to watch this."

"You've got thirty seconds."

Harris scanned the areas between their hideaway and the Earther ore freighter. "Looks clean. I'm ready when you are."

"See that tightened cable? First one is coming up."

"I feel like I'm spotting at some range competition."

"Give me quiet..."

A fifty by ten by twenty meter container lifted out of the top of the dome. Tawn took her best aim. The cable snapped and the container dropped back through the open whole.

Harris nodded as he gazed through his spotter scope. "Nice."

"Wasn't me. Never pulled the trigger."

Harris glared. "You let Emma steal the shot?"

"That, or it just snapped on its own."

"No. That cable was a beast. Could have held three times that without issue."

Tawn smirked. "Since when are you a shipping expert?"

"Had a couple early deployments as the defense squad on a freighter similar to that. Those hoist cables are meaty suckers. Hey... looks like you get a second chance. Another one just tightened."

Tawn took aim.

Harris said, "Don't hesitate this time. You don't want that slug stealing your glory again."

"I got this, now shut it."

The container began to emerge. Tawn squeezed the trigger on her rifle. Harris reacted to the familiar whump of a plasma round exiting the tip. The cable holding the container snapped.

"Nice. That had to be yours. Take that, Emma Costa. You're competing against a level four now."

Tawn grinned. "We got a third one coming up."

Seconds later, as she was squeezing the trigger again, an instant before the familiar whump, the hoist cable on the newest container snapped.

"That one you?"

Tawn sighed. "Nope. She scored another one. She's either a spectacular shot, way better than me, or she's in close like we are."

"Wait. I thought they were going all the way to the south end?"

"They were."

"Then they shouldn't be there yet. They would have at least another hour to go."

Tawn scratched the side of her head. "Yeah... that doesn't make any sense."

"Play back each of those shots through your scope. Zoom in as tight as you can. Tell me what you see."

Tawn complied. "On the first one... cable snapped. Number two... hmm. Small puff of smoke from that plasma round. And the third... nothing again, just a snap."

Harris shook his head. "That's not right. Those cables wouldn't break."

A voice came from behind the blind. "Hey, idiots?"

Harris looked back. "Bax? How'd you find us?"

"You monkey brains got yourselves tagged on the first camera you came across. Lucky for you I had my guy sitting at the monitor when you showed. Don't worry, it's been erased. Nice job finding the blind spot here, but sloppy on getting caught to begin with. I thought you snipers were more thorough than that."

Tawn scowled. "Yeah, well, I've been out of practice for a bit and I'm having to drag the chump around with me."

Bax gestured toward the dome. "Nice shot on that second cable. Impressive from this distance."

"I do what I can."

Harris asked, "What happened with those other two?"

Bax grinned. "You like that? I had one of my guys insert a charge into each of those cables when they were installed on that ship. My investigation is gonna show inferior steel used in the construction. I had the contract for the retrofit. Unfortunately for whatever Earther schmo built those cables, the data will show they took a shortcut. All planted info of course."

Tawn tilted her head. "How were you able to pull that off?"

"By getting myself into a position of trust. Which you two were extremely helpful with."

Harris looked back at the freighter. "Why aren't they hoisting any more?"

Bax shrugged. "Too much to clean up? Don't know. I'm sure I'll be getting called back any moment to deal with the situation. I'm thinking we're gonna send that ship back to have all the cables checked and replaced. Will probably take a week. That sound good to you?"

Harris laughed. "I've got no problem with that. Oh, and thanks for tagging me with that tracker."

Bax smiled. "And thanks for destroying it. Had you not done that I could have stopped you before you revealed yourself to the camera. But I guess you know what you're doing out here, so..."

"Just don't try to sneak stuff on us like that," said Tawn. "Makes you look suspicious. If you feel the need to keep track of us, please ask us and give us a valid reason as to why."

"Fair enough. And before I go, please take out that conveyor. It's causing me unneeded stress."

Bax's comm signaled an incoming connection. "Yes, I saw that. Will be right there to handle it, General. Bye."

Chapter 12

Tawn lined up a shot at the motor control box. To the tune of a whump, bits of metal flew in all directions, and was followed by a distant crack. Two additional shots split the motor casing, while a third tore into its windings.

Tawn slid backward as Harris lowered the blind to level. "This setup isn't half bad. Gives us a bit more room under here. I can almost sit upright."

Tawn shook her head. "It's a problem. If we have to run we leave evidence of this hole we had to dig out."

"Hadn't thought of that."

"It's called training. Never let them know you *are* there and never let them know you *were* there. Makes that mission and future missions a lot easier. Don't give them anything to look for."

"Speaking of that. I know you said these rifles are special and don't leave a beam or trail between the firing tip and target—important for not being seen—but how is it the damage at the other end isn't identified as a plasma strike?"

Tawn replied, "They've done something to it that makes it look different. Don't know what, as that's getting into the physics of it, but I can say it takes two full seconds to recharge between shots. Your repeater is ready in about a third of a second."

"I've seen the damage a sniper rifle leaves. Looks the same to me."

"Instead of a typical plasma burn, they look more like an explosive device was set off. Probably why Bax has been successful at pinning it on sabotage. How the designers pulled it off I couldn't say."

"Never heard about anything like that. How long have we had them?"

"These were new to our side in the last few years of the war. They were designed for clandestine work. The Earthers don't have them."

Harris said, "We have any other targets to hit today?"

Tawn shrugged. "Might take a shot at one of those diggers. Think it best we wait a while though."

Harris rubbed the back of his neck. "One thing I don't get... why aren't they changing their patterns? Why not do things differently if their important equipment keeps getting blown up?"

"They're Earthers. Orders come down from the top. They've been told to do something a certain way and they'll keep doing that until specific orders come down to do it differently. That's the way the Earthers operate."

"I knew they did that on the battlefield. Didn't realize it was empire-wide. Must keep the emperor busy answering menial questions."

Tawn shook her head. "At some level they have designates who are responsible. Those are the people who get rewarded when things go right and executed when they go wrong. And since the Earthers think dying for their emperor is righteous, they have plenty of volunteers for those positions."

Harris chuckled. "Glad we were born into the right side of this war."

Tawn set her rifle to her side, rolled over and clasped her thin-gloved fingers together up under the back of her helmet.

"What are you doing?"

"I'm relaxing, you idiot. I just drove for twelve hours and then we did all this. I'd like to get some shut-eye, if it's OK with you."

Harris rolled up on his side, putting his free hand up in the air. "Fine. Take a nap. Don't need a partner who's being all grumpy."

"Can you face the other way or lay back or something?"

"Why?"

"Because I feel like you're staring at me. It's creepy."

Harris rolled onto his back. "Again with the grumpy."

Four hours passed as Harris stared up at the top of the blind. An alert beeped on Tawn's bracelet.

"What was that for?"

"So I wouldn't oversleep. Pop us up and let's do a target check."

Seconds later, Harris was looking through his scope. "Conveyor is off. Still working on the motor. You want a digger, we have a line on two of them."

"Any patrols forming out there?"

Harris scanned the area. "None that I can see. Wait... I see Bax."

Tawn rolled over, pulling up her rifle and looking through the scope. "That must be the general she's walking with."

Harris chuckled. "He looks like an overweight stump. Short and round."

"So he looks like you?"

Harris smirked. "Yeah. I guess he does. A bit more exaggerated in his proportions than I am, but similar in shape. Although most of mine is still muscle."

Tawn turned with a sarcastic expression. "You keep telling yourself that."

"Hey, when the time comes for action, I won't have a problem keeping up. Besides, the ladies like a guy who's jolly."

Tawn laughed. "Jolly? Where do you keep coming up with these from?"

"Just trying to keep it entertaining, that's all."

"They're checking out the conveyor. Wonder what's on that truck."

"I think we're about to find out."

The duo observed as large steel plates were removed from the vehicle.

"They're shielding it," said Tawn. "Gonna weld those together to protect it. So much for taking out the motor."

"You hit that belt and it comes to a halt also. Plenty of parts on that conveyor that will stop it if damaged."

A voice came from behind them. "You in the blind, don't move..."

Tawn pulled her Fox-40.

"Rumford sent me. Just listen, as I only have a few seconds. They're boxing the vital parts of the conveyor. You'll want new targets. Focus on the diggers for a couple days, and then the transports. Rotate targets if you can.

"The Earther investigators are preparing a report that says they think the damage is coming from snipers. These hills may soon get flooded with patrols. If you see groups of guards forming up, be prepared to evac. That's all. Good luck."

Harris shook his head. "I sure don't like the fact that these people can just walk up behind us."

Tawn sighed. "Our mission here on Eden might be at an end. Kind of surprised it took the Earthers this long to change tactics. I know I said they are slow to change, but I've been shocked by their behavior to date. Bax must really be fouling them up in there."

Harris looked out through the flap. "We have diggers at nine and eleven. Take your pick."

"I'll take the far one at eleven. After, we'll observe for about thirty seconds and collapse again."

Harris asked, "How we gonna handle watching for guard squads forming up?"

"I guess we'll have to pop up every half hour or so for a quick check."

Harris scanned the mining areas. "What we need is a disguised camera we can set out permanently to make observations through. I don't like this popping up and down stuff. We're just begging to be discovered."

"We have a couple cameras in the APC."

"Why aren't we using them?"

"Didn't think we needed to. Wasn't anticipating the need for a constant watch."

Harris chuckled.

"What's so funny?"

I was just thinking about how bored I've been between shots. Had I known we had cameras I'd have brought them out just for that. While watching Earthers work isn't five-star entertainment, it sure would beat staring at the top of this blind for hours on end."

Tawn nodded. "I could see that. How about this. We take out a digger, lay low for an hour, and then one of us goes back to the APC for the cameras."

"I'd be more than happy to make that effort. Where in the APC are the cameras kept?"

"Passenger side, almost to the back hatch, under the bench."

"Fields all look clear. You're free to take your shot."

Tawn lined up the vehicle that was grinding away at the eleven o'clock reference angle. A single round exploded a hydraulic junction, sending sprays of fluid into the hot Eden air. The digger's mighty blades fell silent as all pressure was lost. Workers started scrambling to stop the leak.

Harris nodded. "Nice. That will take some time to repair."

"I think Emma just shut down the digger at nine."

Harris moved his scope. "Flames again. We should do flames next time. Nothing like damage that yields more damage."

Tawn shook her head. "We don't have a shot at the fuel controls from this side. We can do that to a truck next time if you like."

"I like."

Seconds later, the blind was lowered to level and an hour of waiting began. When the alert went off on Tawn's bracelet, Harris was eager to get to work.

He popped the blind up, opened the flap, and the Biomarines scanned the grounds for activity.

"No patrols forming up," said Harris. "Can I go?"

"Give me a sec. No need to rush."

Harris chuckled. "No need for you maybe. For me this is vital to maintaining my sanity."

"OK. Looks clear out there. Stick to the path on your scanner. And keep your eyes peeled for patrols. Just because we haven't seen any forming up doesn't mean they aren't out there."

"That's a six hour hike back to the vehicle. You sure it wouldn't be better for us both to go?"

"For what purpose?"

"For the purpose of us not being separated in case there's an emergency."

"Like you falling in a hole or something?"

Harris chuckled. "Wouldn't you want to be there to see that?"

"We'll have to cover over our hole here."

"We can dig it out again when we get back. Not hard to do. I just think it's better if we stick together."

Tawn nodded. "OK. Let's get this going, then."

The blind was broken down, folded up, and stowed. They filled the hole and double-checked the area for signs of Humans having been there. There were none.

After a six hour hike back to the APC, two hours were taken for sonic showers followed by a quick meal. Another six hour jog had them back at the starting point. Harris began to rake sand out of the hole as Tawn made an effort to place the cameras.

"OK. They're set. Give me the blind and I'll arrange it."

Harris pulled it from his pack.

Tawn said, "Don't think we'll need the matching spray this time. Putting it right where it was."

Several minutes of adjustments saw the blind back in place and its crew inside. Harris connected the camera feeds to his scan device.

"I have connections... and images."

"You should be able to pan and zoom with either one." Tawn lay on her back with her fingers clasped behind her helmet.

"You taking another nap?"

"Yep. I need my beauty rest. And if you make any remarks about that, I'll beat you to within a millimeter of your life and then shove you out where the Earthers can find you."

Harris chuckled. "You don't want snide remarks, then don't make yourself such an easy target."

"Shut it and watch your cameras. I need some rest."

Two hours passed before night began to fall on the Fireburg mine. The cameras switched to night-vision, almost as visible as day.

Harris tapped Tawn on the shoulder. "We have some activity out there. Tell me if you think these are squads."

Tawn took the scanner display in her hand. "Two groups. And they're heading back inside. Wouldn't worry too much about it."

"They've been doing that since just after you dozed off. Probably thirty of those guard squads. What concerns me is the officer giving orders. He's doing a lot of pointing, as in pointing around."

Tawn frowned. "Could be going through the dome and out another entrance."

"If that's the case, these hills might be flooded with soldiers. The diggers and conveyor are still down. Do we take this opportunity to leave until we know what's going on?"

Tawn nodded. "Might not be a bad idea. You can bring in those cameras by the cables, but you'll have to go out and smooth the tracks. Do that and I'll break down the blind."

The cameras were retrieved and the surrounding sand made flat and even. The folded-up blind was stored in Harris' pack along with the cameras. Both Biomarines raked sand back into the hole.

As they turned for the path, a soldier was standing in their way. "Hold here for about two minutes," he said. "Rumford sent me. My squad is already behind you. And just so you know, I could hear you talking from close to a hundred meters. Sound travels in this night air."

After a short pause, the man turned. "Follow me."

Three silhouettes moved between the dunes and rocks, heading away from the dome. The man held out a hand to stop their escape, then waved them to again move forward.

At a second stop, he turned. "Follow your dead trail back out. But keep your eyes open, and movement to a minimum. I don't think we have any squads further out, but I could be wrong. Good luck to you."

The man climbed to the top of a large dune before shouting down the other side. "Hey, wait up."

The Biomarine sniper team made haste, keeping low, and always in constant movement. At the five kilometer mark, they slowed their pace.

Tawn let out a long breath. "That was a lot closer than we wanted it to be."

"We could have waited that out."

Tawn shook her head. "We could if you wanted to lay there in complete silence. I'm guessing those patrols will be a regular thing from here on."

"Should we go back up on the ridge and observe for a bit?"

Tawn stopped, glancing back in the direction of the dome. "I think we've done all we can do here. They catch one of us and they catch us all. That includes our equipment. We'll have to figure out another way to stop production."

Harris chuckled. "That reasoning sounds like something I would say. Could be we're spending too much time together."

Tawn nodded. "I've been saying that since we met."

The trek back to the APC took six hours. Another twelve hours had them on the path back to the main base. An hour into the journey they stopped beside a comm relay. A message was waiting.

"This is team alpha. We cut out yesterday after things got hairy over in our sector. This is for team beta: the other teams have turned back. Head for the main base. We'll see you there. Good luck."

"So we're it, then," said Harris.

"Pull that post and let's go."

The comm relay was retrieved and stowed. Tawn pressed the accelerator to full as a narrow but flat stretch of sand opened up.

Chapter 13

The APC slid to a halt beside the others. Harris hopped out, joining the small group of snipers and their spotters. "What's the ETA?"

"Just under an hour," replied Emma. "Your timing is good."

"I pulled all the comm relays on the way in," Harris said.

"You saw trouble too?"

Tawn came up behind as Harris nodded. "Patrols were walking all around us. Our blind was stellar, but our voices were carrying. We got lucky and had help getting out. One of Baxter Rumford's people helped."

One of the other snipers said, "About her... I had a message for you from the colonel. He said to tell you he hasn't talked to this Baxter person. Whatever they were telling you, they did on their own. And his connection in the DDI says she is not on their payroll and hasn't been since the truce. Before that she was just an informant."

Tawn said, "And now the Bax pendulum swings the other way. If she's doing this on her own, she's playing a most dangerous game."

Harris winced. "She helped us twice. Why would she do that if she's working for them."

"Playing both sides? She's making her fortune working there. Maybe she's using us as a safety net, a way out should things go bad. With her you really can't tell."

The freighter popped over the horizon and settled beside the sniper units. Four APCs drove up a ramp into the cargo hold. The bay door closed as the ship lifted, speeding off toward where it had initially come in. At a point exactly opposite Fireburg on the planet Eden, it turned skyward, blasting up toward the heavens.

Harris and the others took the opportunity for sonic showers before changing into standard clothes and heading for the cafeteria.

Harris grinned. "Cooked food. I can't wait to dig in."

A crewman leading the group turned. "Oh, there's no cooking on this ship. We are strictly fruits and salads."

Harris nearly stumbled. "What? Who does that? Why?"

Tawn smirked.

Harris gave a half smile. "You put him up to that?"

"Couldn't resist. I knew you'd be gunning for that cafeteria first chance you got."

Harris sighed. "All the thanks I get for saving you out there."

"Saving me? When did that happen?"

"When you tried to drive us off that cliff. Had I not gotten that truck back up top you'd have starved to death before reaching anywhere."

"You'd have starved too."

Harris chuckled. "OK, then I saved us both."

The group turned the corner into the ship's cafeteria.

Harris breathed deep in through his nose. "The sweet smell of cooked food." He hurried ahead to an open buffet line. The four other slugs in the group hurried after.

Tawn laughed. "It's like they think we'll run out or something."

A short rumble could be felt through the ship.

One of the stumps said, "Wormhole jump. We should be back in Retreat space."

"How are the domes coming?" Tawn asked.

"Last one is almost complete."

Harris hurried past with three full plates. "Watch it. Coming through."

The meal was eaten while they shared stories of sniping. The freighter landed with Tawn and Harris heading to the colonel's new residence inside dome number two. They turned the corner, walking into a bright new office. The colonel was sitting in his usual chair.

"Glad to see you back in one piece."

Tawn replied, "Had a few close calls."

"That crevasse. Hard luck on those two. Could you see the wreckage?"

Harris shook his head. "Was too deep. Even if they had somehow miraculously survived, we had no way of getting them out."

The colonel frowned. "The risk we take in this job."

Tawn said, "Domes are looking good. The green paint makes them blend right into this valley. That intentional?"

"Nope. Just like the color green. They all have the plating installed, along with the ion inhibitors. Half a dozen of the rail cannons have been delivered. They're being set up and connected as we speak."

Harris said, "Just noticed. You have the grav units working in here? Feels just over normal."

The colonel nodded. "We're sitting at 102 percent standard. Enough to keep us healthy and the regulars from complaining."

"You're letting regulars move here?"

"Just temporarily. We had jobs to do that were best done by skilled labor. Those people are regulars. With the grav units they can come out here to work. Temporarily."

Tawn asked, "We have any new ideas about how to stop the Earthers?"

The colonel shook his head. "Nothing that has any meat to it. DDI says the Earthers will be upping their ship production in a matter of weeks as that titanium makes its way to to their factories."

"Our efforts were only good for stopping them a day at a time. Baxter Rumford is getting rich as their supplier. She's also been a one man army in that dome, pulling off one sabotage after another while pinning the blame on the locals."

The colonel shook his head. "We have a man inside. There hasn't been any sabotage of note. Her efforts have kept you snipers off the radar. That was all changing though. Which is why I called for the withdrawal."

Harris chuckled. "Nobody can make me madder than that woman. At the same time though, I find her ability to stay in the mix fascinating."

Tawn said, "He likes her."

Harris cringed. "I most certainly do not. She's like watching a fighter crashing across a flat plain in slow motion. Parts are flying off, there's smoke and flames, but the pilot keeps riding along unhurt. Fascinating."

"You said you had contact with her. How'd that happen?"

"She found us," Harris said. "Somehow she knew where to look. She said it was because you told her."

"Never talked to her. What do you think her angle was?"

Tawn sighed. "She said she was making a fortune off our destruction. I have no doubt she was. The only angle I can think of is her trying to set up a safe way out should the need arise. Had she shown up wanting a ride, both of us would have been obliged to give it to her. She really did save our asses out there."

Harris laughed to himself. "Sorry. Thought just crossed my mind that she might end up as emperor someday. Not at the moment of course, because they don't allow it, but before this is all done."

Tawn said, "Which brings us back to stopping the Earthers. We need to head home to better work on this. When are the Bolemans due out here again?"

"Tomorrow morning," the colonel replied. "I've arranged for two rooms for you that are about fifty meters from the dome one bar. You two need to take at least one evening of R & R. Unwind for bit. When we're done here, a transport will be waiting in the docking bay to take you."

Harris nodded. "I could go for a good head bashing. I think I might have lost a few kilos out there."

Tawn chuckled. "You didn't lose them. They just moved around back."

Harris half smiled. "Are you saying I have a big tush? And if so, why are you looking at my tush?"

"You can't miss it."

The colonel broke into a roar of a laugh. "You two should take your act on stage someday. Would be a riot."

Tawn scoffed. "A riot to get out of there maybe."

"Regardless, take the night off. Enjoy and relax. All our worries will still be there to deal with tomorrow."

The evening bar in dome one was packed with slugs and stumps. On several occasions song broke out with all parties participating. The now classic Biomarine ballads of "Into the Fray" and "Rosie's got a Fox" were sung repeatedly. The beer and liquor flowed, appetizers were devoured, and cheer was spread.

Morning came early with a knock on Harris' door. The grumpy stump attempted to block out the sound with a pillow over his head.

Tawn yelled. "Get up! It's almost noon!"

Harris let out a long sigh, shouting back from his bed. "Give me fifteen more minutes!"

"OK. Just know they are about to close out the breakfast bar."

Harris rolled his eyes as he sat up. "Not fair bringing food into this."

Tawn laughed. "Get a move on. We have twenty minutes until they close for the lunch conversion and I don't want to be listening to your complaints that whole time."

Harris stripped and stepped into a sonic shower. Jets of air blew the loosened dead skin from his body. A fan sucked it into a grate at his feet. A quick wipe with an absorbent towel removed excess skin oil, leaving behind a clean but pleasant, smell. Skivvies were pulled on, followed by a jumpsuit.

Harris walked out of his room and into the hall. "Let's go. I want some of those scrambled eggs and ribs this morning."

Tawn scowled. "Still don't know how you can eat that mess. Who puts barbecue sauce on scrambled eggs? Your plate looks like you sliced open the head of a bogler and are eating right out of its skull. Disgusting."

"You like eggs?"

Tawn nodded. "Love them."

"And you like ribs. I don't see the problem."

They turned the corner into the cafeteria. A line formed at the buffet, with bins of food being replaced almost as fast as they could be brought out.

Harris glanced up at a clock on the wall, then looked down at the time on his account bracelet. "Wait, it's two hours earlier than what you said."

Tawn smirked. "Yeah. I lied. I knew there would be no other way to get you out here. Besides, we have too much to do for you to be sleeping away half the day. And Trish, Gandy, and Sharvie are on their way in."

Harris shook his head. "You're lucky I'm hungry."

"If that's the case, then I'm always lucky."

They wolfed down a hardy breakfast. The *Bangor* landed on the tarmac and the Biomarines hopped aboard. A grinning robotic pet greeted his master.

"Farker! Hey, boy!"

Harris looked up. "Did you miss us?"

Trish replied, "Up until now, yeah."

"How was it?" asked Gandy. "The colonel told us nothing. And he ordered us to not go to the base there. Said it was too big a risk and we could get any info we needed from him. Then he told us nothing."

Tawn nodded. "He had his reasons. The sniper mission was a success while it lasted. Unfortunately, they eventually wised up and chased us off. Unless Bax has figured out a way to stop the titanium shipments, that ore is flying to New Earth as we speak."

"Bax?" Trish asked. "What does she have to do with this? She resurfaced?"

Harris said, "She has the arm and ear of the Earther general in charge there. She saved us a couple times, which leaves us a bit confused about her motives."

Tawn smirked. "The lady knows how throw out a smokescreen. She does things you despise and then she ups and saves you. At the moment we really don't know where she stands. She's definitely in the in crowd over there."

Gandy again asked, "So what happened?"

The next ninety minutes were spent giving a detailed account of the happenings on Eden.

As the *Bangor* settled on the grass outside the bunker, Tawn asked, "Anything new from inside?"

Gandy said, "Sharvie is up to the 1600s of Earth history. Trish and me are about seven hundred years behind."

Harris chuckled. "Sounds like you haven't been doing much."

Trish stood as the hatch opened. "Not true. It seems the accounting of Earth's history gets more expansive as time goes forward. There is so much to read and see. It's fascinating to learn about because it seems like this whole other world and species, but it's our history. It's definitely us."

Sharvie nodded. "It's hard to not want to jump ahead to see what happens, but the AI in there dictates what we can see and read. Unless you soak it in and comprehend what was happening, you don't move forward."

Harris scowled. "There's testing?"

"Yep. And it's pretty in-depth at stages. You aren't far enough along to have hit any of those, but they're coming, so pay attention."

"Personally, I can't get enough of it," said Trish. "Earth was full of kings and emperors. There were slaves. And everyone fought against everyone at some point. Interesting stuff. And glad I wasn't there. Most of the history reads as if it was a much harder life."

Harris asked, "You make any visits to Jebwa?"

"No. We loaded up on food before you left. I did open a comm and order more equipment for my shop. Might be there by now."

Harris gestured toward the controls. "Let's make a run out for a check. When we get back we'll talk about Eden and what we could possibly do out there."

The *Bangor* settled on the tarmac just outside Haven. A delivery vehicle was waiting with the shop items Trish had ordered. A transport was taken into town.

Along the short ride, Harris said, "You know what I don't see? Cats."

The transport driver said, "The cat problem has been solved, at least somewhat. Stations were set up around the city and outside the farms and ranches. They emit an ultrasonic sound. The cats have been driven out of town."

Trish asked, "What about the pets?"

"Each home was provided with a noise canceling system for that ultrasonic frequency. Our house-cats now enjoy a feral-free zone around their homes, and as an added bonus, they no longer wander off, as the noise picks up as they approach the edges of their properties. Was really quite the ingenious method to stop the ferals without using the suggested barbarous method of bringing in coyotes."

"You said somewhat solved. There are still issues?"

The driver nodded. "It seems the feral cats, now out in the wild, are devastating our bird population further. Steps are being taken to study and preserve the myriad of species native to this planet. I just hope we're not too late for some of them."

Harris said, "I would have suggested bringing in dogs instead of coyotes."

The driver huffed. "Dogs... such needy animals. They require constant attention. Whereas a cat can be ignored and they largely don't care. They give attention when it's asked for."

Trish laughed. "The war between cat and dog lovers has been going on for thousands of years. I had friends with cats, friends with dogs, and friends with both. The cat people hated the dog people and the dog people the cat people. And both of those groups looked down on anyone who had both."

The driver scowled. "Cats are dignified. Dogs drool and lick their... wherever."

Harris smiled. "My dog does neither, do you Farkie?"

Three farks were returned.

The driver pulled to a stop while looking over his shoulder. "Your dog is not a dog. It's a machine."

The group got out of the transport and it sped away.

"He seem kind of rude to you?" Harris said.

Trish replied, "He doesn't like dogs."

The group walked into the government building and into the council hall. Two speakers were on the platform yelling at each other. Members of the crowd shouted out in support of one or the other. The topic was about standardizing fences around the ranching properties.

Harris winced at some of the language being used. "What happened to the happiest place in the galaxy?"

A man sitting near them scoffed. "Be quiet! I can't hear."

Harris led the others out into the hallway. "What's up with these people? They all seem hostile."

Tawn looked around. "There aren't any cats in here. Didn't they use to bring their pets with them?"

Harris asked, "Farker? Do you detect an artificial high frequency noise in here?"

Three farks were returned.

"Can you generate a cancellation wave to neutralize that sound?"

Three farks were again returned.

"Do that please."

Trish looked around. "Wow. I couldn't really hear that before. It was like a quiet whistle. Seems silent now."

Sharvie nodded. "I think it had me a little on edge."

"Might be what's affecting them. Farker? Can you broadcast enough to cover that chamber out there?" Tawn asked.

Three farks were returned.

Harris shook his head as he chuckled. "You can't ask, you have to tell. Farker, broadcast enough to negate the signal in that chamber."

The dog trotted into the room, heading to the stage in the center. The high-pitched, nearly inaudible whistle stopped. The pacifists who had been arguing quieted, instead looking about the chamber for whatever noise was now missing.

Harris stepped in. "Listen up. I think your feral cat repeller has been driving you all nuts. You've turned into an angry people. If you plan to continue to use the signal outdoors, I would suggest adding some cancellation gear in all your buildings. You people used to be pleasant. You all seem irritated now."

Fifteen minutes after the change, the pacifists in the meeting hall were all apologetic and smiles. Several meetings were had and supplies ordered before the team returned to the ship. A jump back to Midelon had them settling on the grass.

Chapter 14

Harris said, "Farker, open a comm to Domicile for me. I'd like to check in."

"Mr. Gruberg," said Bannis Morgan, seconds later when the channel had connected. "Glad to see you've returned from Eden. I hear your success there has come to an end."

"They were onto us and we had to leave. That mine is turning out massive amounts of ore now. Probably enough for a new ship every day. We need a way to stop it."

I have a team working on a new weapon. Are you familiar with a gamma ray burst?"

"Not really."

"It's a natural phenomenon where a tremendous amount of gamma rays are released due to a cosmic event. We believe we can mimic that with a nuclear explosion."

Harris shook his head. "Bombs are useless unless you can sneak them in. And I don't see that happening. Try to drop one and it just gets vaporized before getting close enough to do damage."

"If this weapon proves functional that won't be a problem. At the moment we are attempting to shape the reactions so that the resultant gamma burst escapes as a beam. With such a weapon, you could detonate it a light-year away from the target and expect the destructive energy to arrive a year later. The target would never know it was coming."

Harris cringed. "Can't say I like the thought of that. A weapon that can't be defended against? What if it falls into the Earthers' hands? They would use something like that in a second if they had it. We wouldn't be safe anywhere."

Bannis nodded. "We've considered that as well. And I don't think that is a near-term concern. At the moment we are in the concept phase. We don't yet know if it's possible. And if it is, we may not be able to generate the amount of energy needed to make it viable. We are talking about things that currently happen with the collapse of a star. Not an event we can replicate."

Gandy sat forward. "Mr. Morgan? Could we shield a ship enough that it could withstand being close in to one of these events?"

Morgan thought. "Possibly, although I would have to consult with my teams. What are you proposing?"

"We jump a ship to one of these events and then open a wormhole to Eden space, let the gamma rays travel through."

Harris furrowed his brows. "You just come up with that?"

Gandy shrugged. "It popped into my head when he said gamma ray burst."

Bannis rubbed his chin. "I'll run that concept by my team."

Harris asked, "How are the rail cannons for the Retreat coming?"

"Excellent. We've managed a few modifications that should increase their power by at least 50 percent. It's an exciting development, with potential for more improvements to come. Those updates are being installed on the cannons that have already been deployed."

Tawn cut in, "How is it you're doing this without the DDI coming down on you?"

Bannis smiled. "Simple. They are not classified as weapons. They are defensive devices whose purpose is to prevent meteor strikes. The power of the weapons being reported to the government offices is two orders of magnitude lower than actual, so we don't anticipate generating any alarm.

"That concept came from the colonel's team, as they had a meteor strike that missed the Retreat by only a few hundred kilometers. Prior to that, we were struggling with how we might deploy such systems. The papers we filed made it look like a business proposition where we would build and sell these units to the outer colonies, some of which are prone to meteor strikes."

"Those improvements, could they be done to the *Bangor*?" asked Harris.

"My team is looking into that. If the rails can be removed and modified, I don't see why not."

Harris nodded. "That kind of increase would definitely help. Double that again and we could almost compete with the plasma cannons."

Bannis replied, "We're aware of the potential, Mr. Gruberg."

"What's happening with the budgets? The colonel told us some major programs were on the chopping block."

"It's a dark time for the Domicile defense industry. They continue to cut military personnel and are pushing a 50 percent cut to acquisitions. Ships, weapons, even research, will see drastic budget hacks. We're expecting to have a vote in the Senate in the coming days. It's not looking good for our side.

"Several of my associates are talking of shuttering their manufacturing permanently. These are critical components that will be in high demand should war return. They are also on the verge of retiring up to 70% of the fleet, with nearly a quarter of that to be sold off as scrap. If successful, we will be left with more of a police force than a military."

Harris sighed. "The news just keeps getting better, doesn't it? Maybe we should just negotiate a full surrender now. I'm sure we would get better terms."

"Our home fleet will be less than half the size it has been for the last ten centuries."

Harris shook his head. "Idiots, the lot of them. How are your new freighters coming?"

"All manufacturing has been halted. We don't have the funds to complete the first of them. We'll be needing titanium, even though it looks like we might have plenty if they downsize the fleet."

Tawn asked, "How much would you need to finish that first freighter?"

Bannis tilted his head from side to side in thought. "Oh, probably forty million credits. The consortium has no further interest in funding that project without the mines of Eden."

"Would they be willing to sell out their shares?"

"I would say so. At the moment they consider it a complete loss."

"How much should I offer?"

Bannis chuckled. "I know you and Mr. Gruberg did well with the arms trade. And the funding for building out those domes and defenses at the Retreat have been overly generous, but we are talking large funds."

"Just tell me how much."

Bannis rubbed his forehead. "Well, I suppose if you threw twenty million credits at them they would jump at it. Scrap would only be worth a quarter of that."

Harris said, "Offer them ten million for a complete buyout, including any debts they currently owe on them."

Bannis replied, "Give me a few minutes. I'll be right back."

The comm channel closed.

Harris turned to Tawn. "If we build these, what are we going to do with them?"

"Use them to steal titanium from the Earthers."

Harris laughed. "And what do we do with that?"

"We're gonna use all the refining equipment we have sitting at the Retreat. We'll turn out our own plating again. And we'll use it to beef up those freighters."

"And then what?"

Tawn smiled. "And then we get more."

Gandy asked, "Are we talking about being pirates again?"

"Yes. If that's the only way we can stop the Earthers. We have our own planet. We don't fall under the jurisdiction of Domicile. If we declare war on the Earthers, that's our business."

Harris again laughed. "Declare war? With what? The *Bangor*? Our one ship fleet?"

Tawn replied, "For starters. I just happen to know where we can get a few freighters we can arm."

"With the rail cannons? Doesn't that seem a bit lightweight to you for a fleet?"

"We're attacking a freighter, so no, it doesn't seem light-weight. A few of those rail cannons and the ore is ours."

"And what are you planning to do when the next shipment has an escort?"

"We'll have to figure that out when we get there. Are you saying you're opposed to doing this?"

"No. Just questioning your sanity."

Tawn crossed her arms. "We have to do something. With every ship they build we get closer to war."

Harris said, "What we need is evidence. Something showing the Earthers are building a new fleet. That should put the government on alert."

"And what would that evidence be? You think they will accept images, something that can be doctored? We'd have to steal a new warship and shove it in their faces."

Harris began to grin.

Tawn asked, "What? What's going on in your mousetrap of a mind?"

"I'm thinking we do just that. We steal a brand new Earther warship, we fly it to Domicile, and we park it in the skies right above Post London. They wouldn't be able to deny a New Earth buildup is ongoing. The people would demand action."

Tawn shook her head. "And you were just questioning my sanity?"

Tawn stared at Harris' continued grin. "You're serious about this?"

"I am. And I think we could pull it off. The Earthers would not be expecting something so brazen. With a couple dozen Bios we could take a ship. Maybe when it was just released for trials with only a skeleton crew aboard?"

"I like it," said Gandy.

Tawn turned. "We aren't taking you into a fight like that. This would take hardcore Marines."

Gandy crossed his arms. "You'll need people to take control of the systems and fly it. Which probably means you'll need Sharvie to break into their systems. And you'll want Trish or me flying it."

Tawn chuckled. "Why would we need you to fly it?"

"OK, you'd need us to fly the *Bangor*."

Harris raised a hand. "Look, nobody's flying anything until we plan this out fully. If we decide it's too high a risk we can always abort. Nothing says we have to go through with it. Although... it would make one heckuva statement to the baboons in the Senate. A new destroyer would be undeniable."

The comm was reconnected to Bannis Morgan. "Twelve million credits, that includes assuming all debts, which amount to just under another two million. If you can come up with that, the freighter manufacturing is yours. That includes the orbiting shipyards, which are old, but fully functional."

Tawn nodded. "We'll take it. Can those yards be moved out to the Retreat?"

Bannis scratched his head. "Would take some effort. A tear down and reassembly. Probably adds several million to your costs. Not to mention the workers. You have a big pool of machinists and assemblers available on Domicile. Many of those are highly skilled people."

"Don't they sign up for year-long contracts where they live up on the space-dock anyway?"

"They do."

"Then what's the difference? Why would they care if it's orbiting above Domicile or out at the Retreat?"

"They often take short trips to Chicago Port or back down to the surface with their time off."

"Not a problem," said Tawn. "We can provide shuttle service at minimum to no cost."

"You offer that and you are likely to have more applicants than positions to fill."

Tawn said, "Now for the hard part. Would you be willing to take on the management of this effort? At least until it's up and running."

"I suppose I could make that happen."

"Good. And what I'd like to do when you have it reassembled out at the Retreat is to load up that first freighter with rail cannons. We'll provide the funds."

Bannis frowned. "You do realize the President and Senate would consider that illegal, right?"

"Are there any laws specifically forbidding the building and arming of your own warship?"

Bannis thought for a moment. "No... I suppose there aren't. It's not something most of us would have the means to do. Nor would we want to."

Harris asked, "What kind of time are we talking to get that shipyard moved, staffed, and operational again?"

"What kind of budget do we have?"

Tawn said, "What would your expedited budget require?"

"Five million credits versus two million if we took our time."

Tawn nodded. "Then make it happen. We'll provide the funds as soon as you need them. When could you start?"

"I can have the paperwork done today and begin work on the move in the morning."

"Excellent. Hold up your credit store for me."

Bannis chuckled. "You don't waste time, do you?"

Twenty million credits were exchanged. "That should cover everything you need, plus a small contingency fund should anything of immediate need arise."

Bannis bowed his head. "Give me an hour and you'll be the proud owners of a freighter factory."

Bannis reached out and closed the comm.

Tawn said, "So we'll have an armed freighter, and the ability to produce more. Now we just need a plan as to how to make use of them."

Gandy asked, "When do we start planning our raid on the Earther factory?"

Harris shook his head. "Tawn and I need a bit more time to contemplate what that entails. In the meantime, I think we pay a visit to the bunker to continue our history lessons. Maybe some of our past Human struggles will point us toward a solution to the Earther situation."

Several hours later, Farker followed his master as the group moved back into the bunker and down the hall. Harris settled in his usual room, Farker lying at his feet. The image of a smiling Alexander Gaerten showed on the display in front of him.

"Hello, Alex."

"Hello, Harris. I am glad you are here. I have news for you about my research."

"Hit me."

"The maximum speed achieved with the current drive systems is one-sixteenth the speed of light. I believe we can enhance the drives to achieve a faster speed."

Harris sat forward. "That would be fantastic. How much additional are we talking? 50 percent?"

Alex shook his head. "I'm afraid that is not possible at this time. The theoretical limit of those drives is calculated to be nineteen thousand two hundred meters per second. Currently our systems are able to achieve 97.135 percent efficiency. I believe we can safely add nearly half a percent to that number."

Harris sat back, crossing his arms. "Half a percent? So just barely faster than we have now?"

Alex nodded. "It will give you the ability to outrun any foe."

Harris huffed. "Outrun? You mean still get shot at for ten minutes while putting enough distance between us to get out of cannon range, right? Ten minutes is death at the moment. Come back with 50 percent speed improvement and then we're talking."

"I am sorry, Harris. We are limited in this endeavor by our knowledge of physics. Are you indicating you have no interest in implementing this upgrade?"

Harris sighed as he set his hands on the table in front of him. "No. We want it. What's the amount of effort needed to get this done?"

An image of the drive with several parts exploded showed on the display. "Minimal. The tools and materials in Trish's shop should be adequate to make the necessary changes in under an hour. And I will continue my research into the drives on the *Bangor*. If there are any other improvements that can be made, I will notify you at the time."

"Too bad you can't design an entirely new drive that gives the 50 percent speed increase I want."

"Would you like me to add that to my research list?"

"Uh, sure. Any other discoveries you've made?"

"I am sorry, that was it. The other items requested are proving most difficult to enhance."

"Where were we with my Earth lessons? Oh, wait, I have one more thing first. If you get a chance, open a portal to Jebwa space and scan that planet for life forms. They have a feral cat problem over there. At the moment they are keeping them away with a high frequency sound wave. Any better way to handle that in a natural way? They aren't interested in doing a massive cat hunt. Goes against their non-violent ways."

"I will add that to my task list. As to your prior question, we were reviewing the records of your ancestors. The Germanic tribes had stormed out of Northern Europe, taking control of much of the western half of the Roman Empire. Numerous emperors rose to power, attempted realignment of their forces, and were subsequently murdered by rivals."

For the next four days, maps, timelines, cultures, and empires were discussed. The Roman Empire gave way to Medieval Europe in the west and the rise of Islam in the east.

The Tang Dynasty reunited China with their influence, expanding to cover most of east Asia. The Polynesians settled much of the Pacific islands, and the Pueblo culture took hold in the American Southwest.

Harris emerged along with the others for a much needed break. "Fascinating stuff. Sharvie? What era are you up to?"

"What they called the nineteenth century. It looks like our ancestors were constantly warring. There were always small fights going on somewhere. I also found out that eventually the globe is divided into camps in the east and camps in the west. The eastern coalition became the Earthers. We're from the western coalition."

Gandy said, "Well, don't spoil it for the rest of us. I want to know how it turns out while I'm reading it."

Trish laughed. "Turns out? We know how it turns out. That's us, you numbskull."

"I was talking about before we left Earth. What exactly happened and why. And why were the two ships of people at each other then?"

Sharvie shrugged. "Don't know yet. But we'll find out."

A meal was shared, followed by a half day of sleep and relaxation.

Chapter 15

Harris called the others into the cabin of the *Bangor*.

"We're making a run out to Eden. This is for a check of their progress. Sharvie, you'll come with us. I want you to hack into the Earthers' systems if possible. Trish, you and Gandy will stay here. Alex has an upgrade to our drives that needs to be fashioned. Do it on the shuttle. If it checks out we'll do it here as well. I don't expect us to be gone more than half a day."

Gandy and Trish headed for the shop. A short time later, the *Bangor* slowed as Eden came into full view from the nighttime side.

Sharvie said, "I'm picking up Earther comms. Give me a few minutes and we should have those cracked."

Tawn looked over the nav display. "I count five warships up in orbit, two down below, one at Fireburg, and one at Bax's old mine."

"They reopening her mine?" asked Harris.

"Hang on. I'm zooming in... yes. I count eight buildings under construction at that site."

"Just for grins, take a look at the other sites we had mapped. Any activity at those?"

Tawn moved the alignment of the camera. "Yep at that one. And... that one too."

After the fifth confirmation, Tawn stopped. "They have the beginnings of operations at every mine sight. This is blowing up in our faces exactly as we hoped it wouldn't."

"Any ships guarding those other sites?"

"Not at the moment, but we aren't getting close without them spotting us. They have a mine starting about four hundred kilometers from our old sniper base camp. Doubt we could even make it to the surface without being detected now."

Sharvie said, "I have a comm. It's between their command ship and the ground. Pushing it to the speakers."

"General, are you certain of your security?"

"I am. Baxter Rumford has been critical in this regard. Since I gave her control, the attacks on our equipment have ceased. We captured a cell of five spies yesterday. One who was sent to us by our own bureau. I was suspicious at first, but the information we found was undeniable. The cowardly offender then killed himself before we were able to fully question him."

The other voice replied, *"The results Rumford is getting are pleasant news to the emperor after such a slow start to this operation. The royal family has taken notice. Her opening those other mines was at first frowned upon due to the production shortfalls at Fireburg. That move is now being looked upon with great favor."*

The general nodded. *"I hope to increase our production threefold in the coming months. And double that again before year's end. The emperor will have all the titanium he desires. What is the word coming from manufacturing?"*

The highly-decorated officer on the command ship pursed his lips as the video portion of the comm appeared on the display. *"I cannot release that information other than to say it is going extremely well. I now believe we can meet our production targets with ample time to spare."*

The general returned a broad smile. *"Admiral, that is music to my ears. My time is best spent conducting war, not industrial management. I look forward to the day when that once again happens."*

"Soon, General. We are all looking forward to that day. This new threat has everyone on edge."

Tawn asked, *"What new threat? They talking about us?"*

Harris shrugged.

"Admiral, have there been any more talks?"

"No contact whatsoever. They moved into the new colony. That is all the intel I have."

Tawn winced. "You think they're talking about the Retreat?"

Harris shook his head. "If you'd hush, maybe we could find out."

The general leaned back in his chair. *"If they're arming that colony, Admiral, it makes this effort to rebuild our fleet that much more critical. That is not something we can allow."*

An aide came into the image, whispering into the ear of the admiral.

The Earther fleet officer said, *"I am sorry, General. I must go. The emperor has called me home. Keep up the good work out here. We need all the titanium you can produce."*

The general bowed his head. *"I will do my best, Admiral."*

The comm closed.

Tawn sighed. "They know we're arming the domes. This isn't good. We need to complete our work there before they have a fleet big enough to attack."

Harris said, "One way to help with that: throw credits at the problem. We have enough to spare. Sharvie, didn't you say your friends emptied the accounts of another Earther spy unit?"

"Yes. We have just over a billion credits in our accounts now."

Tawn narrowed her eyes. "What? How much?"

"Just over a billion."

Harris chuckled. "Can you imagine being the Earthers who lost those funds? Talk about quick executions."

"My friends don't think there is any more to be had. They've changed out their systems and firewalls. And the spider-web of account trails have all gone cold. They said the one they were following had all the monies moved into a single account and then withdrawn in person. At the moment they're out of leads."

Harris shook his head. "A billion credits. There's only a couple people on Domicile with that kind of money behind them, and both are in the defense industry, so those billions may not last, if they still even have them."

Tawn said, "Take us back to Midelon. I'd like to talk to the colonel."

Harris looked over the displays. "Not sure what else we can do out here besides listen."

Sharvie come forward from the bunkroom console and sat.

"We could leave a recording device, but there are hundreds of comm channels running all the time. Would be a mess to decrypt and sort through them all."

Tawn said, "Why not just keep a comm wormhole open and record everything?"

Harris shook his head. "We'd run the risk of being detected and compromised. There's only been one wormhole I've detected coming into Eden, and that was from New Earth. Not like on Domicile where hundreds are coming in from the outer colonies at any given moment."

Tawn replied, "Then a recording device might be just what we need. Mr. Morgan could probably help us with acquiring one of those."

The *Bangor* returned to Midelon. Trish and Gandy were finishing the update to the shuttle when Tawn stepped up into the shuttle's cabin.

"We're about to test it out," said Gandy. "Want to come?"

Tawn shook her head. "Just checking in. When you're finished, the *Bangor* is waiting."

Harris was sitting in the supply hut with Farker in front of him. An image of Bannis Morgan floated just above his pet.

"I will check with my satellite division. That sounds like something they may have available."

Harris said, "And cost is not a problem. Just give us a quote within reason."

Tawn sat. "Connect us to the colonel when you're done."

Harris turned back to face the image. "Are we done?"

"We are."

The comm closed.

"Trish and Gandy are about to test the shuttle. If this works I think we also apply it to those freighters after they come off the line."

A comm was opened to the Retreat.

An image of Colonel Robert Thomas appeared. "You have news?"

"We do," said Tawn. "The Earthers are opening all the mines we had mapped out. They're expecting to triple their ore output in three months. And to double that again by the end of the year. They won't have any restrictions on meeting their needs. Actual ship construction will be their only holdup."

Harris said, "And there's more."

The colonel chuckled. "There's always more."

"We think the Earthers know you're arming the Retreat."

The colonel sighed. "I knew this would happen when we let regulars come out here for the construction. I'll pass the complete list of those workers we had to the DDI for screening. If someone in there is working for the Earthers, they'll find them."

Tawn said, "Attention out there at the Retreat was not what we were looking for. Sorry we brought this to you, Colonel."

"Nonsense. You are only trying to protect Domicile and all her citizens. It's what all of us have sworn to do. You didn't cause this, and you aren't responsible for the Earthers' actions. You are responsible for building these tremendous domes, arming them, and bringing most of the Bios out of poverty. You have absolutely nothing to be sorry about."

Harris smirked. "Unless you want to count our gunrunning."

"Given the circumstances, that can be overlooked."

"So what can we do about any of this, Colonel?" Tawn asked.

"I have a group that meets every day to discuss this very issue. Unfortunately we haven't settled on a workable solution. Every suggestion has been high risk with little chance of actually stopping production for more than a day or two. Our own government has been the major stumbling block in all this. It's like we're fighting against ourselves."

Harris said, "There's a solution out there, Colonel. We've just yet to find it. One of the things we commed you for today is financing. What would you need, credit-wise, to expedite the projects you have working? Give us a number that would cut your timetables in half."

The colonel leaned back in his chair, crossing his arms. "Half would be a tall order. I suppose four of five million credits might smooth out some of the rough spots. I don't know that half is an achievable goal, even with those credits."

Tawn said, "How about twenty million?"

The colonel leaned forward. "Where are you getting all this money? No, forget that. I don't think I want to know."

"Thirty million?"

"Twenty would be more than adequate. We already have funding for the ongoing projects. That amount to throw around would certainly push things along."

Tawn said, "Hold up your credit store and I'll send it through."

The colonel chuckled as the transfer was made. "The bank of Freely, where nothing is impossible."

"Just get your build-out finished, Colonel. I think we're gonna need it. You might also look at how to make those domes self-sustaining. If the Earthers do come this way, they will most assuredly set up a blockade. You would be on your own."

The colonel nodded. "We've already taken those considerations into account. Protecting and feeding six or seven thousand Bios here at the Retreat will be a much simpler task than doing so for the billions of regulars on Domicile."

Tawn nodded. "We just want you to be ready in every way we can. Who knows, a prolonged fight here might be just the thing that gives Domicile time to get their act together."

"Let's hope so."

The comm closed. With no more activities on their short list, the drive speed enhancements were tested on the shuttle and added to the *Bangor*. Both ships performed as Alex had predicted, now slightly faster than any other ship available from New Earth or Domicile. The group made their way into the bunker to continue with the Earth history education.

Tawn sat in front of a display. "Alex, not that this isn't all interesting, but what's the point? Why are you taking us through this exercise?"

"To best chart one's path to the future, it is imperative that one knows their past. As Humans, you have the ability to learn from your mistakes. Not only in a physical, reactionary mode, but as reasoning, thinking beings who are driven by emotions as much as the physical world around us. While knowing about Tawn Freely is undeniably important, knowing where Tawn Freely came from, her environment and what shaped it, is equally as important."

Tawn chuckled. "Well, I know where I came from. That would be the DNA of about a hundred fifty other people all being assembled in a Petri dish."

"I am referring to the Human species of course and not your own humble beginning. By knowing and understanding your specie's past, you will make better decisions for the future."

Tawn continued her discussion as she moved through screen after screen of historical data. A common theme had emerged. Man did not always play well with Man. Empires and kingdoms, along with almost every other form of government, had been tried. Some had been successful over short periods of time when administered by the right person. Others failed miserably, forcing that misery on their people.

Across the hall in another room, Harris was having his own conversation. "Looks like the Europeans are exploding around the globe with exploration and trade."

Alex nodded. "Trade fleets and caravans brought wealth to the region, which at the same time was experiencing an understanding of science and health. This was happening in other parts of the Earth at the same time. Trade accelerated the exchange and adoption of many of those ideas."

Harris rubbed his chin. "So I could equate the exploration of the Americas with our expansion into the outer colonies. Many of us seem to always be looking to make our fortunes outside of the watchful eye of government. I'm guessing it was the same for many of these explorers and the settlers that followed."

"There are many similarities, but most of humanity's experience out here has been unique, if only for the fact that no other beings have been encountered. In the Earth Americas, there were sparse populations of peoples who had come before. They were of course conquered, just as Man has done to weaker groups and cultures throughout his history."

Harris sat back. "So thousands of years there, followed by a couple thousand out here, and there have been no encounters or even hints of other sentient civilizations. Looks like we have an entire galaxy all to ourselves."

"Our exploration knowledge of the Milky Way covers less than one thousandth of 1 percent of what we know to be out there. We've encountered many different species of animals, including your favorite, the bogler. One would have to reason there are other sentient species among our stars."

Harris chuckled. "Well, let's hope we can settle our own differences before they show up. So tell me more about these explorers..."

The better part of a week was spent in the bunker before Harris declared a recess. The group of five were gathered in the supply hut after having finished a meal.

Trish said, "They call it a world war, but it wasn't. Was kind of a Western war."

Sharvie replied, "Just wait, there's another one coming."

Gandy said, "Anyone else fascinated by their flying machines?"

"Speaking of flying," Harris said, "Mr. Morgan promised us the recorder today. I've asked him to drop it at the Retreat. Trish? You and Gandy up for a run in the shuttle to pick it up?"

"We leave and we can't get back in without Farker."

"Not sure why I keep forgetting that. OK, anyone who wants to go, let's go now. Trish, you can pilot the *Bangor*."

The others glanced toward the bunker.

Harris chuckled. "Fine, go back to your edutainment. Trish and I will go it alone."

Ninety minutes later, the heavily modified Zwicker class ship pulled to a stop in front of the newly constructed shipyard.

Trish said, "Wow. That is really coming together."

Harris nodded. "The colonel released a few million extra credits to the contractors. Mr. Morgan said they expect to restart the assembly of the first freighter this week. That should put us about three weeks away from initial trials. He thinks we can take possession of it in about six weeks."

Trish half smiled. "Then what do we do with it?"

"We'll figure that out in six weeks, I guess. Go ahead and take us down to the Retreat. The colonel is waiting. He promised us lunch."

Trish shook her head. "While I respect him for all he's done, he's just as bad an eater as you. Every time I look over at you I want to get up and wipe off your face. You Bios are disgusting eaters."

Harris chuckled. "We just like our food, that's all. And if you want you don't have to sit with us."

"No. That would just be rude. Besides, I want to hear what you're talking about. I just don't want to watch you eat."

The meal went off just as disgusting as Trish had expected. The recording device was collected and a jump to Eden space followed.

"So what do we do with this thing? Dump it out the airlock?"

Harris nodded. "Yep. We enable it, check that it's functioning, and then release it. We should record wormholes opening and to where, ship navigation data, and of course comm conversations."

"And why is it they won't detect it?"

"Shielded and passive."

Why don't we have these positioned all around New Earth? And why don't they have them around Domicile?"

"I suppose the ship traffic might be useful. And you know what? They probably both do have them. They just don't have the decryption we have. At least not that we know of. I tell you though, had we had this during the war it would have given us a huge advantage. Nothing like knowing what the enemy is planning before they take action."

The device was tested and released at Eden. A jump was made to Midelon, with the *Bangor* soon settling on the grass. Tawn came out to meet them.

Harris asked, "What's up?"

"I contacted Haven to check on a few things we ordered. They said they've had a number of unidentified ships popping into orbit and then leaving."

Harris scowled. "Earthers. Hope they aren't planning on bothering them. There's nothing there to be had for the emperor. Their trade barely supports that colony as is."

Tawn scratched the side of her face. "Yeah, I was actually a bit shocked they even reported it to us."

"You think they're finally starting to trust us?"

"Maybe."

Harris said, "Maybe it's time we went out and mingled with some of the colonists on the other truce worlds. Could be the Earthers are already scouting those colonies for a takeover."

"That's what it has me thinking. When do we go?"

Harris gestured toward the cabin. "No time like the present."

The *Bangor* rocketed up through the sky as a fireball.

Chapter 16

The ship settled on the tarmac beside the Massington III colony town of Tinea. The Biomarines were greeted by a shuttle that took them into town. Tinea was home to a mix of miners and farmers. Land was plentiful and the atmosphere tolerable. The slightly heavy gravity had kept it from being popular with regulars.

The transport driver said, "You in on business?"

"Of sorts," Harris replied. "Who here would know about ship traffic in this system?"

"That would be our port chairman, Mr. Winkeford."

"Can you take us to see him?"

The driver chuckled. "That would be easy. He has a permanent stool at our local pub when not conducting port business."

The transport stopped and Harris tipped the grateful driver a generous twenty credits.

Dimber Winkeford was seated where the driver had indicated.

"Mr. Winkeford? My name is Harris Gruberg."

"Biomarine?"

"Yes."

"First one of you I've seen out here. What can I help you with?"

"Was curious as to the ship activity in this system. Have the Earthers been active out here?"

"Usual activity from them, I'd say. We have had a few unmarked ships come through recently though. If I was to guess, they would be Earthers, but it might just be someone who doesn't want to be known as belonging to either side. We tend to get a lot of independents out here."

Harris nodded. "You wouldn't happen to have recordings of comm traffic, would you?"

"Recordings?"

"I know you probably keep nav records. Any chance those are kept along with any comm data?"

"Well, that's all encrypted. What good would it do us to keep that?"

"Was just a question. If you don't have it you don't have it."

"I'd have to say we don't, then."

"How are you folks set for supplies out here?"

Dimber rubbed his chin. "Could be better. We have a supplier who goes to New Earth and another who makes runs to Domicile. Both seem to take their time and charge some hefty fees for doing so though."

Harris glanced over at Tawn. "We happen to run a supply business from Domicile. You have any specific needs at the moment?"

"I do. My cousin is operating a mine. He's in need of some refining equipment, and a few months after he gets it he'll be looking for transportation of the product. He has a buyer lined up on Domicile, but he has to deliver."

"Sounds right up our alley," said Tawn. "Tell you what, Mr. Winkeford. Put out the word and take a list of orders. We'll be back tomorrow to give you a quote on fulfillment. Probably looking at somewhere in the neighborhood of cost plus 25%, plus our fuel and labor costs spread over the whole delivery. So the more items under order, the cheaper the delivery cost."

Harris nodded. "We often get wholesale pricing as well."

"This first shipment might be a doozy. We have a lot of pent-up demand out here."

"Just make the list. If we can buy it, we'll do it for what I just said. If things work out, we'll try to set up runs on a regular schedule."

Handshakes were made and pleasantries exchanged. The original mission of coming out to the truce colonies was about to be fulfilled.

As they walked a sidewalk in the town of Tinea, Tawn said, "I have a question."

"Shoot." Harris replied.

"How are we gonna make this work? We don't have the time to be making regular deliveries out here."

"We won't have to."

"What do you mean?"

"I mean we'll sub this out. Our new freighter will be perfect for this. We'll just need a captain and crew. And we'll only service the Domer colonies. Will give them a chance to grow and spread their influence. We're no longer trying to be spies for the DDI."

"I like it. And if we can turn a profit we might even be able to pay for that freighter."

After getting a ride back to the Tinea spaceport, Harris pushed open the hatch and hopped up into the cabin of the *Bangor*.

"I wonder how long it would take Mr. Morgan to make up a couple dozen of those recorders? Wouldn't mind dropping one in each of these systems out here. We could retrieve the contents, have Alex decode them, and pass them off to the colonel's analyst team. Imagine having the big picture of what the Earthers are up to."

Tawn sat in the copilot's seat. "Sounds good as well. I think this has turned out to be a good trip."

The duo returned to town the following day. An order sheet of more than fifteen hundred items was passed from Dimber Winkeford to the new suppliers. After a jump to Midelon, a comm was opened to Domicile.

Fritz Romero answered. "Mr. Gruberg, good to hear fro you."

"How's retirement?"

Fritz laughed. "Boring actually. I seem to go from boom to bust. I can't believe I'm saying this, but I actually miss the challenge that Fireburg brought."

Harris smiled. "Good. Then you'll like what I have to say. Remember us talking way back about opening up a supply business to the truce worlds? Well, we believe that time has come. I have an order sheet in hand for fifteen hundred items. I have a freighter that should be coming online in a couple weeks. She needs a captain and crew, and we need an administrator to run this new trading company."

"You have my full attention."

"We'd like you to be her first captain, to hire a crew, and to start making deliveries to the truce worlds. And only to Domer colonies. We should have two additional freighters following this first one, all brand new and top-of-the-line. Sound like something you'd be interested in?"

Fritz nodded. "Very much so. You stated this was to begin in a few weeks?"

Tawn replied, "Actually we have the orders in hand. I was thinking we could lease a ship for the first delivery or two."

"And you're certain this new freighter will be ready in a few weeks?"

"We've given Mr. Morgan the go-ahead to expedite it. With this first order we now have a purpose for it."

Harris said, "You'll also be doing some data retrieval for us, but I'll get into that later."

"Send me the list and I'll get to work on leasing a warehouse and putting together a staff to manage acquisitions and shipping."

Tawn held up her credit store. "Here's a mil to get you ...ed. If you need more, just ask. There are fifteen inhabited ... worlds if you exclude Eden. All have Domer colonies. ...e if we can feed them a little growth hormone with ...ently-priced goods deliveries. I'll pass you our contact ... this first order."

Harris said, "While you're getting things set up there, we'll be paying a visit to some of the other colonies to get the ball rolling. Once you have your crews in place, you can take over that effort as well."

Fritz grinned. "Thank you for rescuing me from the boredom of retirement. I used to fixate on the time when I would one day be able to kick back and put my heels up. Now I can't think of anything more revolting. Living is to have a purpose."

The conversation continued for a short while before they signed off and the comm was closed.

Harris said, "That went better than I expected."

"And we got the right man for the job. His work at Fireburg was outstanding."

Harris sat back with a sigh.

"What?"

"You and me. A slug and stump. Regular Joes. We have a billion credits at our disposal. We have a small fleet of freighters being built for us. We managed to fund a retirement planet for Biomarines that now has three hardened domes with rail cannon defenses.

"We're working every day to see to it that New Earth does not take over our worlds. And we're sitting here on a planet that no one else in the galaxy can reach. How fantastical is all that?"

"Very. Which is why I try not to think about it in those terms. It becomes overwhelming. An awful lot of that is just from dumb luck, but a lot is from our hard work too."

Harris chuckled. "Wasn't long ago we couldn't afford a meal between us. Both our credit stores were almost dead empty. You couldn't pay your rent and I couldn't make my payment on the *Bangor*."

Tawn winced. "You aren't getting ready to try to kiss me or something, are you?"

Harris shook his head. "Not even remotely. Just saying we've managed to come a long way as a team, that's all. This partnership, it works. And not like some creepy relationship thing if that's what you were thinking. That's a repulsive thought, by the way."

Tawn laughed. "For both of us."

Harris grinned. "What does my partner say to me springing for some chow?"

"Where we going?"

Harris pointed. "To the supply hut. It's time for lunch."

"Nothing says 'springing for lunch' like an MRE."

"You're not coming, then?"

"Didn't say that."

Trish, Gandy, and Sharvie were finishing up.

"Sent you a message that we were eating," said Gandy.

Harris nodded. "Thanks. Got it. We were on a comm with Fritz. We're finally setting up that supply business we originally went out to Eden to do, starting with the Tinea colony. We'll be making runs out to the other truce worlds to see if we can set up the same with each of them. We plan on getting one of those recorders to drop in each system. Should give us the big picture of what's going on out there."

Sharvie said, "That's a lot of data to decrypt."

"Nothing as compared to when we drop one in New Earth space," said Tawn.

Harris raised an eyebrow. "When was that decided?"

"Would be idiotic to not do. Even if we just decode it and give it to the DDI."

"We're finally going to New Earth space?" asked Gandy.

Harris shook his head. "Not until after we've eaten."

After lunch, they opened a comm to Bannis Morgan and ordered two dozen of the passive recorders, receiving promise of a one-week delivery time. On the fifteen truce worlds in question, twenty-two Domer colonies of greater than a thousand residents had been settled. Visits to each saw fourteen eager to trade with the new corporation, freshly named Bio Trading Galactic.

Gandy shoved a recorder into the airlock. With a press of a button, the quarter-meter-diameter sphere tumbled out into space.

"That's the last of the truce worlds, Mr. Gruberg. We going to New Earth?"

Harris stared at his nav display in hesitation for fifteen seconds.

Gandy asked, "Well?"

"Let's go."

A jump was made to New Earth space. The wormhole was opened three hours' distance from the second-furthest planet in the system.

Harris said, "It'll take us a full day to get in and place this device. We can't risk detection or they'll come after us with everything they've got."

"So we just jump back to Midelon, where it's safe," Gandy replied.

Harris shook his head. "I don't think it's that simple. We get caught and they'll flood the truce worlds with ships looking for us. This isn't like throwing a rock at their window. This is like breaking into their home. That device is clearly from Domicile. Placing it in their territory is an act of war."

After an extended flight, the *Bangor* moved into position. "Gandy, let her go."

The recording device was placed in the airlock. A button press had the air inside the lock vacuumed out. The outer door opened, releasing the device, then closed and sealed.

"It's away. What's next?"

"Now we go collect the one from Eden. When you pull this next one in, deploy another. We'll be taking it back for Alex to play with."

A short run and a jump had the Eden device in the cabin and a new one deployed. A second jump returned the ship to Midelon.

Harris picked up the recorder. "I'll be in the bunker talking to Alex while he works on the decryption. I suggest the rest of you move on with your history lessons. I'll let you know if anything important comes up."

Harris placed the device on the table in the main room and sat in the chair. The image of Alexander Gaerten came to life.

"Mr. Gruberg, I see you've returned a recorder. Is this ready for decryption?"

"Yep. Should have a good bit of comms and nav data on there. If you crack the comms, can you screen the messages for ones that involve or mention Baxter Rumford or the general?"

"I can. Do you have any other specific instructions?"

Harris thought for a moment. "Actually, yeah. If the nav data has Bax's ship coming or going, highlight those occurrences and link them to any relevant comms she was having at the time."

The image nodded. "Very well."

"What kind of turnaround time are we looking at?"

"A full day. There are four thousand two hundred twelve recordings to evaluate. Would you like me to begin?"

"Please. And notify me when you're done so I can return the device to the *Bangor* for deployment elsewhere."

"The device is ready. All records have been copied."

Harris stood, grabbing the recorder by a pair of handles on its side. After returning it to the ship, he made his way back into the bunker, sitting in his now familiar chair in his usual room. The history lessons continued.

An eight hour session saw two Biomarines emerging with hunger on their faces.

Tawn ripped open a packaged meal from the pacifists at Haven. "How far you gotten."

"Early twentieth century. You?"

Tawn replied, "Late twentieth. They have nuclear weapons, the first Human astronaut walked on their moon, and a cold war between two of the superpowers of the time just ended."

"That reminds me, I wonder how that gamma burst bomb is coming?"

Tawn bit into a piece of condensed bread. "If we had it, would we use it?"

Harris nodded. "On Eden? Yeah. Anything to stop that production."

"We still have spies down there."

"That would be a sacrifice they signed up for."

The meal was followed by another eight hour session, more food, and then rest. As the sun came up the following morning, Harris met the others in the supply hut.

Tawn asked, "We checking in with anyone today?"

Harris nodded. "Mr. Morgan. I mentioned that gamma bomb yesterday. Want to know if they have made any progress. Also want to check with him on things there at Domicile. How are the budget cuts shaping up now that he's seen the legislation."

Sharvie said, "I finished the history lessons last night."

Tawn turned. "You've moved to the next level?"

"No. I've been told I have to wait for the rest of you to catch up."

Trish said, "I've just passed the all electric vehicles mandate. And it looks like east and west are on the verge of war again. That Islamic war in Europe was bloody. Didn't seem to end well for anyone."

Gandy added, "I'm at the same spot. We just landed astronauts on another planet. I can't believe it took months to travel that distance. Can you imagine if we had to do that?"

Tawn asked, "Sharvie, how were the details leading up to our coming out here?"

"I was kind of shocked. It all made sense though. And I'll let you work your way through it so you're not biased by any of my thoughts. I want to hear what the rest of you think anyway."

"Shocking?"

"Maybe not shocking, but not what I expected from the stories we've all heard since childhood. And I'll leave it at that."

Harris opened a comm to Domicile. "Mr. Morgan, just checking in. Was wondering how your research on the gamma bomb was coming?"

"Moving forward. They've managed to overcome several major hurdles. To my knowledge, only two remain. If those can be conquered, we have a viable weapon."

"Give us a rundown again of what you expect this weapon to do."

Bannis nodded. "It will send an intense burst of gamma radiation in a single direction. That radiation would be powerful enough to penetrate the shields of any ship we have ever flown, killing all who fall within the beam."

"What kind of radius are we talking about?"

"At fifty kilometers, a hundred meters. At five hundred kilometers, a kilometer. At five thousand kilometers, the power has dropped by 90% while the area effected moves out to fifty kilometers across, although it may no longer have the energy to penetrate some of our better shielding.

Harris smiled. "A thousand kilometers. I can almost get the *Bangor* in to that before being detected. Is there a delivery mechanism for this?"

"There is. A hyper missile. It can reach the speed of our ship drives for a short burst. We can work another thousand kilometers of standoff if utilizing the missile for propulsion."

"That sounds fantastic. When can we have a couple?"

"Once the research is complete, we can evaluate the production side of this endeavor."

"What's the word on our freighters?" Harris asked.

"Moving along nicely. The schedules remain the same. The entire space factory is operational and work on the first unit continues. Installation of the cannons at the Retreat are almost complete. And while we're on the subject, I have a new pair of rails to be installed on the *Bangor*, along with a few circuit updates. This will increase the power again over our latest update."

"Music to our ears, Mr. Morgan. Do we pick those up or do you install them there?"

"Not here, Mr. Gruberg. I can have them out to the docks at the Retreat in say... four hours?"

Harris nodded. "We'll be there."

"When you arrive, wait for my signal before coming in. The DDI have had several ships out there of late. Would rather you not have an encounter if possible."

"Consider it done. And thanks again for all you do, Mr. Morgan. You've kept us in this game."

"Let's just hope time doesn't expire before we achieve our goals."

The comm closed.

Chapter 17

Four hours later, the *Bangor* and the shuttle, newly named the *Gooch*, popped through a wormhole from Midelon. After a short wait, a signal was received from an associate of Bannis Morgan. The docks were clear, and a host of workers were ready to implement the rail update.

Harris and Tawn, followed by Farker, stepped down onto the deck of Bay 14. Bannis Morgan's man was standing at the wait.

"Mr. Gruberg?"

"That would be me."

The man waved a hand. A dozen workers moved several large pieces of equipment, parking them just in front of the ship.

"We'll have those changed out in about twenty-five minutes. Mr. Morgan had us practice on an old hull that he has. Looks like this one is in good shape."

Harris nodded. "She does the job. Hopefully with this update she'll do it a little better."

The man held out his hand. "Karl Stromber. This update should help more than a little. The rails alone should allow the transference of three times the energy to those pellets. With the circuit updates you'll likely be taxing your reactor's ability to provide power for the first time."

"Sounds more like a major update."

"It is. And it cost the lives of two of our engineers during our one and only test fire. Best we can figure is a rail was misaligned and the energy transferred to the housing instead of the pellet. Aside from the lives lost, it caused extensive damage to our testing facilities. Has taken a lot of credits and much of our pull in the capital to put off an investigation."

Tawn said, "Mr. Morgan didn't mention any of that to us. We'd be happy to assist with financing the rebuild."

"No need. The facility was being closed due to the budget cuts."

Harris asked, "So what kind of power should we get out of this new system?"

Karl shrugged. "We aren't certain. Theoretically... almost five times the speed. But there are several variables associated with those estimates. It could be off by a factor of two in either direction."

Tawn said, "That would put us on equal footing against a cruiser or destroyer as far as standoff distance. Only our destructive power would be far greater."

Karl nodded. "It's almost terrifying. Such a weapon would way unbalance the scales. If in the hands of the Earthers, it might mean the end of us all."

Harris scoffed. "End of us all? Of them maybe. Why would we not implement this fleet-wide?"

"Earther spies are everywhere, Mr. Gruberg. We roll out something like this and three months later it will be on half their fleet. Our side won't make use of it. They will. Mr. Morgan contemplated not bringing it out at all. So he asked me to tell you that whatever you do, you can't allow this ship to fall into the hands of the Earthers. Understood?"

"We understand."

Karl moved on to direct the workers performing the update.

Harris stood with his arms crossed. "How about that. Our little *Bangor* might just be able to take out an Earther warship in a one-on-one fight. If this works, we may have to pay another visit to Eden. Draw out those ships parked there and we could take them out one by one."

Tawn shook her head. "Let's not get ahead of ourselves. As Karl said, they aren't certain of what it will achieve."

Harris nodded. "I guess we'll find out just as soon as we're out of here."

A comm came in from Gandy. "Mr. Gruberg, we have a ship just showed on the nav display. It's big."

"Big as in warship or freighter?"

Trish replied, "Positively identified as the *Ceclips*. DD destroyer 1447N."

Harris frowned. "Crap. We're in the middle of this. How long before it reaches here?"

"Twenty minutes maybe."

Harris called out, "Karl! We have an incoming warship!"

The Hosh-Morgan engineer nodded and turned back to the task at hand. The workers began to scramble.

Trish came over the comm: "Hang tight. We're gonna try to distract them."

Tawn replied, "What? That's a bad idea."

Trish said, "Too late. I just flipped our distress alert. They are coming our way."

"And when they get there?"

"I'll tell them I didn't realize it was on. Gandy is disconnecting the interior circuits for the horn and lights. And... they're off."

Tawn said, "You do realize the DDI is looking for both of you, right?"

Trish was silent for a moment. "I thought they didn't care about us."

"They care because you're associated with two persons who assaulted a DDI agent."

Trish took a deep breath. "Too late to turn back now."

Harris said, "You can outrun them in that ship. It should be faster."

"Sorry, too late for that. We were kind of heading toward them."

Harris asked, "Karl, what's your time to complete?"

"Twelve to fourteen minutes."

Tawn said, "Gonna be cutting it close if they come on in."

Trish came over the comm. "I just talked to one of their officers. Told her we were fine and we didn't realize the alert had been triggered. They wanted to board to check, but we were able to convince them it wasn't necessary. And I added that if we didn't get our daddy's ship back on time he would be furious. They've just waved us on. Sorry, that's all the time I could buy you."

Harris walked over to Karl. "What can we help with?"

Karl shook his head. "Circuit updates are in. All we have left is rail alignment."

"Will she fly?"

"Yes."

"Then button everything up. We'll get the alignment done later. We can't be here when that destroyer arrives."

"Two minutes. Get aboard. I'll yell through the door when you're ready. And, Mr. Gruberg, whatever you do, don't fire that weapon until that procedure is complete. I've left a copy of it on your system just in case."

"In case what?"

"In case you can't return. This team is the only one we have trained to do this. We'll be leaving following your departure. We will have to arrange a time for us to return."

Harris followed Tawn aboard. "This is turning into a mess. We should have hauled them out to Midelon and let them do it there."

Tawn sat, strapping herself into her seat. "Not a good idea."

"Why's that?"

"We have a DD destroyer bearing down on us. You think that's just bad luck? One of Karl's crew could easily be DDI. Or somebody on this dock facility."

Karl slapped the side of the *Bangor*. "Move out!"

The hatch closed and sealed as the drive came online. Karl Stromber's team hustled away, heading for their own ship as the *Bangor* rose to a hover. After moving through an airlock, the small cargo-shuttle blasted out into space, moving away from the incoming destroyer.

Trish opened a comm. "We're jumping to the other side of the Retreat. I'm sending the coordinates. Come get us when you're ready to head home."

A hail came over the general comm. "Unidentified ship, this is the Domicile Defense destroyer *Ceclips*. Stop your drive and prepare to be boarded."

Harris asked, "How we looking?"

"Just out of range," said Tawn. "Keep going. We can jump back to get the *Gooch* when ready."

Harris chuckled. "Whose name was that?"

"That would be Sharvie's. It was her first ship name. She named it after her cat."

"She had a cat? She a pacifist like the rest of that warped colony?"

Tawn smirked. "Warped colony. Can't believe you said that. You actually like those people."

"I kinda do, when they aren't bent outta shape. We're due for another run back there to check on the equipment we ordered."

"I think we need to handle this rail thing before going anywhere. I don't like being completely unarmed."

Harris returned a half smile. "Not completely. We have a slug and a stump on board. That has to account for something."

"Only in our minds."

Hails continued until the *Bangor* was safely away. Jumping to the coordinates provided by Trish, they collected the brother and sister. A further jump had the outlaws back at Midelon.

Gandy read the alignment instructions. "We could do this."

Trish glanced over his shoulder. "I don't know. Looks complex. And we'd have to build our own tools."

Harris said, "Let me give Mr. Morgan a comm. We can meet his team out there whenever they're ready to finish up. Would rather have it done the right way."

Gandy crossed his arms. "OK. But I think we could handle this. And what if we need to do it in the future?"

Harris chuckled. "When would that be? You planning to update those rails for us?"

"No. Just saying it wouldn't hurt."

"Unless you mess up and we explode into a million pieces."

"Fine."

A comm was opened to Bannis Morgan.

"Mr. Gruberg," said Bannis, "I have bad news. Mr. Stromber and his crew were detained. They are all being held for questioning as to what they were doing out there working on your ship. It's a felony, and will put each of them behind bars for up to two years. The techs don't know about the capabilities of those new rails. Mr. Stromber does."

"You think he'll talk?"

"Don't know. He's a good man, but he has a family to support. I was sent a status that the alignment wasn't completed. If so, I no longer have a team capable of doing that."

Harris looked back at Gandy with a half scowl. "Looks like we fall back to you. You sure you can do this?"

Gandy nodded. "Fairly sure."

Harris chuckled. "Great. Mr. Morgan, thanks for your efforts. Looks like we'll be doing this here."

"Good luck, Mr. Gruberg. I would suggest you triple-check your work on this. And then check it again."

The comm closed.

Harris let out a deep breath. "You two are up."

Gandy stood. "We can handle this."

The better part of a day was spent studying the alignment procedure. The twins argued repeatedly, putting Harris on edge. The fighting ended as the actual work began.

Tawn stood in the bay doorway of the shop. "Cats and dogs until they get working."

"We need this to work," Harris said.

Tawn laughed. "Yeah. If it doesn't though, we're not gonna be around to care."

"I guess that's true."

"Maybe we deserve this."

"What?"

Tawn chuckled. "Well, we've left quite the trail of destruction behind us. Loads of Earthers, our own spies getting killed, Morgan's engineers blown up—this latest crew heading to jail. All because of us."

"Not because of us—other than the Earthers on Eden we killed, they were directly because of us. But the others... we can't control everything that happens around us. We just have to do the best we can and keep trying to move forward."

Gandy looked up from several pieces of equipment. "These say the rails are already in alignment."

"Check it again," Harris said.

Trish replied, "We've checked twice."

"Again." Harris pointed.

Gandy stood, walked the perimeter of the ship, and hopped up into the cabin. Two minutes later he emerged. Manual says the rails are self-aligning."

Tawn said, "Check again anyway."

Trish came back a minute after. "Calibration check shows exact numbers. Down to a hundred-thousandth of a millimeter. They are dead-on."

Harris sighed. "I guess that only leaves us with a test."

Tawn began to follow, bringing Harris to a stop. "Only one of us needs to go. You stay here with Farker and the others. I'll take a few practice shots at the moon up there. I'll keep a comm open where you can watch."

Tawn returned a scowl. "Check all the parameters before pushing that trigger. We don't want a foul-up to be because of *your* foul-up."

Harris nodded as he sat and strapped himself in. "Take Farker to the supply hut and have him display the comm image. You might as well be comfortable while I blow myself up."

The hatch closed as the *Bangor* levitated. A slow flight away was followed by the usual fireball as the ship raced up through the atmosphere. The others settled in the supply hut as an image came to life above their robotic dog.

Harris said, "Six minutes. Grab yourselves a beverage."

Trish took a seat on a bench. "You should power on the rail circuits. Read back what they're reporting to me."

"OK. Circuits are on. Currents show 'Balanced.' Feed is active. And our mystery gauge is... down. Hmm. Only shows two hundred twenty. We were at a thousand."

Trish frowned. "That doesn't sound right. Wait... the alignment procedure says to turn off the safety-lockout when done. Is it still on?"

"Yes."

"Off please."

"Done."

"What's it say now?"

"Two hundred and thirty."

Trish sighed.

Gandy said, "There's a symbol on the bottom of that gauge. What's it read?"

"M."

"Big M or little M?"

"Big."

Gandy turned to face his sister. "That can't be right either. Two hundred thirty megajoules?"

Trish figured in her head. "Over a thousandth of a second? That's insane power. Mr. Gruberg, make sure that lap belt is tight."

Gandy added. "And I'd take that first shot from a distance."

Harris nodded with a smile. "I like where this is going."

Tawn said, "Just be careful. We need that ship in one piece."

"Thank you for the concern over me."

Harris took aim at the Midelon moon. "Slowing for the shot. OK. Here we go. Pellet is in the breach. And..."

The image on the display shook violently for only a moment before going blank. The comm had been lost.

Tawn stood. "Farker, reestablish that comm if you could, please."

A single fark was returned.

Gandy stood. "We should go up and check."

Trish nodded. "Yeah."

Tawn sighed. "Come on."

They boarded the *Gooch* and were soon on their way toward the moon.

Trish asked, "Anything on the nav sensor?"

Gandy shook his head. "If the ship's still together, it's doubtful we'd see it anyway. That's good, right?"

Five minutes of anxiety passed before the ship came into view.

Tawn said, "His bracelet should work from here. "Harris? You there?"

Nothing but silence was returned for what seemed like an eternity. "Sorry, was trying to get my power back on. Cabin's full of smoke."

Chapter 18

Several runs were made planetside to retrieve the tools needed for a short-term repair. After a transfer from the shuttle and an hour of rewiring circuits, the *Bangor* again came to life.

Gandy sat in the pilot's seat. "I'll take us in."

Trish yelled, "Hold up!"

Gandy turned. "What is it?"

"Dampener field is down. You hit that throttle and you'll flatten us all."

"Controls shouldn't allow that."

"Except for the fact that we just bypassed half of them."

A switch was flipped. "OK, what's the indicator say?"

"Green."

Trish nodded. "Take us home."

The *Bangor* settled on the grass beside the bay door of the shop. Harris hopped out, heading toward the supply hut.

Tawn asked, "You OK? Where you going?"

Harris glanced over his shoulder. "Hungry. I assume they'll be at that for a while."

Tawn looked over at Trish.

"Go ahead. Gandy and I have this. Sharvie, unless you're hungry, you can keep us company. We're gonna be here for a while."

Harris sat in the hut with a packaged meal in front of him. "Should have done this beforehand."

"Never go to war on an empty stomach?" Tawn quipped.

Harris took a large bite from a log of compressed food. "Exactly."

A scowl came across his face. "What is this?"

Tawn replied, "It's a vegetable medley. Sun-dried, hydrated and then compressed into that log."

Harris shook his head before taking another bite. "Hideous."

Tawn laughed. "And yet you continue to eat it."

"Not gonna waste good food. That's a crime."

Tawn snickered. "OK. That's not really food. It's meant to absorb moisture from that package so the rest of it stays fresh."

Harris stopped mid-chew. "Like a desiccant?"

Tawn nodded. "Exactly."

Harris turned with a scowl to throw it away.

Tawn laughed. "Wait!"

"What?"

"I might have just made that up."

"So it's food?"

"It's food. Weird pacifist food... but food."

Harris sniffed the log still in his hand before taking another bite.

"Wait! It's a desiccant."

Harris let out a long sigh. "Keep it up and I'm gonna make you take the next test shot."

Tawn shrugged. "I'd do that. Looked like you shook for a moment before the comm went dead."

"Shook is not the right word. I actually flipped forward so hard I banged my head on the console. I think that plate has a slight depression in it now. It went from there to a violent backlash. Pitch black by then."

"You hit the target?"

"You didn't look?"

"We were kind of busy saving your ass."

"Saving me? Didn't need saving, just a ride. So you didn't check the moon surface for damage?"

Tawn shook her head. "Didn't know if it actually fired."

Harris chuckled as he stood with the veggie log still in his hand. "Oh it fired."

"Where you going?"

"Up to look."

Tawn sighed. "Hold on. I want to see this too."

A quick run in the shuttle had the Biomarines hovering five kilometers above a newly developed crater on the moon.

Tawn said, "You did that?"

"That is where I was aiming. What's that... five times the size of what we used to get?"

"At least ten."

Harris rubbed the back of his neck. "Did we just create a monster?"

"How so?"

"As Mr. Morgan said, what if this fell into the Earthers' hands? Our ships couldn't defend against something like that."

Tawn nodded. "First shot would rule in that scenario. We'll just have to be extra cautious if we get near any Earther ships."

Harris said, "I'm kind of eager to get near an Earther ship. If we get these hiccups worked out, it might be time for us to pay Eden a visit and clean house. With that kind of firepower we could shoot them before they had a chance to do any damage to us. And one shot would devastate a destroyer."

The shuttle landed. The two Biomarines walked into the shop.

Harris took another bite of his veggie log. Tawn looked down at it in disgust.

"What?"

"You've had that in your hand for something like forty-five minutes," Tawn said.

Harris chuckled. "So? Not like it's gonna go bad that quick."

Harris turned. "Trish, what's our prognosis?"

"We need a bunch of new parts."

"Like?"

"Like power feeds. Reducers. Limiters. Transformers. Filters. That power surge fried parts all up and down the power line. We're gonna have to make a run to Domicile."

Harris shook his head. "Can't do it. Make a list of what you need and we'll order it through the pacies. We can have Mr. Morgan expedite it for us."

Trish shrugged. "Whatever. Just know that it's gonna be a lot."

The list was drawn up and a run made to the Haven colony in the shuttle. Tawn followed Harris and Farker as they walked into the government building. A meeting with the trade minister ended with the parts order being placed.

They next took a short walk to the meeting hall. A dozen pacies were camped around the center stage, listening to a fellow citizen happily blather on about what a wonderful crop year he was having.

Tawn said, "Quite the difference from that stage as compared to last time."

Harris nodded. "They're back to being happy people. While I wholly disagree with their lack of defending themselves, I do admire their accomplishments."

Tawn chuckled. "More like our accomplishments."

"We set it up but they're running it. Trade minister said they just started exporting food to Domicile. Sounds like they're accomplishing something on their own. And they're happy."

Tawn shook her head. "Never would have taken you for a pacifist."

Harris chuckled. "I'm not. I just admire their ability to achieve happiness. How many smiling faces did you see on Domicile last time we were there?"

Tawn patted him on the shoulder. "Come on, let's get you out of here before there's a full conversion. We can't afford to lose you at the moment."

Harris turned with his partner and began to walk toward the door. "At the moment? So you can afford to lose me later?"

"Let's hope."

A jump was made back to Midelon. As Trish and Gandy enlisted the help of Sharvie, Tawn and Harris walked back into the bunker and into their respective education rooms.

Harris sat in his chair and an image a Alex popped into view.

"Greetings, Harris."

"Hello, Alex. Let's see if we can make some good headway today. Where'd we leave off?"

"You were just entering what was called the First World War. Six of the major European powers of the day had divided into two camps. Germany, Austria-Hungary, and Italy comprised the Triple Alliance, while Britain, France, and Russia joined into the Triple Entente. The war itself is said to have been triggered by a single event.

"A Serbian national, rumored to have been a member of a militant organization known as the 'Black Hand,' assassinated Franz Ferdinand, the archduke of Austria-Hungary. This led to a further alliance between the Triple Alliance and the Ottoman empire, followed by Germany declaring war on France."

Harris nodded. "Go Germany. My ancestors were from there."

"Yes, well, the Germans would fall on difficult times when an armistice was signed, as it soon became apparent that their economy was in shambles. It was a redefining time for many of the old-world empires..."

The historical accounts continued through the day. Harris emerged after another eight hours in the chair. Having advanced into the late twentieth century. He joined Tawn and the others in the supply hut for a meal.

"How far did you get?" Tawn asked.

"Late twentieth century. Cold War has just ended."

Sharvie said, "There's a lot to come, but you're nearing the end."

Harris rubbed his lower back. "Good. I've had about enough of those chairs."

"What have you learned?"

"I learned ancient Humans weren't much different than modern Humans. We'll all fight at the drop of a hat. Empires boom, become gluttonous, then weaken... and then collapse. Happened over and over. And why? Because each new generation seems to have to relearn many of the lessons of the old."

Sharvie nodded. "I find it interesting how quickly the political pendulum can swing. Seems to go hard right immediately following a war and then trend left as prosperity takes hold. That leads to the gluttony and eventually another war."

Tawn said, "I'm in the early twenty-first. The spread of Islam has the world divided into three camps: the Islamists, the democracies, and the communist-leaning party dictatorships. World seems headed for the Third World War."

Sharvie replied, "I won't comment so I won't give away any spoilers."

Harris asked, "How are the repairs coming?"

Trish answered: "I think we have most of the damaged parts pulled. Probably another half day. Will take another day or so to replace them, and probably another couple after that to do any needed calibrations. And that just brings us back to where we started. If we fire either of those railguns again, we'll be right back to where we are today."

"So what do we do?"

Trish shrugged. "Too much power going into those rails. Something will have to be redesigned."

"Do we still have that limiter we took out when we put that gauge in?"

Trish thought for a moment. "We should."

"Would it be worth trying that out?"

"Actually, it would. That's an excellent idea, Mr. Gruberg."

"He gets lucky every once in a while," said Tawn. "The cage door up there will open up and an idea will roll out. Usually, though, you have to take care that you don't step in it."

Trish half smiled. "This one was actually a good one."

Harris grinned. "Thank you, Miss Boleman, for recognizing genius when you see it."

Tawn leaned back quickly, startling Gandy. "Watch out!"

Gandy replied, "Why? What's happening?"

Tawn pointed. "His head. It's growing bigger. Could explode all over us at any moment."

Gandy pushed a chuckling Tawn back upright. "Don't scare me like that."

Trish said, "Seriously, it was a good idea."

The back and forth between Tawn and Harris continued for much of the break, each getting in a number of digs. When the break had come to an end, the partners returned to the bunker as Trish, Gandy, and Sharvie worked to complete the pulling of damaged parts.

On the history front, wars in the Middle East gave way to a spread of Islam through much of Africa, with early indications of it beginning to take hold on the South American continent and in Europe. Those pushing its spread were militant, opting too often to use force instead of persuasion.

Harris said, "So there were three camps. These Islamists, the Russians and Chinese with their satellites, and the democracies. All appear to be heading toward conflict."

Alex replied, "Correct. This will all change rapidly as a new battery technology ushers in the viability of the electric car, rapidly replacing the internal combustion engine and roiling the oil for energy markets. The Western countries were no longer reliant on the east and the Islamists for their energy needs.

"This brought about a new alliance between the east and the Islamists. The march toward a global war was taking shape.

"War is what we do."

"That all changed when two wormholes between Earth and this region were discovered. Those discoveries coincided with the additional discovery of an imminent supernova explosion.

At first the alliances rushed to send probes through the wormholes, which had opened at only a month's traveling distance from the Earth. The eastern alliance focused on one while the West placed their interest on the other. Those interests exploded when each of the probes returned data that a habitable planet was just on the other side of each. Efforts quickly turned to focus on manned exploratory missions.

"That would again change as it was determined the supernova explosion was sending a tremendous gamma-ray burst toward Earth. It was declared an Earth-killer event by the scientific communities of both factions. Plans were quickly drawn up for colony ships.

Harris asked, "How much time did they have?"

"That was the big unknown. Estimates ranged from days to decades. In a strange turn of events, both sides came together to assist one another, believing that it was better if some of both lived than if everyone died. A huge space dock was created and the assembly of two massive colony ships was begun.

"The ships were originally designed to hold fifty thousand passengers each, with a sustainable bio-section where food could be grown and used materials recycled. The journeys through the wormholes and to the respective planets would take five years."

"So how did we come to have our wormhole drives?"

"The ship projects were scaled up to accommodate five million citizens each. To quell the anxiety of the populations, additional hull structures were being assembled. Leaders on each side promised that all citizens would be taken through—a near impossibility given the circumstances. Materials had been stripped from existing facilities to construct the ships in as rapid a timeframe as possible.

"As those efforts were ongoing, my team discovered several secrets about the wormhole and how one could be replicated.

This was the discovery of the boson field and of how it could be manipulated. Those efforts eventually led to the creation of this complex."

Harris sat back in his chair. "Wait, I thought you were in here after the first few hundred years. How is that possible?"

The image of Alex smiled. "Upon arrival at Domicile, twenty-four members of our science team were selected to be future guardians. Our bodies were flash frozen, with one new member thawed and put into service every twenty years. I was the last of the guardians."

Harris returned a skeptical expression. Our early history here is sketchy. Why wasn't any of this preserved for us to know?"

Alex shrugged. "I cannot speak for the early leaders and their decisions of what should be preserved. Our archives here contain a minimum of information about that period as well. What I do know is we had a tremendous population explosion following our arrival. Domicile was a planet that was ready to be colonized, and we had the right people along to do just that.

"Upon arrival, the ships were dismantled—as designed—and used to build our first city. For reasons not afforded to me, our scientific discoveries accelerated in those early years. A boson generator was constructed and travel throughout the Domicile System became instantaneous.

"That generator was scaled up, with the result being travel to the nearby star systems. A third such enhancement brought travel to New Earth and a rekindling of our relationship with our fellow Humans. Shortly after that accomplishment, it was decided that the boson field should not be controlled by either party, but instead reliant on each.

"The two bosom complexes were constructed and manned by a science team from each colony. Travel and exploration of the outer colonies commenced, with each colony experiencing nearly unbelievable growth. Families of a dozen children or more were not uncommon.

"For security reasons, the systems were put in place at each complex that would preclude travel to and from them without authorization. The general population, including the politicians, governors, and such, were kept in the dark about the existence of the complexes. They were controlled and run by the scientific community. Probably the only reason they exist today."

"How is it they continue to function after nearly two thousand years?"

Alex smiled. "Automation and artificial intelligence. I was constructed to maintain this facility, and to train any future scientists who might somehow make their way here."

Harris chuckled. "From what I was told, Cletus Dodger was no scientist. How is it he made it here?"

"Cletus was allowed to visit because the complex was in dire need of items we could not reproduce. He was fed. Enhancements were made to his ship, and he was educated in our history. In return for his assistance with the trade, he was given Farker as a companion. Cletus Dodger's kindness, and his willingness to assist, have given this complex another thousand years of sustainability."

"That's a fascinating story. It also explains a lot. We came here, we prospered, we expanded, and of course we fell back into our normal Human habit of fighting."

Harris tapped his fingers on the table. "A few things I don't get. Where did those original wormholes come from? And how was it our early settlers were so wildly successful? I mean, going from five million to close to a billion in a handful of generations. I would think they would have required help."

"Domicile is a fertile planet, Harris. As is New Earth. As to the origins of the wormholes... those indeed remain a mystery."

Harris pursed his lips. "So what's next?"

"You have completed this level and will be given access to the next once the others have finished."

Harris stood. "Guess that means I go back and wait. Getting hungry anyway."

The image of Alex remained in view.

"Wait. Why are you still here? You usually disappear when I get up from the chair."

"That action is no longer deemed necessary. Welcome to the always-on me."

The holographic image grinned.

Chapter 19

Harris walked out to join the others. Tawn was sitting on a bench with her arm up across the back. "Finally."

"I have to say that was interesting. Where are the others?"

"Trish and Gandy are finishing up their educations. Sharvie is just in talking with Alex."

"You think the pacies have our parts yet?"

"I talked to Mr. Morgan this morning while you were in there. He said he expected them to ship within the hour. That was three hours ago. So yeah, they might be in."

"I think I'll head over to pick them up."

Sharvie walked into the room. "Can I come?"

"Sure."

Tawn nodded. "I'll wait here for the Boleman kids."

Harris made his way aboard the shuttle, with Sharvie following and Farker at his heel. Ninety-five minutes later they were settling on the tarmac at Haven.

Sharvie said, "Why no controller today? Don't they normally request identification or something?"

"They do." Harris shrugged. "Not like them to not have someone here to greet us."

The hatch opened. A quick inspection of the tarmac building showed no one to be there. A vehicle was commandeered for the ride into town.

Sharvie shook her head as they drove. "We've usually passed a half dozen people out walking or in their fields or something by now. This is creepy."

Harris replied, "Must all be in a grand meeting or something. Probably trying to determine what to do with all this blue sky."

"The weather here is always nice."

"It usually clouds up and rains for about an hour in late afternoon."

They pulled to a stop in front of the government building.

Sharvie frowned. "I don't like this."

She followed Harris and Farker as they walked the hall into the meeting chamber. "See, nobody here either."

Several cats were roaming about the meeting room. One had been slaughtered and hung beside a door.

Sharvie grimaced. "Who would do that! And you got blood all over you. You backed into that dead cat."

"If it's still bloody, then whatever happened must have *just* happened."

"That's horrible!"

"Power is still on."

Sharvie shed a tear for the slain animal. "They're all gone, Mr. Gruberg."

"Let's head back to the ship. We'll do some scans and see if we can find them."

As the vehicle pulled out onto the tarmac, a freighter dropped through the sky, landing fifty meters from their shuttle.

The pilot stepped out. "No one at the control station?"

Harris shook his head. "Nor in town."

"Anyone here that can sign for this cargo?"

"What'cha got?"

"A large order of parts and a handful of miscellaneous items."

Harris waved him over. "I'll sign."

"You have credentials?"

"You carrying those for Mr. Morgan?"

"I am. You Gruberg?"

"That would be me."

"Since there's no one here, I guess you'll have to do. Is that blood?"

Harris nodded. "Backed into a slaughtered animal down there. Not sure what to make of all this yet. The pacies always did refuse to defend themselves."

"Well, I don't want to get caught up in whatever's going down here. I'll just be on my way. Give me a hand and I'll help transfer the cargo."

Fifteen minutes later the small freighter was lifting off.

Harris said, "Let's get up there and see if we can figure this out."

Sharvie worked the sensor controls as Harris flew the shuttle. "I'm not seeing anything Human. Tons of cats on the outskirts of town."

"Nav display is showing some meteors or other debris coming down as fireballs. Let's check it out."

As the shuttle moved closer, Sharvie said, "Thousands of pieces."

Harris zoomed in on a fireball with one of the forward facing cameras. "Burning up completely, whatever it is."

Sharvie stood with a look of horror as she worked another camera.

"What is it?"

Sharvie slowly shook her head in disbelief. "It's the pacifists... I think." Tears began to roll down her face as she looked at a floating body.

Harris growled. "What the...? Somebody spaced them. All of them. We have to get back to Midelon."

A jump was made, followed shortly thereafter with a landing. Harris hopped out, hustling over to the supply hut, where the others were sitting.

"They killed the pacies!"

Tawn returned a confused look. "What? Who?"

"Had to be the Earthers. All twenty thousand pacies. Took them up and spaced them all. Left them to fall back through the atmosphere and burn up so there'd be no evidence."

"You sure?"

Sharvie stepped forward, tears flowing. "We saw them... the bodies. Just over twenty thousand. All dead and floating in orbit. They were still in their robes and wearing their sandals."

Tawn scowled. "All of them?"

Harris nodded. "We scanned. Nothing left but a few farm animals and thousands of cats."

"What are we gonna do?" Gandy asked.

Harris gestured toward the shuttle. "We have the parts. We're gonna repair the *Bangor* and we're gonna go kick some Earther ass. There's no reason for what they did. Those people weren't hurting anyone."

Tawn shook her head. "Senseless act. Right up their alley. Harris, come on. Let's get those parts while they get to work."

The team moved with a mission to bring their fighting ship back online. The myriad of parts were unpacked, identified, and laid out for installation. Trish and Gandy worked like machines on the repairs while Sharvie, Tawn, and Harris were their gophers. Four and a half hours later, Trish shoved the railgun limiter circuit back in-line.

"Done."

"Power it up."

Trish pushed several buttons. The gauge on the console read "23," with the big M illuminated.

"Twenty-three megajoules. Wanna see what it will do?"

Harris nodded as the hatch closed and the *Bangor* lifted from the ground. "You people better strap yourselves in."

Gandy slowly raised a hand. "Uh, should we split up and some of us follow in the *Gooch*, just in case?"

Harris looked back with an irritated expression. "Couldn't have prompted for that before?"

Tawn shook her head. "Just put us back down."

The *Bangor* returned to the surface and the transfer was made. A comm was opened to the shuttle.

Harris said, "You should be seeing what I'm seeing."

"We got it," replied Tawn.

Trish said, "Make sure the security-lockout is off."

"It's off. Rails are powered on and the pellet is in the breach."

Before the *Bangor* exited the atmosphere, Harris pulled the trigger. A fireball shot forward as a bright streak.

"First test is positive."

Ten minutes later, after a run out into space, the ship slowed to a stop fifty kilometers from its target. "Here we go. Pellet loaded... and..."

The *Bangor* shook as the tungsten round was propelled to nearly half the speed of light in a thousandth of a second. Dust exploded up from the surface of Midelon's lone satellite.

As the dust began to settle, Tawn said, "Wow... just wow. That crater is twice the size of the last one. What's your status?"

Harris looked over the console. "Everything is green. I think we're good for a multi-shot test."

Trish said, "Do us all a favor and do them one at a time first. Maybe three or four in succession."

The next minute saw four new craters created on the moon's surface. "All indicators are still green."

Tawn said, "Put it on auto. Let's see what we've got."

Harris made the adjustment. "Hold on to your britches."

The *Bangor* shook violently and began to move backwards as a steady stream of hypervelocity pellets emerged from the rails.

Tawn raised her eyebrows as she watched the results. "Whoa."

The comm feed from the *Bangor* shut down. The shuttle moved in close.

"Harris? You still with us?"

"I am. We lost power. No smoke this time though."

Trish said, "Good. The new breaker must have worked. Go to the panel back in the bunkroom. Next to the console there. Open the panel to the right and flip the breaker back on."

Twenty seconds later the *Bangor* came back to life. "Done."

Trish replied, "Run a check on your console. If everything is green you should be back to where you were."

Harris sat. "All looks good."

Trish smiled. "We at least have manual. The circuits and feeds can handle the discharge for that."

Harris took a moment to review the devastation left by the weapon. "This has got it all over a plasma cannon."

Tawn said, "We take this out to Eden, are you prepared to unleash a firestorm? The Earthers may declare war on us."

Harris nodded. "Let them. They can't touch us here."

Tawn replied, "They can rebuild, you know."

"Let them do that too. We'll just follow up with another assault."

"They still have twice the standoff range we do."

"Won't matter. We can handle what they're dishing out long enough for us to get within range and take them out. And with the slight speed advantage we have now, we don't have to worry about them catching us."

"You seem confident."

"More angry than confident."

Tawn sighed. "Let's go back, get some food in our bellies, and then discuss this between all of us. That mine at Eden isn't going anywhere in the next few hours."

Harris returned a scowl. "You set on that order of business?"

"I am."

"I'll see you back on the surface, then."

Lunch was had and the discussion began. Twenty minutes into arguments being laid on both sides, a decision was made. Tawn and Harris would attack in the *Bangor* while the others safely watched from the *Gooch* with Farker.

Systems and supplies were checked before a comm was opened to Bannis Morgan.

Harris said, "We just wanted to inform you of what's going on."

"What did you do out on Jebwa?"

"We didn't do anything on Jebwa. We got there and the pacies were all gone. Found out later they had all been taken up and spaced. All twenty thousand. Every citizen. What have you heard?"

"What I heard is that you are responsible. The freighter pilot said you were acting suspicious, you had blood on you, and you stole the cargo he was delivering."

Harris returned an angry stare for several seconds as he digested the news. "We weren't acting suspicious. We were wondering where they all were. And the blood was from a dead cat we found butchered in their meeting hall. It was hanging and I backed into it. As to the cargo stealing, how can you steal what belongs to you?"

Bannis held up a hand. "Don't shoot the messenger. I know it wasn't you. But the media has already sent a crew out there and have come back with footage."

"That fast?"

"That fast. Images of you, Tawn, Trish, and Gandy are being shown non-stop. It's already being called the 'Jebwa Atrocity.'"

Harris frowned. "Not like we could go back home anyway."

"You can't go near the Retreat anymore either. The DDI has several ships parked out there on a permanent basis, specifically looking for you and your crew."

Harris' frown turned to a scoff. "Let them look. We'll be over at Eden solving our problem there. This Jebwa incident has to be the work of the Earthers. Probably still mad about the pacies' time on Eden."

"Whatever the cause, the DDI now has firm orders to bring you in. As does every law enforcement agency at every outer colony. Will likely follow on the truce worlds. So I would look for all your supply deals to fall apart there."

Tawn said, "Mr. Morgan, you have to use your influence to shut this story down. It's a lie. We didn't do it."

Bannis let out a long sigh. "Unless you have evidence of that there's not much I can do. The pacifists here are in a feeding frenzy over this. Even though claiming to be non-violent, they want your heads on a pike."

The comm was closed and a new one opened to the Retreat. A similar conversation was had with the colonel. He was understanding, and believed in their innocence, but there was nothing he could do to assist any further without putting himself and the colony at risk. The comm was closed and Harris turned with a dejected look on his face.

Sharvie said, "Maybe the recording device will have some conversation evidence on it?"

Harris looked at Farker. "Open a comm to Alex, please."

The familiar image appeared. "Greetings, Harris. I was expecting happiness, but I see forlorn faces. Has something happened?"

Harris nodded. "The pacifists on Jebwa were murdered and the authorities on Domicile think we did it. We need evidence that it wasn't us. Have you finished the decryption of the recorder we sent you?"

"I have another 12 percent to complete. Why?"

"Can you search through what you have for any references to Jebwa?"

"One moment."

Harris turned to the others. If this batch doesn't have anything, the next one should."

"Jebwa is mentioned in three conversations. The first is in reference to the pacifists being moved out there. The remaining two appear to be jokes about joining the pacifists on Jebwa. Is there anything more specific you are looking for?"

"Yeah, like orders telling some captain to round them up and kill them."

"I am sorry, Harris. There doesn't appear to be any records indicating any such activities. Perhaps it is included in the remaining 12 percent?"

Harris sat back and waved a hand. "No. There would have been more than one reference. We have another recorder we'll be picking up shortly. Maybe we'll find something on there."

Harris closed the comm. "Let's just go and get this over with."

Tawn shook her head. "This is big. I say we wait until morning."

"What difference will that make?"

"It will hopefully let you calm down some. And I'd rather go at this fresh just in case it turns out to be a prolonged engagement."

Harris huffed. "Fine."

Trish stood. "Gandy and I aren't done with level four. We should head in there and finish up so we can all advance."

"Yeah, the Earth seems to be in disarray," Gandy said. "I'd say another war is brewing. Big war, I mean."

Tawn said, "You're close to the end. I'd guess only a couple hours away."

Sharvie stood with a thumb pointed over her shoulder. "I'm gonna follow them in and just talk with Alex."

Tawn sat on a chair across from Harris. "Tough day. I know you were fond of them."

"I was fond that they were happy without abusing someone else to get that way. They just wanted to exist and be left alone."

Tawn returned a half frown. "In the long run they probably wouldn't have been successful anyway."

"Why would you say that?"

"Their education system. It consisted of meditation and a small dose of telling each other how things are done. We set them up for success, but they wouldn't likely end up that way. If you hadn't noticed, there were no kids. Another thirty or forty years and they'd have been nothing but a bunch of old codgers, probably in failing health, with a town around them that was collapsing because nobody knew how to repair it."

Harris let out a sigh. "They were happy though. At least for a while. And I think they were smart enough to have learned what they needed to do to keep going. As far as kids go, they could have had a steady stream of new recruits from Domicile."

Tawn shook her head. "Those kids coming out just want to be left alone. They wouldn't come out here if they knew it meant having to care for a bunch of old people."

Harris asked, "You purposefully trying to bring me down?"

Tawn chuckled. "No, just trying to calm you down. What happened was atrocious. Tomorrow we'll make the Earthers pay for it. I just want you going in there with a clear head. Vengeance might bring parties to war, but it doesn't make for good war-fighting."

Harris let out a single laugh. "What was that? Sixth grade they taught us that?"

"I believe it was."

Chapter 20

Harris downed the last of his breakfast.

Tawn asked, "How you feel this morning?"

"Better. You were right to make me wait. The lions of vengeance were roaring in my head yesterday. That would not have made for good decision making. Thanks for putting them to sleep."

Tawn nodded. "Well, you can wake them back up now. It's time to even the score. So what's your plan? I know you've been thinking about it."

"We go in, straight for the command ship. If we can line up two of those ships we might even be able to take them out before getting fired at. After that we break away, try to lure one out and hit it. And we'll keep doing that until there aren't any left."

"What about the dome?"

"When we have the warships out of the way, we go down and kill it. Two or three well placed rounds from those rails and the inside of that dome will be scrambled. Then maybe I strafe the pits a time or two."

"And the other mines?"

"Then we can go after the other mines."

"OK."

Harris asked, "OK, what?"

"Sounds like a plan," Tawn replied.

Harris let out a long breath. "You ready to do this?"

Tawn smiled. "Don't you know? I was born ready. Got the DNA to prove it."

Trish, Gandy, and Sharvie boarded the *Gooch* with Farker as Tawn and Harris manned the *Bangor*. Ninety minutes later they were stopped, just within view of Eden.

Harris opened a localized comm. "This is it. You three go fetch that recorder and then come back here and wait. No going closer, no snooping. Give us four hours. If we aren't back by then, you take that recorder back to Alex and come back to check for us right here at this time every day until you feel it's reasonable to stop. Understood?"

Trish nodded. "Understood."

Harris zoomed in on the nav display as the localized comm closed. "Four ships. Three more down on the surface, one at Fireburg, and a couple at other locations."

Tawn swirled the display around in front of herself. "Best we can do is two at a time. I could do a wide spiral before we take on the command ship. Might get lucky and clip one of the others."

Harris shook his head. "We don't have the spiral shot. No autofeeder, remember?"

"Hmm. So I guess we're going straight in then."

Harris manipulated the display. "If we come in at this angle we'll have a decent shot at this second ship. Ten degrees right and we have a third shot at this one. If it's not already throwing everything it has at us."

"I like the looks of that. Make it happen."

Harris entered two waypoints into the nav computer before pushing the throttle to full. "Twelve minutes to the first turn. Another eight and you can power up those guns. Three after that and it's happy time."

The Biomarines were silent until the *Bangor* reached the first waypoint.

Tawn said, "Funny how you remembered that vengeance saying yesterday."

"They drilled that into us pretty good, didn't they."

"They did. Along with a thousand other good lessons. I mean, think about it... all the battles we've been in, and we survived.

Even with the fiercest of fighting, the survival rate of a Bio was way above a regular's. I'd have to say they taught us well."

Harris chuckled. "You're not going back to thinking about your wanting-to-be-a-farmer days, are you?"

Tawn smiled. "Actually I was. Only now I'm glad I was born Bio and not a regular. We have such an advantage with what we're doing here right now. Terror is replaced with determination. Nervousness with anticipation. Self doubt with overwhelming confidence, but not arrogance."

Harris turned with a nod. "I guess they packaged us up pretty good."

Tawn held her hand up in the air with the palm facing Harris. "Not pretty good. The best."

Harris looked up at her hand. "You expecting something with that?"

Tawn grabbed his hand by the wrist, picked it up and slapped it against her own. "Weren't you paying attention to history back there? It's called a high-five. It means 'oh yeah,' 'great,' 'excellent,' 'for sure.'"

Harris chuckled. "I don't recall seeing that. Thought you were trying to do that wave like the Queen of England or something."

Tawn shook her head. "Don't remember seeing that. I wonder if our educations were largely based on the questions we asked or the responses we gave?"

"Sounds like a question for Alex."

Tawn grinned as she held her hand up in the air again. "And you know why it will be a question for Alex? Because I have extreme confidence that we will be victorious here and return."

Harris stared at her open palm.

Tawn huffed. "Come on, don't leave a girl hanging. Slap it on!"

Harris reached up for a minor tap.

Tawn shook her head. "I hope you've got more than that waiting for the Earthers."

The second turn was made. "Three minutes and we're gonna find out."

Tawn flipped several switches. "Rail circuits are on. Security-lockout is off. Pellet is in the breach. All we need is a target."

"Ninety seconds."

"That look like the same command ship to you?"

Harris shook his head. "The back end is different. You think that's a new ship?"

"Could be. Wonder if it's made with Eden titanium?"

Harris chuckled. "They aren't turning them out that fast. Sixty."

Tawn checked-over the railgun settings. "We are ready and set."

"Thirty. At fifteen we can expect the possibility of plasma fire."

Tawn nodded. "Bring it on, big daddy. We aren't going home empty-handed today."

"Fifteen... ten. We have plasma..."

Tawn nodded. "Just have me aligned for zero."

Harris pulled hard left to avoid the first two rounds before swirling around on the original line. At zero, Tawn unleashed the first tungsten pellet. Two seconds later the second pellet flew.

A burst of six plasma rounds came their way as Harris cut ten degrees to the right. "In line for number three in two... one... mark."

Tawn unleashed another round. The first struck the command ship dead center. A cone of debris jetted out the far side as the remaining energy from the hypervelocity tungsten round impacted the second ship, causing major exterior damage.

The *Bangor* rattled and shook as repeated rounds found her hull.

Harris said, "We have quality hits on command and number two. Three is falling in line after us. Our shot there just missed aft. It moved on us too fast."

Tawn replied, "Should have aimed us forward."

Harris nodded. "Would have been a nice forethought. Wasn't sure we'd even get a shot off."

The *Bangor* shook violently for several seconds.

Harris swerved and juked to avoid the plasma rounds that followed.

Tawn scowled as a pair of hits rumbled on the back of the Zwicker class ship. "I'm finding this weapon a bit useless at the moment. Maybe we should consider building it into a turret before coming back out here."

Harris said, "You wanting another crack at that destroyer?"

"Can you make that happen without killing us?"

Harris grinned. "We're about to find out."

The *Bangor* spun to face backward, aligning perfectly with the pursuer. Tawn squeezed off a round as Harris flipped the ship forward again. Three plasma rounds jerked the attackers back in their seats and then side to side as the hull-breach indicator sounded.

Tawn yelled, "They've opened up those welds! We just bled off a quarter of our cabin air!"

Harris flipped down the visor of his helmet. "Doesn't matter. You just ripped their guts out and took the ass end off that ship. Scratch one destroyer."

Harris turned the *Bangor* back. "Thirty seconds until we're in range of that fourth ship.

"Do your jukes before they start shooting this time. Might spread them out a bit for us."

Harris chuckled. "You want to drive?"

"Just do it!" Tawn growled.

"On it. Fifteen... ten... five... mark."

Repeated plasma rounds struck the hull of the *Bangor*, although not at the same instant. Three seconds later, the nose of the approaching destroyer caved and rolled backward as the tail end of the ship fragmented into a spray of debris.

Harris nodded. "Scratch four."

Tawn said, "Two more coming up from the surface."

Harris nodded. "We'll be passing that command ship on the way in. I'll line you up. See if you can throw them another bone."

"Another bone?"

Harris chuckled. "Hey, I'm concentrating here. You'll have to live with my lame metaphors."

Tawn smirked. "Surprised you even know what that means."

Harris half frowned. "Only because Alex used it on me and I had to ask. I've been schooled now. Thirty seconds."

Tawn nodded. "Looks like those other two destroyers will be coming in one at a time. Perfect. We might just pull this off."

"Fifteen... ten... five... mark."

"Our fury has been unleashed."

"Forty seconds to the next mark."

The two approaching destroyers met with the same fate as their brethren. Harris turned the *Bangor* toward the surface, taking aim at the Fireburg dome.

"Ninety seconds."

Tawn yelled, "Crap! Dozen wormholes opening behind us! Get us out of here!"

Harris hesitated as a small ship rocketed away from the dome below. "Wait, that's the *Fargo*. This time I'm taking her out!"

Tawn reached over and grabbed his shoulder. "We don't have time!"

Harris scoffed as he turned the *Bangor* away. "Again, she skips away."

He reached over, flipping the trigger on the railguns. The ship rumbled as two tungsten pellets raced out into the atmosphere as long stretched-out fireballs, burning up before reaching their target.

Tawn scowled. "That make you feel better?"

"Yes."

"We have a hail coming in from Bax. You want to answer it?"

Harris enabled the incoming connection. "We *are* gonna get you, you traitor."

Bax replied as her image came into focus. "I must implore you to stop. You don't know what you're doing!"

Harris laughed. "Kicking your Earther asses is what we're doing."

"They aren't your enemies. At least not right now."

Harris shook his head. "We know you're building ships. And I think we both know those ships will be used against Domicile. You'll kill everyone just like you did with the pacies on Jebwa."

"What happened on Jebwa?"

Harris growled. "I can't wait to either vaporize you or snap your skinny red neck. Your people rounded up all twenty thousand pacies and spaced them. I know it was you. That has Earther written all over it."

Bax sighed. "If Jebwa was attacked, it wasn't the Earthers. And we're in deeper trouble than I thought. If the Denzee have already come that far, we're only months away from a full-on invasion."

Harris returned a sarcastic chuckle. "Denzee. And I'm supposed to believe these Denzee did this? I suppose next you're gonna tell me they're a breakaway faction of radicals that have separated from the other Earthers?"

Bax shook her head. "No, they are actually small brown furry beings. Kind of a cross between an Earth monkey and a Domicile braza. Only smart. They've already taken over one of the Earthers' outer colonies. Came in and spaced a quarter million settlers before setting up house there. Already more than a billion have landed."

Tawn cut in. "Oh my gosh! A monkey invasion! Our worst nightmare! For some reason we aren't believing you."

Bax scowled. "Listen, you morons. I'm not making this up. And to prove it to you I'm calling off the Earthers and coming to you. Unfortunately for your vengeful egos, we're all gonna have to work together on this if we want to live. The Denzee have no use for us. They will space both Earthers and Domers alike."

Tawn gave an uneasy look to Harris. "Earther ships just dropped off. And Bax is heading this way."

"Has to be a trap."

"It's not a trap, you idiots. This is real. Your friends on Jebwa have already paid the price for being unprepared. You want the rest of the Human race to go out the same way?"

Harris slowed the *Bangor* as the *Fargo* pulled up alongside.

"Look, I'm serious here. Our space is being invaded. I only found out when you were down there on the surface sniping. Just like you, I needed to be convinced. I didn't believe it until the emperor took me out there himself."

Tawn asked, "If this is such a big deal, then why haven't you told Domicile?"

Bax sighed. "I've done my best to convince the emperor to do just that. He's prideful. He thinks the Earthers can handle this on their own if they can build enough ships."

Harris huffed. "And then he'd gladly attack us when he's done. You've picked the wrong side, Rumford."

"I can prove it to you."

"And how would you do that?"

"Follow me out to Rumanta III. You can see for yourself."

Harris chuckled. "I bet you have a couple dozen Earther ships just sitting there waiting for us. You think we're stupid?"

"Yes I do think you're stupid. But it's not a trap. You can jump anywhere in that system and see for yourself."

Tawn crossed her arms. "And just where are these Denzee from?"

Bax let out a long sigh. "We don't know. Could be from anywhere out there. If their raider ships are already reaching the truce colonies, none of us have long to live, unless we can meet them at Rumanta and push them back. Show them Humans aren't to be messed with."

Tawn rolled her eyes. "Now you're sounding like those old corny recruiting videos. 'Protect Domicile. Be the freedom fighter of tomorrow.'"

Harris chuckled. "We used to make so much fun of the regulars over those."

Bax glared. "Idiots. Focus. We're being invaded. We need that titanium, not to attack Domicile with, but to build a fleet to defend us all."

Harris scratched the side of his face in thought for several seconds. "Rumanta III?"

"Rumanta III," Bax replied. "Just make the jump. This is something you will want to know. And just so you also know, the emperor is probably gonna have my head for this. So go. See it. Report it. We're gonna need the help if any of us are going to survive this."

Harris sat silent for most of a minute.

Bax raised her hands. "Well?"

"I'm thinking."

"Before you strain yourself, think about this: you liked the pacies—thought they were dumb, like I do you, but you liked them. I know you want revenge on whoever did that to them. The furry little beasts on Rumanta III are waiting for your vengeance. Harris Gruberg wants his pound of flesh. Go there and you'll see billions of those pounds to choose from."

Harris looked at Tawn. "What do you think?"

"Maybe we go have a look. I'm sure if she's lying we're gonna run into her again at some point. Would make offing her that much more enjoyable."

Harris nodded. "I like your reasoning."

Bax shook her head. "I can't fathom how you two morons are still alive out here, but you are. And you may just be solving a huge problem for me. Go see. Report. Get the Domers involved. This concerns us all."

The comm closed. The *Fargo* turned and headed back toward the dome.

Tawn gestured toward the heavens. "Let's go check it out. We can always off her later."

Chapter 21

The *Gooch* was ordered back to Midelon before the *Bangor* jumped to the Rumanta System. Hundreds of unknown ships showed on the nav display.

Tawn frowned. "She was telling the truth."

Harris powered the ship forward.

Tawn asked, "What are you doing?"

"I'm taking us in for a look. The DDI will need as much intel as we can provide."

Tawn flipped on the circuits for the railgun.

Harris glanced over. "We're not gonna need that."

"Just in case."

The display in front of the console was filled with images of Denzee ships. Harris quickly compared their shapes to a fleet of "baby rattles" A small forward sphere sat at the end of a long tube. On the other end, a much larger sphere made up the remainder.

Harris shook his head. "Bright yellow. Not the best if you want to remain unseen out here."

"Don't think they care."

Harris gestured toward the comm console. "See if you can pick up any communications. If we can record a sufficient amount, maybe Alex can translate it for us."

Tawn flipped several switches, turned dials, and pushed buttons. "Nothing. Not a peep."

"Check the light-speed frequencies."

Seconds later, Tawn sat back. "Wow. Chatter like crazy."

"You recording?"

"Yes. I'm picking up what appears to be thousands of simultaneous comms. Maybe our FTL comms will give us a big advantage.

Harris zoomed in on one of the ships. "Those would be gun turrets. Question is, what do they shoot?"

Tawn pointed. "Those look like missile tubes?"

Harris nodded. "If those are conventional, I'm a lot less worried than I was."

"Hmm. The Earthers are worried. That tells me they've already engaged with these ships and lost. Which is why they're going all in on those mines."

Harris frowned. "I'm starting to think this isn't gonna work out in our favor."

"How so?"

Let's say we team up with the Earthers, build up their fleet and ours. If we defeat the Denzee, which of us will be left in the power position? I doubt it will be those idiot politicians at home putting us on top."

Tawn chuckled. "Well, don't get yourself all worked up because of one possibility out an infinite number. You're looking too far ahead."

"Am I?"

"We just found out about these invaders. Let's take this in for an hour or two and then head back. I'd like to get that crack in our ass fixed."

"It's not leaking. We're fine."

"We're fine unless we get in another fight."

Harris waved his hand toward the nav display. "You see anything heading toward us?"

Tawn stared. "Actually? Yes. You best get us out of here. That has to be a third of their ships coming this way. And they're fast. Faster than us."

Harris turned the *Bangor*. A wormhole was opened and the small vessel slipped through. A second jump had them in

Midelon space. Forty-four minutes later they were landing in the grass outside the bunker.

Trish, Gandy, and Sharvie were waiting as the hatch opened.

"What happened?" asked Gandy. "Was that Baxter?"

Tawn nodded. "It was."

"Why'd you let her go again? She's working for the Earthers."

Harris shook his head. "There's been a new development. We might all be working to help the Earthers build more ships."

Gandy returned a perplexed look. "Why?"

Tawn said, "Humans have lived our whole existence as the dominant and only sentient species. We're smart. We craft tools and use them to do the work we can't naturally do. No other animals have had that ability other than making use of a stick or a rock… until now."

"Until now?"

"One of the Earther colonies has been attacked and overrun. Bax thinks one of their scout ships may be responsible for killing the pacies. We've just been out to that Earther colony. The invaders are real."

Harris said, "We have to send this info to the colonel and Mr. Morgan. They'll have to feed it to their contacts at the DDI. As Tawn said, we may be helping the Earthers build ships now."

Tawn brought the others aboard the *Bangor*, replaying the video they had captured at Rumanta. Stunned stares looked on in disbelief.

Harris said, "Farker, comm Alex for us."

The image of Alexander Gaerten flashed into view. "Good morning, Harris."

"We've got problems, Alex."

"Explain."

"I'm sending you some comm recordings done at light-speed frequencies. We've encountered another species of sentient beings and they've invaded our happy little space."

"You must be referring to the Denzee."

"How'd you know?"

"You advised me to open comms to New Earth and Domicile to gather information. I determined that might be a good idea for each of the colonies. The Denzee are a fascinating species. Very hive-like in their behavior. They have a queen, workers, and warriors. They are intelligent, although I would place that at just below that of Humans.

"Unlike Humans, however, they are committed to their tasks. And their queen, from what I've been able to gather, is of much higher intelligence than the standard human. The colony at Rumanta consists of multiple minor queens and a single major queen. Their warriors and workers follow orders exactly as given."

"Why didn't you tell us any of this before?"

"My programming enables me to answer questions or take on specific tasks. I was not programmed to inform or alert based on external events. If you would like, I can do so. I will however need very specific instruction for that mission to be effective."

Harris sighed. "Fine. And since you already know about the Denzee, do you have an understanding of their language?"

"I do."

"And do you know what they are planning?"

"I do."

Harris shook his head. "Can you... wait... just tell us what they're planning."

"Orders from the major queen are to conquer this section of the galaxy and to subdue and exterminate all Humans."

Tawn rolled her eyes. "Well, that's just great. We're moving from one disaster to another. You wouldn't happen to have an image of what they look like, would you?"

"Yes."

"Please show it to us."

The hologram floating above Farker's back turned to an image of a small, brown, furry animal that stood upright on two legs. Its hands and feet consisted of two long, taloned fingers and opposable thumbs. A ridged, bald skull-plate ran from their forehead around to the back of their neck. Despite their small stature, they appeared to be both sturdy and muscular. A pair of beaver-like incisors highlighted an otherwise flat and featureless face.

Trish said, "Other than the talons and the teeth, they're actually kinda cute."

Harris asked, "Do you have an image of one of their queens? And if so, please show us."

The image changed. The Denzee queen, other than the ridged skull-plate, looked nothing like her minions. Her body was devoid of fur, covered instead by a pale blue skin. She was also taller by a third and appeared to be obese.

Harris said, "She's a big girl."

Tawn chuckled. "If we painted you blue, you'd be a perfect match."

Harris sighed. "I'm not much bigger than you. And certainly nothing like that. Alex, what else can you tell us about their queens?"

"They are continuously pregnant. From what I have been able to gather, they have multiple uteri that are generally at different stages of gestation. At birth, broods commonly consist of eighteen to twenty-two offspring. A single uteri pregnancy takes approximately ten weeks."

"What do we know about the others?"

"The warriors are fiercely protective of their queen, as would be expected. The workers perform the tasks given, regardless of the complexity or danger. If the queen orders work to be done, they are compelled to do exactly as she asks."

Gandy asked, "What about their ships?"

"They refer to the standard ships as Dulons. The workers move about by use of the Dulons. The ship itself consists of two spheres of differing size, and a long tube connecting those spheres."

Harris nodded. "The baby rattles."

"Yes. That would be a fitting description of their external shape."

"You said the worker ships. Are there others? Those rattles were all we saw at Rumanta."

"Yes. The warrior ships."

A new image was displayed.

Harris said, "Looks like the head of a claw-hammer."

"The Ratoon is four hundred and twenty meters in length. Each Ratoon holds at least one queen and as many as a hundred thousand warriors."

Harris smiled. "Given the size of their warriors, we should be able the kick the crap out of them on the battlefield. What kind of weapons do they carry?"

"The translated language refers to them as shock weapons. Pistols and rifles, not unlike our own. A ball of energy, similar in nature to our plasma rounds, is emitted by these weapons. The rounds are slightly less powerful and move more slowly, but they appear to be guided, making them highly accurate."

"Ours are accurate enough."

"The Denzee hand weapons, once a target is selected, may be fired up in the air if so desired. The guided round will arc and seek out the target, making it difficult to hide behind obstructions if looking for cover. There do appear to be limits to that arc, so they are not 100 percent effective in that manner."

Tawn asked, "What about the weapons on the Ratoon? On the rattle we could see turrets and what looked like missile launch tubes."

"The armaments on the Dulons consist of a maser cannon, and missiles as you suggested. The masers have a range equivalent to our plasma cannons. The destructive power is also similar. The missiles provide defense for close combat. Raider ships attempting to board either the Dulon or the Ratoon would find that feat difficult."

"Those look like turrets on the Ratoon. What are we up against there?"

"Again we have a maser, only an order of magnitude more powerful."

Sharvie asked, "Where are you getting this information?"

"From their conversations and data. One can construct an accurate image of many of their systems from listening to not only their conversations, but also by analyzing their data transfers. I can provide a somewhat complete layout of a Ratoon, although it fully lacks information on the ship's power systems."

Tawn frowned. "So they're coming to wipe us out. Do we know anything about their history? Where they're from? How many of them are there?"

"I can only interpolate numbers for you with regards to the number of known or suspected queens. I have one communiqué that refers to the 'Council of Queens,' with an attendance number being close to a hundred thousand. Each of the queens at Rumanta has approximately a hundred thousand workers and fifty thousand warriors."

Gandy did the math. "That would be fifteen billion. They outnumber us, but not by a huge amount."

Alex's image returned, replacing the Ratoon. "Also in that communiqué was the mention of the council being only one of many such councils. We may be vastly outnumbered. I will add that I have been unable to gather any reliable information on the number of planets or ships they may have. We don't know if this is an advance fleet, one of many, or their entire garrison."

"What about their drive systems?" asked Trish.

"From the information I've gathered, their ships are capable of reaching 62 percent light-speed by conventional means. I do not believe they have the ability to travel through wormholes. Although I suspect they may have already acquired that technology from the dozen Earther ships they have captured.

Harris winced. "Captured?"

"Given the fact they were likely the culprits at Jebwa, they may have already perfected or adapted the wormhole systems."

Harris crossed his arms. "If they can do 60 percent light-speed, they will run circles around us in battle."

"I don't believe that to be applicable in a wartime situation," Alex's image replied. "Indications are this speed can only be obtained over several hours at full throttle. Their combat speed capabilities are similar to ours, limited by their inertial dampening fields."

Tawn asked, "You said their queen is constantly spitting out pups. What about their workers and warriors?"

"There are worker spawners as well as warrior spawners. The queens themselves give birth to spawns and elites. Within a queen's realm of a hundred fifty thousand subjects, several thousand births and deaths happen every day. A worker will be fully mature in fifteen weeks and live for approximately seven years. A warrior for twelve.

"The elites are specialized workers such as engineers, scientists, even mathematicians. The elites are highly educated and are tasked with overseeing much of the daily activities, ranging from farming to shipbuilding."

"How about the queens and spawners, or elites as you called them? What life expectancy do they have?"

"A spawner becomes fertile at twelve weeks and will continue to be impregnated and give birth for the remainder of her life, approximately seventeen years. Elites have a similar longevity. A queen, on average, may live for seventy years."

Harris asked, "What does their colony look like? Buildings? Businesses?"

"The hive is one contiguous building. Contained within are the birthing rooms, care facilities, housing for all, manufacturing—virtually everything except food growth. Their food consists of a smaller species that is not dissimilar in appearance to themselves. They call them bogwem."

Tawn said, "So they're carnivores, like Harris."

Harris chuckled. "I eat bogler. They're big and ferocious. Not some helpless little rat."

Tawn shrugged. "Bogler, bogwem, whatever."

"As I said, the hive is a contiguous building. The breeding houses for the bogwem are separate."

"What are these buildings made of? We didn't get close enough to see out at Rumanta."

"Dirt, laced with secretions from the workers. The resulting substance hardens to equal the strength of concrete. Their buildings are a maze of tunnels and rooms. Interestingly enough, they construct the ships within the hive. When complete, the hive is destroyed, allowing the ship to leave. Construction of a new hive is begun immediately thereafter."

The conversation about the Denzee continued for several hours before a slew of questions had been asked and answered.

"Wow," said Tawn. "Wasn't expecting any of this. I know we're trained to avoid such thoughts, but this is almost back to overwhelming."

Harris nodded. "Not what I was expecting out of today either. Our mission has definitely changed. I think it's time we called the colonel."

"He won't be happy with this news. They were just starting to get settled there at the Retreat. I wouldn't doubt they'll all get called back to active duty, maybe even in the next few days."

"That would include us too. If they don't lock us up."

Tawn sighed. "Yeah, I guess it would. At this point though, I'd have to think we could do far more from here than stomping around in some Biomarine unit again. We have a lot more to offer than quick reflexes and muscle."

Tawn chuckled. "Especially you. You've probably got an extra forty kilos to offer."

Harris shook his head. "You just keep digging in with the digs. One day you'll be sorry."

Tawn nodded. "Maybe, but the rest of those days I'll be happy."

Gandy said, "I hope the two of you can stop joking long enough to get serious about this. This is big. We can't afford to let them get a foothold on our worlds."

"We have no intention of letting that happen," said Harris. "We'll talk to the colonel and get a strategy going of what we might do. Between him, Bannis Morgan, and the DDI, we'll figure something out."

Tawn asked, "We tell the colonel or Mr. Morgan first?"

"This is war. That goes to the colonel."

Chapter 22

"**G**ruberg. Tell me what happened. My contacts out there at Eden aren't replying."

"Things have changed on us again, Colonel. And not for the better. And that includes for the Earthers."

"Something new?"

"Very new. And very big. Our little corner of the galaxy is being invaded by an alien species."

The colonel chuckled. "Good one. I like the straight faces the two of you are putting on. Very convincing."

Tawn said, "They're convincing because they reflect reality, Colonel. A species called the Denzee have attacked and taken over Rumanta III. They already have a billion occupants setting up a colony there. And the Jebwa Atrocity... it was these Denzee and not the Earthers who are responsible."

The colonel's expression turned from a modest smile to a serious stare. "This is real?"

Harris nodded. "As real as it gets, Colonel. We've been out to Rumanta. It's surrounded by hundreds of ships. Both of us hate to say this, but we need the Earthers to build as many ships as they can. The Denzee are coming for all of us."

Tawn added. "And they don't take prisoners. We're talking complete extermination of all humanity."

The colonel frowned. "What intel do we have on them?"

"I'm sending over a session we just did with our AI. We'll dump in all the data we recorded. And if we could ask a favor, have your analysts scrub everything down to the raw intel, leaving us and our AI out of it, before they turn it over to the DDI. We'd also like all that initial data to be destroyed."

The colonel replied, "That may be difficult, Mr. Gruberg. The DDI has agents here in-house now. We don't get to have a meeting where they're being excluded."

Tawn held up a hand. "Fair enough, Colonel. We'll handle the scrubbing on this end."

Harris asked, "How we gonna do that?"

"We ask Alex to do it for us. This is the sort of thing he's good at. We can send along the raw recordings Alex took from Rumanta as well. And the translations."

"Colonel, we'll comm you back when we have a package ready."

"I'll get to work on that with Alex."

The colonel asked, "What happened with your raid at Eden?"

"We destroyed five Earther ships. Which reminds me. Trish, Gandy?"

"Yes?" Gandy replied.

"The *Bangor* took damage to her tail again. We'll need the two of you to patch her up. Same thing that happened last time."

Harris turned back to the image of the colonel. "The rail upgrades worked far better than expected. In fact, I almost killed myself when testing them out. We ended up installing a current limiter in-line that reduced the surge enough for us to take manual shots with it. Those pellets come out with far more energy than before."

"So you were successful at destroying Fireburg?"

"Not exactly. We took out their ships and turned toward the mine. We saw Baxter Rumford exiting in the *Fargo* and broke off to take her out first. And it's a good thing we did. Otherwise that dome and the mine would be in shambles right now. Instead, they're still ramping up production."

"These Denzee are that much of a threat?"

Harris nodded. "I believe so. The intel we have at the moment points to us being under-prepared and ill-equipped to deal with this. All the cutbacks going on with our military need to be fully reversed. And, Colonel, you'll probably have to prepare everyone there for the possibility of a reenlistment. Our services will probably be needed."

Tawn came back a few minutes later. "Alex sent a package to your comm. Contains everything we talked about and more. Should get the colonel rolling."

Harris looked back to the image of Robert Thomas. "Sending you the data now, Colonel. You'll want to act on this immediately. Not that I even need to say that. But please do."

"Haven't we come full-circle on this? Our greatest enemy is suddenly our friend."

Harris nodded. "Yeah. Well, maybe we'll get lucky and survive this and all Humans can finally *be* friends."

"Big dreamer, Mr. Gruberg. We'll just have to deal with that when this is over."

"Have a look over the data, Colonel. I'll comm you back this evening to see if I can answer any questions you might have. And If I don't have the answers, I'll try to get them."

The comm closed. A second channel was opened to Domicile. Bannis Morgan popped into view above Farker's back.

"Mr. Gruberg, wasn't expecting you again so soon."

"I have some big developments that I need you to pass on to the DDI, Mr. Morgan. Much bigger than the titanium at Eden. And it exonerates us from the Jebwa Atrocity."

"That does sound big. What has happened?"

"We are no longer alone in this galaxy. A new species has invaded the Earther outer colonies, and has come as far as the truce worlds at Jebwa. The Earther colony at Rumanta III has been completely wiped out and the planet overrun."

Bannis was silent for several seconds. "A new species?"

"They call themselves the Denzee. Small brown furry things. Anyway, more than a billion of them are camped on Rumanta and they're looking to spread through this entire section of the galaxy. I'm sending you a data package to forward to your DDI contacts. As I said, this is big. And it's immediate."

"If true, this is grave news."

"It is. And it's up to us now to convince our government they need to turn things around. We aren't prepared for this threat. And we now need to assist the Earthers in any way we can to build ships. They are the first line of defense. If we can work together to stop them there, maybe we can all live on in peace."

"Has contact been made with this species?"

"Supposedly the Earthers have tried and failed. These Denzee don't take prisoners. They don't appear to have any interest in ruling over anyone but their own. It's not a good scenario, Mr. Morgan. And we aren't prepared to fight it out right now."

"I'll have a look and pass it along, Mr. Gruberg."

"Any progress on the gamma bomb? This might be where we need it."

"Nothing new to report at the moment. Were you able to solve your power issue with the new rails?"

"Oh yeah. Wow. We installed a limiter that originally came with the ship when it was decommissioned. Knocked the power down just enough to allow manual firing. On auto it blew a breaker we installed almost instantly. The speed and energy of the pellet are way up though. If you can solve that power issue I would definitely recommend making those updates at the Retreat. Who knows, that might just be what saves us from the Denzee."

"I will pass that information along to my designers and engineers."

The conversation continued for several minutes before they closed the comm.

Tawn said, "He always seems calm, no matter what the news is."

"I guess when you reach his age you have a different perspective on things. Anyway, where are Trish and Gandy? They started on that repair yet?"

"They were looking it over when I came back in."

Tawn and Farker followed Harris out and behind the *Bangor*.

Gandy said, "Back up. She's moving it over so we can get started."

The group followed the ship to the shop. Trish hopped out and immediately headed for a piece of equipment that would identify and highlight the damage caused by the plasma strikes. Gandy followed, readying a welder.

Sharvie stood by Harris. "What are we gonna do, Mr. Gruberg?"

"Don't know yet. We get the *Bangor* back together and I suppose we might head out to check the place over again."

"I know Gandy wanted to steal an Earther ship. Would it be worth the risk for us to steal one of these Denzee ships?"

Harris glanced down. "You willing to storm aboard with a blaster?"

Sharvie returned a nervous reply. "If I have to."

Harris chuckled. "Don't worry, I don't see that happening. If we decide to do something like that, I'm sure I'll have plenty of volunteers to pick from at the Retreat."

"Good. I don't think I'd make a very good assault Marine."

Harris smiled. "Actually, I think you'd do as well as any other regular. With a little training we could have you storming the decks of one of those Denzee ships."

"I'd much prefer to work behind the scenes."

Harris pointed. "Excellent idea. Head back to the bunker and see if Alex can work with you. Maybe even tap your friends at Domicile. Try to break into a Denzee ship or system."

"Really?"

"That's what you and your friends are good at. This fight needs to involve everyone. Maybe you can take control of a ship and fly it out to us where we have a boarding party ready?"

Sharvie grinned. "I will storm that deck, Mr. Gruberg."

Sharvie turned, waddling off toward the bunker.

"She really respects you," said Tawn. "Not sure why, but she does."

"She's a smart girl, that's all. And of course she's drawn to my good looks and charm."

Tawn laughed. Harris chuckled.

"So when we get the *Bangor* back in the air, do we want to make a run back to Eden to talk to Bax? She might be able to give us some insight into the emperor's plans."

Harris shook his head. "The emperor's plans are to build a fleet and to defeat the intruders. After that I have no doubt he will want to come after us. Not you and I, but Domers in general. And why wouldn't he? If he goes headlong into this and starts to fail, he can always call on his Domer brothers and sisters."

Tawn nodded. "Makes perfect sense. So how do we activate the politicians back home to get involved?"

"That info we sent should be enough. That was twenty thousand Domer citizens that got spaced. Pacifists. If that doesn't rile them up we're in trouble."

"They *are* pacifists you know. They might end up spending six months trying to get the Denzee to talk to our diplomats, all the while with military cuts continuing."

Harris shook for just over a second.

Tawn laughed. "What was that?"

"Don't know. I guess just the thought of that happening is so revolting it sent a shiver up my spine."

"You are one interesting character, Harris Gruberg. Just when I think I've peeled away the last layer of the onion and seen your core, there's a new surprise. You must have some Human DNA in there after all."

"Now you have me wondering if we *should* try to contact Bax."

"Maybe. Or maybe we go take another look out there first and wait to get a response back from the DDI. Would really like to know where they stand before taking any action one way the another."

"You know, Sharvie may have had a good idea. Stealing one of those rattles might be just the thing we need. If we determine they aren't all that, we can turn our focus back to making sure the Earthers don't come clobber us after dealing with the Denzee."

Trish walked around the side of the ship. "Crack's a lot shorter this time. Give us an hour and she'll be ready to fight again."

Tawn asked, "Anything we can do to prevent that? Twice now doesn't give me a comfortable feeling about our survivability."

"I could weld another plate on there. Would probably just blow right off the first time you took a hit, but at least that would be something."

"Waste of time," said Gandy. "I went over this with Alex last time. If we cut a plate into two centimeter strips and weld those on, it will be much stronger. You might lose part of a strip or two, but the crack, if you got one, would be limited to the short length between them. Not the long splits we have seen twice now."

Trish frowned. "That's two solid days of welding to do that right."

Harris nodded. "Let's go ahead with that. We aren't going anywhere at the moment. If Tawn and I need to go back out to Rumanta to observe, we can take the shuttle. Won't be able to go in as close, but we probably don't need to."

Gandy said, "I gave Alex the specs on our railgun update. He said he'd evaluate how we might be able to use the full-auto mode of the feeder. If he comes back with anything for us between now and when she's finished welding, I can install it."

Trish scoffed. "Me? Why am I doing the welding?"

Gandy replied, "Because you're good at it. You called my welds crap last time and pushed me aside."

"Well, they were."

"Which is why you'll be doing them."

Tawn said, "If there's an issue, I would prefer the better welder."

"Fine. But at least make him cut the strips."

Tawn nodded. "Fair enough."

Sharvie waddled out of the bunker, joining the others. "My friends are in. They said they would do it. Only thing is I would have to provide them a comm bridge between Domicile and Rumanta. If we use our current ship it would leave Alex's systems open to intrusion should one of them get the notion to do so. And once they were in we might never get them out."

Harris rubbed his forehead. "How well do you trust them?"

"Mildly. But this may be different considering what it is we're dealing with. Most of them didn't believe it was even real. One wouldn't stop laughing until I showed him a piece of the video you took when you were out there. Now he's all for it."

"Farker, connect us with Alex please," said Harris.

An image appeared, floating above the dog. "Good afternoon, Harris. Do you have a need?"

"I have a lot of needs. The immediate one is a comm bridge going from Domicile to Rumanta. Sharvie's friends want to attempt a hack of the Denzee systems. Any way you can provide that link without compromising your own systems?"

"If my services are used I would indeed be vulnerable. Since we are using a ship just in free space as our comm link, might I suggest one of you travel there to authorize their use of that ship? It would allow me to block all access attempts from there should any of Sharvie's friends want into my systems."

Harris nodded. "Let's go with that, then. Sharvie, we'll take you up and drop you off. Give us a comm when you're ready to be picked up."

The image of Alex slowly shook its head. "That would be unwise. Any contact would open your own vessel to unauthorized entry."

"Fine then. We'll drop you off and come back in a half day to pick you up."

Alex smiled. "That would prevent an intrusion."

Sharvie shrugged. "OK. I'm ready whenever you are."

The shuttle was powered up and Sharvie taken to the comm shuttle parked in free space near Midelon. A case of MREs were left as a contingency if longer than half a day would be required.

The *Gooch*, with Tawn aboard, jumped out to the Rumanta System.

Chapter 23

Harris said, "There's more here than there was last time."

"And we have two of the warships. Those are intimidating."

Tawn sighed. "And they're coming this way. That tells me their sensors are at least as good as ours."

Harris returned a frown. "Take us home then."

"Should we dump out one of the recorders?"

"I have to think they would come out and find it. How about we jump further out, then come back at a different location to drop one?"

"Sounds reasonable. Wait, several of those warships are jumping."

"So they do have jump technology. At least we know how they're getting around now."

Tawn looked over the sensor data. "I have a location. The Barrier colony."

"Let's go see what's happening."

A jump to Barrier colony space was followed by a half hour ride to come within sensor range. Four of the Denzee warships were engaged in a firefight with a dozen New Earth destroyers. The Denzee weapons appeared to have a slight power advantage while their shields held firm against the New Earth plasma cannons. Debris fields for two other New Earth destroyers were spreading out in high orbit.

Harris shook his head. "This doesn't look good. The Earthers' hits aren't doing significant damage."

Tawn said, "Look at that. All the lights coming from that Denzee ship just shut off. You think they lost power?"

A disc on the front of the warship glowed blue-white, followed by an explosion on a New Earth destroyer, a strike that penetrated several bulkheads.

Tawn shook her head. "Not coming back from that. Looks like the Denzee have a superweapon."

Harris nodded. "We need to take this info back immediately."

A jump was made to the Retreat.

Tawn said, "The DDI see us out here and we have to leave right away. They still have warrants out for us. And if we get caught, I don't think it would go well."

"The colonel needs this data. We'll leave immediately after."

An hour passed before the shuttle was within comm range of the colony of Retreat.

"We have a DDI ship here in the area," said the colonel.

Harris replied, "We have important news. The Denzee are attacking the Earther colony at Barrier. A dozen NE destroyers are engaged with four of the Denzee warships. The attackers have some kind of superweapon. I'm sending you the data we have. See to it the DDI get this as soon as possible."

"This is bad news, Mr. Gruberg. It seems they are on the move, which shortens the time we have to react. I just got word this morning that the President's advisers have told him to not take action, as the Earther ambassador felt they had the situation under control."

Tawn said, "We can confirm that is not the case. The Earthers' plasma cannons are exacting minimal damage. Two destroyers were nothing more than debris fields. We watched as a third took a devastating hit from one of those weapons."

"I have the data. Let's have a look," Harris said. "Jump about two minutes into the recording."

Nearly a minute passed before the colonel replied. "I see."

Tawn added. "And they have jump drives. We confirmed a wormhole opening. Looked just like one of ours on the sensors."

"Could be they're adopting our technology. Do we have any indication of how long they've been on Rumanta?"

Harris replied, "We think a month or so, but we don't know the timeline leading up to that. The emperor could have kept this quiet for however long he wanted to. Could be they showed up a year ago and have been in negotiations since then. We don't know."

Tawn nodded. "But we may be able to find out. We could go back to Eden and try to contact Baxter Rumford. She indicated before she was mostly in the dark, but that may have changed."

The colonel took a deep breath, letting it out slowly. "You won't find her there. She's been taken to New Earth under escort. The emperor was not fond of her giving you information about the Denzee. I just received that intel from the DDI this morning."

"Sounds like we *won't* be talking to her."

"Not necessarily. We do have contacts on New Earth. It's possible the DDI could arrange a meeting if it was determined to be a priority."

Harris chuckled. "The only thing the DDI want to arrange for us is a prison cell. We have Midelon. They want to know about it. We aren't telling."

"I'll talk to my contact and see what I can find out. The DDI may already have full information with regards to what's known about the Denzee."

Tawn shook her head. "Don't stick your neck out, Colonel. You get too involved and they'll put you in a compromised position just to get to us. Let's just keep our contact at a low level. If we learn anything we feel is critical, we'll bring it to you."

Harris asked, "You have any word from the shipyard out here?"

"I do. Two days until flight testing of the first freighter. You'd have to talk to Mr. Morgan about any issues it may have. I understand the rail cannons are not functional."

"Thanks for that, Colonel. Say, you wouldn't happen to have a spare shuttle we could take, would you? We've had to repurpose our comm shuttle and are in need of a new one."

The colonel frowned. "Hmm. I just took possession of a personal craft yesterday. Haven't even taken it out yet. I'll have someone bring it out to your current coordinates. And don't worry about returning the pilot. I'll have the shuttle follow to collect him from the drop point."

Harris gave a single nod. "We'll be here... unless the DDI chase us off."

The new ship was collected and returned to Midelon space. As an added security precaution, it was parked at a location just out of comm range of the other comm shuttle currently in use. Harris and Tawn returned to the planet's surface.

"The welds are going faster than expected," said Gandy. "Alex gave us a design for a jig that allows a faster and more accurate weld. The crack has been repaired and the plate strips are going on now."

Harris nodded. "Well, that's at least good news."

"Has something happened?" Gandy asked.

"The Denzee are assaulting the Barrier colony. We need to get the *Bangor* flying again."

"Are you thinking about engaging with the Denzee?"

"Possibly. Would like to have that option if I feel the need to take action. Oh, and we discovered they have sensors at least as good as ours. They spotted the shuttle from maximum range. Gandy stepped over to a console and typed. "Estimates place that colony at thirty thousand inhabitants."

Tawn said, "First, I think there's way more than that. And second, where'd you get that info?"

"Alex has been compiling a database of all the information he's been able to retrieve from Domicile and New Earth. It may not be the most up to date, but it does give us something."

"The sensors showed three cities of what would be fifty thousand colonists each. I bet we're looking at close to a quarter million."

Gandy typed away on the console. "Could be. That data was from a twelve-year-old report. Those thirty thousand were primarily from a military outpost."

"Good to know we have that kind of data available, even if it's old."

"Is anyone going up to get Sharvie?"

Harris nodded. "I'll go. She should be done with whatever she's doing."

Forty minutes later, the *Gooch* arrived at the comm ship.

Harris walked through the docking tube. "Were you able to make a connection?"

Sharvie nodded. "And then some. The translator and firewall structures Alex provided almost made it easy. Their systems are not to unlike our own. Digital, I mean.

"Once in we crashed four of those rattle ships into the atmosphere of Rumanta and all the way to the ground. During the chaos that followed, we managed to guide away a fifth. We have it parked about an hour outside their sensor range and have complete control of the ship's systems. It has a crew of about five hundred on there right now. We believe the normal contingent of workers are down on the planet."

"What are your plans for it?"

"My friends aren't sure what to do with it. The front runner at the moment is to shut down the environmental systems until the crew is dead or incapacitated. We're getting pushback from a couple members who don't want to go to that extreme."

"They do realize these things have already attacked and killed Humans, right? The entire Rumanta colony of Earthers. And our pacifist friends on Jebwa."

Sharvie nodded. "They understand. And unfortunately we need them and their skills on the team."

"How about this: see if you can convince them to lower life support to a level that makes it difficult to survive, but doesn't kill them."

"You aren't thinking of attacking it, are you?"

Harris nodded. "If I can convince the colonel to give us a dozen Bios. If you fully control that ship, and do that with the environmentals, I feel confident I could take control of it with a large squad. We do that and we can fly it back here to study."

"I think I can convince them of that."

"Can you do it now?"

Sharvie hopped on a comm. After a five minute discussion, the effort Harris had suggested was made. The Denzee crewman would soon find life aboard their ship a struggle.

"Are you OK up here? Want to come back down?"

Sharvie shook her head. "Would rather stay here to oversee the team and make suggestions. I finally feel like I'm making a contribution."

"Any hint at a counter effort by the Denzee?"

"To break into our comm?"

"Yeah, anything that would give them access to our systems or networks."

"Not a chance. I don't think they have the personnel with the experience for that. At least not on this particular ship. These are your standard crewmen."

Harris half smiled. "Good to know. Just keep doing what you're doing. And look for us coming into your connection from the other end. We'll show you how a Biomarine squad storms a ship."

"I'll be watching. Oh, and when you get there, you'll find the main docking bay open. You should be able to fly right in."

A trip to the Retreat in the *Gooch* gathered a squad of a dozen Biomarine volunteers who were eager to get-in-the-mix. The group was returned to Midelon, where the *Bangor* was undergoing a final inspection of the new welds. Once finished with a battery of tests, Trish gave the thumbs-up.

Harris turned to Trish and Gandy. "You two remain here and provide support to Sharvie."

Gandy said, "How about we pilot the *Bangor*? I assume you'll be taking your team aboard. Who's gonna watch the ship?"

Trish nodded as she pointed at her brother. "What he said."

"OK, that's a reasonable suggestion. One of you stay and one come with us. The two of you decide."

After a short discussion, Trish raised her hand. It'll be me. He wants to be here if Sharvie needs him. Besides, I'm the more experienced pilot with the *Bangor*."

"Good enough by me. Grab whatever you need. We'll be leaving in three minutes."

Harris was waiting in the cockpit when Trish stepped into the cabin with an armload of tools.

Harris chuckled. "You planning on a rebuild while we're out there?"

"No. Just like to be prepared. If needed, with these items I could repair most of our systems. The standard toolkit isn't bad, but it has a few shortcomings."

Harris nodded. "When we get back, think about what you might want to move aboard as a more permanent set."

The drive was powered up and the *Bangor* was soon racing up through the atmosphere. Once in free space, they opened a wormhole to the Rumanta System, and more specifically, to the location of the hacked, rattle ship.

Harris stood as Trish piloted toward the vessel. A hologram display of the ship floated above Farker's back.

Harris said, "We call these rattles, because they look like a baby rattle, if you've ever seen one. We'll be going in through the main aft docking bay. The outer door will be open.

"You'll be using your suit environments as we've had the environment on that ship cut back to the minimum sustainable level for oxygen breathers for the last several hours. We have a short list of the hand weapons they have in use, but I would expect the unexpected here as we don't know their strategies, tactics, or fighting capabilities for that matter."

One of the squad members raised her hand. "Will we be taking prisoners?"

"Not certain as of yet. I'll make that determination depending on the resistance we encounter once we're in that bay. If they fight, which I totally expect they will, we fight to the bitter end. If they lay down arms, well, we'll have to set up a two-man team in the bay to accept prisoners.

"If we go the prisoner route, any Denzee coming in with their hands raised will be treated in a humane manner. One of you will pat them down while the other keeps vigil. If they check as clean, park them on their ass right there on the deck.

"Trish, you'll be monitoring the nav to make sure no ships are approaching from outside. Last thing we want is to be trapped aboard that ship with one of those warships coming in."

Trish nodded. "Got it. And what do I do if you lose control on the ship?"

Harris returned a confident look. "Use your best judgment. Although I'd suggest you back out of that bay and wait for word from one of us to return."

"I can handle that."

Harris zoomed in on the various decks of the ship, using intel from Sharvie and her team of hackers. The sphere that made up the aft of the ship would be secured first, followed by the long tube connecting it to the smaller sphere.

"Any final assault will be geared toward taking the bridge. After that, we'll be reliant on our hacker team to fly it back to Midelon space."

Harris took control of the *Bangor* as it approached the enemy ship.

A comm hail from Sharvie was accepted. "What's our status?"

Sharvie replied, "We remain in control. Although there's a group up forward who continue to work against us. I'm forwarding streams from the deck cameras, which cover almost every square centimeter. Five of the forward cameras have been disabled. You'll be able to see which ones. And just so you know, they all look to be armed. All of them."

Harris nodded. "Keep this comm open."

Sharvie shook her head. "I don't think that's a good idea. Someone on our own team is trying to hack through my firewalls here on this ship. If successful, the *Bangor* will be next, and you don't have anyone there to monitor that. I'm working with one of the people I know personally to try to find out who on our team is doing this. So far they've avoided our traces."

"How do we keep the camera feeds running?"

"I'm passing you the data for a direct link. Have Farker make a connection and run as your firewall. If he detects any intrusion attempts, have him switch comm channels with you every few seconds. That should at least be a deterrent for a short while. Hopefully it will give us time to uncover their identity."

Harris turned to face his team. Weapons were checked and rechecked, as were the supplies in their suit-packs. As a final effort, complete diagnostics were run on their combat suit systems. A video stream of the docking bay was brought up as a hologram, floating above Farker's back.

"I want two mini-squads. I'll take one with six of you, while Miss Freely will lead the other. As you can see, we can expect some resistance as we enter the bay. We'll be going in with the hatch pointing toward space, so we'll be using the *Bangor* as a shield until we're fully out and on the deck. I'll be taking my squad to the left while Freely's team moves right. We'll need to secure this bay before we can move forward."

An image of the hallways just outside the bay was pulled up. "Coming out, we again go left while Freely's squad goes right. Clear all rooms down this hall. At the end you'll find stairwells. Make your way to the top deck. When we meet up there, we'll start our way back down, clearing every nook and cranny. We can't afford to leave stragglers behind us. The *Bangor* will be passing us bioscan results to assist with this effort."

Tawn asked, "Should we leave someone in the bay once it's been cleared?"

"No. Trish will be here in the *Bangor*. If she needs help she can let us know. I don't anticipate them having weapons powerful enough to damage this ship. Shields will remain up once we've landed."

"What about the main tube leading forward? How do we prevent the Denzee from coming through once we pass it on our way to the lower decks?"

Harris replied, "We'll be leaving one member from each squad at those entryways. There are two decks running through that tube, hence two guards."

Harris shut down the hologram. "Anyone unclear about what we're doing? No? Good. Let me add that we're on a timer here. We should expect the Denzee to be out looking for this ship.

"If we get an indication they've found us, we'll have no more than eight minutes to fight our way back to the *Bangor*. At that time, the *Bangor* must leave. If you can't make it, well, you know the protocol."

Harris again took the controls as the raiding ship closed, pulling into the docking bay while turned to the side. The hatch was opened and the two squads exited in a flurry of blaster fire.

Chapter 24

Harris dove to the deck at the front edge of the *Bangor*, firing two plasma rounds at a pair of Denzee crewmen who were standing in the open. He rolled and dashed to the cover of a loading vehicle parked in the bay. The loud cracks of blaster rounds impacting the machinery in front of him were countered by the familiar whumps from the Saxon Repeating Plasma Rifles.

Tawn's squad took out another Denzee crewman as they made their way behind a stack of containers on the far wall. Harris was quickly joined by the remainder of his squad.

"Genna, you and Harpwell move down this way. The rest of us are heading straight for that door."

Trish came over the comm. "Five bios showing in here. Two left and three right. Five more moving down the hallway toward the door."

Harris' charge cleared the left side of the bay, ending by taking the door. The five crewmen coming down the hall met with quick deaths as two slugs dropped through the door, blanketing the approach with plasma fire. Tawn's squad made short work of the remaining three.

"Bay is clear of bios," said Trish.

Harris glanced back at the ship. "You're on your own in there. You have trouble, you comm us. If it gets bad, just take her out and wait for further instructions."

Harris looked at Tawn. "Let's keep it moving but keep it safe. They're crewmen, not warriors. They'll make mistakes. Exploit them. See you on the top deck."

Tawn led her squad off in the other direction.

Trish said, "Bisocan shows fourteen Denzee down this hall on either side just in front of you, Mr. Gruberg. Two behind the first door on the right."

The door was blasted open. A stump ducked behind the doorframe, dodging several rounds before charging inside. Two whumps saw to the end of the crewmen attempting a defense. The remainder of the hall was cleared in the same manner. Trish highlighted bioscan data, passing it to either squad as they moved forward.

The stairwells going up saw minor resistance. All were dispatched with minimal effort on the part of the Biomarines. Their moves were precise, their efforts determined, and their tactics spoke of their extensive training and experience. Nine minutes into the assault, the top deck was reached and cleared.

Harris said, "We have two stairways on either side of this ship. Post someone at each of these two. Tell me when you have the stairwell covered and we'll move down a deck. You move down two. When you have it cleared, wait for my signal that we're ready to drop another level. I'm giving us twenty-two minutes to clear this sphere. We have Trish's help. Let's see if we can shave a few minutes off that allotment."

Tawn nodded. "Show the way."

The twenty-four decks of the larger sphere were taken without casualty. A run back up the stairs saw the two squads converging on the two halls in the tube leading forward.

Trish came over the comm. "Bioscan counts sixty-five crewmen in the rooms along those halls. That's all the info I can give you. The hacker is close to penetrating our firewalls. I have to disconnect."

Harris nodded. "Just follow our prior instructions. We still have the camera feeds running to our helmet displays. Be safe."

The comm closed.

Harris looked to his second. "Turkey shoot is over. We'll have to work for these."

The slug standing beside him grinned. "An honest fight? I prefer it, sir."

Harris' squad moved down the upper tube. The first two rooms were empty. The third erupted in blaster fire as the door was opened. Shrapnel from a disintegrating doorframe dug into the arm of a slug. After a coordinated series of plasma rounds, the room was cleared.

"You OK?"

"Just in the meat, sir. Cut through the suit. Could use a bandage... and a good stiff drink."

Harris waved her back. "Dothan, see what you can do to patch her up. You two up front, keep that injury in mind going forward. Make certain you're as far around the corner as possible when the door is opened."

As the squad moved ahead, Harris leaned against the wall. A slug and a stump moved to the next door. The wall behind Harris buckled outward violently, pushing him across the hall and into the far wall. He slammed to a hard stop and dropped.

The door was blown open and the room filled with plasma fire. Any fight from those inside was quickly over.

Dothan knelt beside a stunned and shaken Harris. "You'll live."

Harris held up a hand. "Give me a minute to clear my head."

Dothan glanced up at the others. "Hold up. Chief has cobwebs."

Harris stood, rotating a shoulder that had taken the brunt of the initial hit. "I'll be OK. Move us forward."

Dothan waved to the two Biomarines in front. "Move out. We're good. Sir, I'd suggest you hang back for a few minutes. We've got this."

Harris nodded. "I think that best."

Ten minutes of continued action saw the team reaching the end of the connecting tube. The smaller of the two spheres, eight decks tall, held the bulk of the Denzee crewmen. Harris enabled a translator that had been loaded into his helmet system. The commands that would follow would be spoken in Denzee.

"This is Harris Gruberg. I'm in command of the force you are fighting. We have control of the rest of this vessel, including all systems. Surrender now and you will be allowed to live. Attempt to resist further and you will die."

The footsteps of small boots could be heard coming from around a corner along with hushed voices.

Dothan leaned back toward Harris. "I don't like this, sir. We're exposed."

Harris nodded. "Listen up. Fall back to those first two doorways. Dirgess, you and Scalese stay out here, but be ready to move back should things get dicey. I'll give them one more chance to respond. If they don't, we'll press forward."

Harris stood in a doorway with the two Biomarines on either side of the hall in front of him. "This is Harris Gruberg. We're giving you one last chance to comply with our request for surrender. Enough of you have died. There doesn't need to be any more."

Again the thumping of small boots was heard, along with whispers in Denzee.

Dothan said, "Sounds like a lot of boots out there, Chief."

Harris opened a comm to Tawn. "What's your status?"

"We're at the hall's end. I've given the ultimatum as we discussed. Haven't received a reply."

Harris nodded. "Hold tight."

A comm was opened to the *Bangor*. "Trish? What's the bioscan telling you?"

The comm closed before an answer was given.

Harris sighed as he looked over his shoulder at Dothan. "Hackers must have her tied up still. Looks like we're doing this the hard way."

As Harris leaned out into the hall to give the order, the loud cracks of blaster fire filled the audio in his helmet. Dirgess and Scalese opened fire immediately as a rush of Denzee flooded their position. Plasma and blaster fire quickly gave way to hand-to-hand fighting with knives. The two Biomarines were overwhelmed by numbers before a respectable fight could be put forward.

Harris repeatedly expelled explosive rounds into the horde of Denzee crewmen filling the hall in front of him. Dothan reached up, pulling him back by his shoulder as the first of the Denzee reached their position. Plasma rounds split bodies wide as their taloned fingers clawed gouges into the lower suits of the Biomarines.

Tawn came over the comm. "They're pushing us back down the hall! It's a bloodbath but they keep coming! We lost Lopez in the initial surge!"

Harris countered as Denzee body parts filled the hallway just outside his door. "Dirgess and Scalese are gone! We're trapped in side rooms! There are hundreds of them!"

"The numbers are thinning down here. You must have taken the brunt. Hang tight. We're on our way up!"

Tawn yelled into her comm. "Push forward! We're taking this hall!"

Harris, Dothan, and a stump named Ferris fired a constant stream of plasma toward the door and into the hall beyond. The whumps of their rifles was followed by the rumble of explosions in the hall. An equal maze of similar noise emanated from just down the hall at the next room as the two slugs trapped inside attempted to defend their position.

Several minutes of mayhem passed before the forward assault stopped, the rumbles and explosions of plasma rounds coming from the near end of the hall.

Tawn yelled over the comm. "Charge out! We've got 'em pinned!"

Dothan shoved Harris forward, high-stepping over the remains of dozens of dead Denzee just beyond the door. Forty seconds later, the hallway fell silent.

Harris stood, knee deep in body parts. "Your squad?"

"I lost Bellamy coming up. You?"

Harris glanced back down the hall. "Shaw? Drumford?"

Dothan came from their doorway. "Gone, sir. Both took blasters to the head, so it was fast."

Harris sighed. "We have eight decks to clear. Let's move."

Two stairwells went up and down through the levels of the smaller spherical section of the Denzee rattle ship. The team, this time staying as one unit, fought their way to the top deck. Five minutes later, the single vast room at the top was cleared of belligerent defenders.

Harris pointed at the far stairwell. "Take your team that way. We'll meet you in the middle of each deck. Leave one behind to guard the stairwell as we clear the rooms."

Tawn nodded with a smile. "Exactly as I would have called it. I'll race you to the center."

Harris frowned. "We've probably taken out 60 percent of their crew. I wouldn't get too cocky if I was you. That leaves a couple hundred still. Pick your battles and bring your four friends back alive."

"You concerned that we haven't heard from Trish?"

"I am. But at this point our only real choice is to finish the job. We do that and we can jump this ship out of here."

"And where would we take it? We don't have Farker with us."

Harris nodded. "A fact I'm aware of. Worst case, we jump it to the Retreat and leave it with the colonel."

Tawn took a step toward the assigned stairwell. "Let's get this over with before we have visitors."

An explosion coming from the stairs knocked a squad member off her feet. The roar of small boots followed.

Harris pushed Tawn toward the other stairs. "Come on!"

The duo slid, spinning around to face the other way as the rest of their team stepped over and past them onto the stairs. Harris was the first to pull the trigger, catching the lead Denzee as it charged out with a blaster in hand. Eight plasma rifles focused a continuous stream of bolts into the stairwell opening. Screams were heard and chaos ensued. The fallen quickly blocked the path upward.

Harris stood, charging forward. "Over here!"

The team followed, again taking up positions facing the other way. The rumble of small boots echoed with the first Denzee coming into view after reversing their attempted assault.

Several hundred plasma rounds later, the second stairwell fell silent. The remaining Denzee were in retreat.

Tawn hopped over her friend, jumping into the pile of bodies on the stairs behind them as she forced her way down. The remaining squad members followed. The second level saw light resistance, as did the third.

When the fourth was reached, Harris moved back to the entrance for the upper tube. "Tawn! Check out the boot prints! They're headed for the docking bay!"

Tawn grabbed one of the remaining slugs. "You stay with me. We're gonna clean this place out. The rest of you go with him!"

Harris hustled down the tube with six others just behind. As they approached the doorway leading into the bay, they encountered a dozen Denzee and quickly dispatched them. Burns on the wall just outside the doorway told of a fierce fight.

Harris slid to a stop, poking his head around just far enough to get a look at the bay. It was in shambles, having seen multiple large explosions. The *Bangor* raced in from outside, skidding to a stop in front of him with the hatch exposed.

Trish jumped into view. "Come on! We've got four minutes until the Denzee ship arrives!"

Harris vaulted forward and was quickly in the cabin. "How many ships?"

"Just one. But it's one of those warships."

He turned to face the remainder of the team. "Go back and get the others, meet us back here as soon as you can. I'll see what we can do to slow their progress."

The hatch closed as Harris strapped himself in. "You'd better sit and cinch that belt."

The *Bangor* lifted, rushing out of the smoldering bay. "I had to use the railgun. Probably a hundred of them rushed me. Some were still clinging to the hull when I moved outside. I dropped the power down to minimum and fired three rounds."

Harris nodded. "You did good. Only a dozen left when we arrived."

"Are we about to do what I think we're doing?"

"Yep. Dial that power back up to full. We have no idea what the shielding is like on that thing."

"What's the full plan?" Trish asked.

"Delay. We try to slow them down long enough for the others to get back to that bay."

The *Bangor* closed on the rapidly approaching warship. The exterior lights on the Denzee ship went dark as the blue circle on the front began to glow white.

"They're firing!"

Harris turned hard, moving just out of the way of the invisible beam of energy, flipping back in time for Trish to fire off a hypervelocity tungsten pellet. An exterior shielding plate beside the powerful Denzee weapon buckled but held.

Harris growled. "We're in trouble."

Two additional railgun rounds did their damage on either side of the circular weapon. Neither penetrated the ultrathick hull of the approaching ship.

Harris turned the *Bangor* back toward the rattle and the rest of his team. "I hope they're waiting when we get there."

Bolts of bright green plasma energy emerged from the Denzee ship's standard weapons, bolts that were easily dodged as Harris ducked, rolled, and swerved with the *Bangor* on his way back to the rattle ship for a pickup of the others. A rapid deceleration and a hard cut had him landing in the bay only seconds later.

"Freely! Where are you?"

"On our way! One minute!"

Harris shook his head. "We don't have a minute! They're already on top of us!"

Harris held back the impulses from his brain telling him to leave. Tawn emerged from the doorway just as the great ship outside slowed.

"This is gonna be tricky," Harris said as the others boarded. "Strap in!"

The *Bangor* moved out of the bay and around the large sphere, staying just out of direct sight of the titanic Denzee warship.

"We're trapped. They get close enough and we don't have anywhere to hide."

Tawn released her belt, moving to stand behind Harris with her hand on his shoulder. "Maybe our only option is a bum-rush? You think we could make it to their hull, where their weapons can't get to us?"

Harris winced. "Will take all the luck in this galaxy to pull that off. If I can get them to follow us around, I'll put us back in that bay."

"And from there?"

"From there we do whatever comes next."

Tawn smirked. "That has Biomarine written all over it. Let's do it."

Harris looked at Trish. "I'm about to do a roll that will expose us for only a few seconds. Take a couple shots if you can."

Trish nodded. "Ready when you are."

The *Bangor* flipped up and over the edge of the great warship, making it visible just behind the large sphere of the rattle-shaped Denzee ship. Two tungsten rounds found their mark, one entering through an exterior port, no doubt causing tremendous internal damage, the second merely denting the exterior hull. The Denzee ship moved toward them, following the *Bangor* just as Harris had hopped.

A hard push forward had the much smaller ship around and sliding back into the docking bay from where it had only moments before escaped.

"What now?" Trish asked.

"We wait for them to come back around. Flip that rail cannon back to autofeed. Dial the power down by 5 percent. When they come into view, just squeeze that trigger and hold it."

Chapter 25

Twenty seconds of excruciating silence passed before the nose of the Denzee hammerhead came into view. Trish squeezed the trigger, firing three hypervelocity pellets a second. Six pellets mangled a forward cannon and the surrounding shielding before the power breaker flipped off, taking the *Bangor* into darkness.

Trish asked, "Why aren't they shooting?"

As she flipped the breaker on, Tawn said, "They have a prize. They'll be wanting to know who we are and how we took control of this ship."

"Can't we shoot the rail cannon again?"

Harris replied, "Might be our only choice. We can't allow them to take us. We know too much."

An image of Alex popped into existence above Farker. "Greetings, Harris and Tawn. I've been monitoring your situation. It seems dire."

Harris chuckled. "You here to gloat? Doesn't seem like you."

"On the contrary. I'm here to deliver a message of hope."

"Hope? Hope for what?"

Trish said, "We have a wormhole opening. It's... one of our new freighters."

A comm came in from Sharvie. "Finally! We caught the rat trying to hack us. He's been taken care of. I hope the help I sent is enough."

A second comm came in. "Gruberg, Freely, we'll see if we can give you a bit of space."

"Colonel?" Harris asked.

"Miss Withrow said you might need some help. I've brought the newly commissioned freighter, the *Hailstorm*. Major! Bring those cannons online! Full auto!"

Harris shook his head. "The tungsten won't penetrate their shielding, Colonel. We're just throwing punches."

"Then we'll throw punches."

Tawn stepped forward. "Colonel, have your gunners aim for ports or vents. And stay away from the front of that beast. We don't know if that big gun is still functional or not."

The *Hailstorm* slid in for a broadside exchange with the Denzee warship. Plasma bolts pounded the freighter's shields as a half dozen autofed rail cannons opened up. The *Hailstorm* rumbled inside as plasma bolts impacted its shields, jerking its occupants up, down, and side to side. External plating buckled in spots, but held.

Plating punched heavily inward on the Denzee claw-hammer without breaching hull integrity... until a door blew from a small docking bay. As each cannon passed, their aim was altered to take advantage of the opening. Smoke billowed. Flames burst out and quickly extinguished. Debris littered the space surrounding the great ship.

The colonel barked an order. "Bring us around! And target that damage!"

As the *Hailstorm* spun, slowed, and reversed course, the behemoth warship began to move. A second volley of plasma bolts saw two sections of the freighter's hull give way. The bulkheads behind held firm. The newly commissioned ship returned rail cannon fire into the damaged Denzee bay, widening the hole. Decks and interior bulkheads shattered and failed with the second pass.

The colonel yelled, "Take us around!"

The upstart freighter spun and pursued as the Denzee ship continued to pick up speed. Five minutes into the chase, the *Hailstorm* broke away, its speed not capable of matching the much faster vessel.

Harris gave a look of relief. "Thank you, Colonel. We were had."

"You need personnel to clear that ship?"

"No, sir," said Trish. "No bio signs on here but our own."

Tawn said, "We could use a crew though, Colonel. A few of us are a bit beat up from shrapnel."

"Bring them over, Miss Freely. We have a medic aboard... and supplies. I'll send a crew back and we'll see if we can bring her home."

Harris said, "I'd like to take her to Midelon first, Colonel. You take her home and the DDI will sweep her away. We won't have learned anything for ourselves."

"We learned this barge can hold her own against their plasma weapons. That in itself is good news."

"We found a weak point and were able to exploit it. If they have any kind of intelligence they'll be looking to cover that vulnerability."

"As will we."

"Yes, but what you didn't witness was having to fight that main gun. I've seen it go five bulkheads deep into the nose of an Earther destroyer. It would do equal damage to that freighter, if not more. We must have gotten in a few lucky shots to disable it just before you arrived. I'm certain those defenses will be enhanced for our next encounter."

The *Bangor* moved into the small docking bay of the *Hailstorm*. Their medic was waiting to assist the injured.

Tawn gestured toward Harris. "Go get that shoulder looked at."

"It's fine. Just bruised."

Tawn shrugged. "Your body. If it was me, I'd be worried about needing to fight again tomorrow. I'd want to be at the top of my game."

"Fine. I'll have it looked over. Colonel, when your crew is ready over there, let's jump to a neutral spot. From there we'll take the Denzee ship with us. I'll bring your crew back once we're settled."

"So no visit for me to the mystery planet?"

"Not yet. Until I'm given the OK, I won't be allowing any other piloted ships in there. We'll be dropping this rattle short of the planet. We can pick it up on our own from there."

The Denzee ship was moved to Midelon and the colonel's crew returned. Two days later, Harris walked the bridge deck as the massive ship sat on the grass beside their encampment. Trish and Farker walked by his side.

"Alex, have you given their systems a full analysis?"

"I have. I would expect that the vulnerabilities taken advantage of by Miss Withrow's team have been secured. They were intricate finds, but identifiable once an attack happened."

"You find any more we might make use of?"

"Several, but they do not open the systems to the level of access achieved in this last attack. I would qualify them as minor exploits. More nuisance than detriment."

Harris asked, "Anything else of note or interest?"

"Yes."

Harris chuckled. "Well, would you please tell them to me?"

"Their drive systems are considerably advanced. They are able to achieve speeds above 60 percent light-speed. Substantially faster than our own systems."

Harris nodded. "That's impressive. Is it something we can replicate?"

"I believe we can. The major difference is in the containment vessel surrounding the drive. In our systems, 72 percent of the magnetic field is absorbed by shielding. In the Denzee drive, 98 percent of the field is utilized as it is reflected by the containment structure. That single difference, in theory, accounts for 87 percent of the speed advantage they possess."

Trish said, "So we can increase our efficiency by adding this wonder shielding? What is it?"

"An alloy. I will forward the material list to your comm. While we do not have the means to produce this here, it could be done on Domicile."

Harris asked, "You find anything else of value?"

"Yes."

Harris shook his head. "Tell us please."

"The exterior shielding, also an alloy, would add 22 percent to the 'hardness' of our hulls. The emitter tips of their plasma weapons are 14 percent more efficient. And their environmental systems recycle air at only a quarter of the power use of ours."

"How about things like computers or inertial dampeners?"

"Both of ours appear to be superior. I do have one other item that I believe you will find interesting."

"Go on."

"The ion inhibitor boxes we use to add protection to our hulls, they can be adjusted, with a minor software modification, to better inhibit the effects of the Denzee plasma weapons. This one update may add as much as 30 percent to our plasma shielding."

"That's huge, Alex. When can we have this adjustment? Or I guess I should say, give it to us."

"I'm forwarding the update and the installation instructions to Trish."

Harris nodded. "Good. That will at least give us something. You have the designs of our new freighters. I'd like you to enhance those designs with these updates. Let me know when those are ready and we'll forward them to Mr. Morgan."

"I'll let you know, Harris."

"Wait, one last thing. You said the hull plating on this ship is harder than ours. Is there any way for us to strip some of it off here to add to the *Bangor*?"

"One moment while I perform an analysis... yes. The cutting and welding equipment in Trish's shop should be sufficient. I will forward what I consider to be the best plating to remove, along with instructions for its installation on the *Bangor*. I would caution, however, that you will be losing much of your stealth capability. If you'd like, I can work up a design to regain most, if not all of that, but I suspect it will require a visit to a manufacturing facility."

"Do that, Alex. And thanks."

Harris turned to Trish. "When he sends you that plating, let's get to work and get it stripped. I want to turn this over to the colonel and the DDI as soon as possible."

"How long before all these bodies start to smell?"

Harris replied, "Not an issue. So long as we keep the temperature in here below freezing, they'll keep until we turn it over. The DDI can then clean it up if they want."

Trish looked down at her comm bracelet. "I have incoming data from Alex. I'll get Gandy and the tools Alex suggests and get started."

Five hours passed before Trish came to see a resting Harris. "The shoulder feel any better?"

"Not really."

"We have the plating removed. If you want to deliver the ship to the colonel, it's ready to go."

Harris nodded. "You sure you have everything you need? Once we give this over we won't be seeing it again."

"I took what Alex recommended, plus another 20 percent. We should be good."

"You have an estimate of how long it will take to weld that on?"

Trish nodded. "Three days, according to Alex."

"Go ahead and get moving on that. Tawn and I will be taking the rattle to the Retreat."

Harris opened a comm to Sharvie. "How you doing up there?"

"We have twenty ships under various stages of hack right now. Some we fully control and others we are working toward. The rattle ships continue to assault Barrier. We've sent eight of them to the ground as fireballs, but more are coming."

"No troops on the ground there yet?"

"No. And the warships that were there have gone back to Rumanta. Possibly an attempt to protect that colony. We're keeping the pressure up there too, but they're slowly regaining control."

"And you're all set for food and such?"

"I'm good for another week, thanks."

Harris rounded up Tawn. He piloted the shuttle with Farker as she insisted on flying the Denzee ship. Ninety minutes later they were parked in orbit over the Retreat with a comm open to the surface.

The colonel said, "I'll notify my contacts at the DDI. Once they're on their way, I'd suggest you scat as soon as they show on your nav display."

Harris nodded. "Will do, Colonel. The Denzee ship is complete except for a small section of plating. I'm sending you an analysis we performed on it that outlines a number of enhancements we could make to our own fleet, giving us a better edge in a standard fight. We don't have anything that will stand up to the main weapon on their warship. I'm sending what data we have along on that as well."

The colonel replied, "If they don't pull the warrants they have out for you and your crew, I'll be shocked. Between this and the data I just turned over from the *Hailstorm*, they'll be far ahead of the game, without having risked a single agent or ship."

"Having those warrants lifted would be nice, but I wouldn't trust them to not still grab any of us for questioning. We have Midelon, and they want to know what's there. How is the *Hailstorm*, by the way?"

"Extensive hull damage. Lost two of our rail cannons. Mr. Morgan has it back in the dock at the moment. He says two weeks should bring her back to 95 percent, with the remainder being cosmetic. I told him not to put any effort behind repairing the paint job."

"What about production of the other two?"

"Three weeks and both will be ready for flight testing."

Harris nodded. "Can't be soon enough. Any thoughts on producing more?"

The colonel shrugged. "I think that all has to do with the monies available. Bannis told me they're running close to a hundred million credits each. He's put a large part of his personal fortune into this.

"Although... I might have a solution. Instead of the DDI, if I turn this ship and the information you have given over to Mr. Morgan, he might be able to generate enough contract work through upgrades to more than cover his costs. I would imagine the fleet admirals would be keen to have what you've brought us today."

"Excellent idea. In fact, I believe I'll open a comm to him right now and give him the news personally."

The colonel nodded. "Please do."

An image of Bannis Morgan showed on the display. "Mr. Gruberg, Miss Freely, the colonel filled me in on your latest exploits. I'm told you have a Denzee ship in your custody?"

"We do. I have it here at the Retreat, waiting for you."

"For me?"

"I was just discussing with the colonel. We've conducted a quick analysis of the ship's drive, shielding, and systems. I have a number of design updates to offer, not only for our freighters, but for you to submit for contract updates to the Domicile fleet. Enhanced shielding, weapons, and a drive that can propel a ship to 60 percent light-speed. I don't see how they could refuse. Especially given the current threat."

Bannis sighed. "The DDI is fully aware of the threat. Our politicians have buried their heads in the sand and don't want to hear about it. That's partly because the New Earth emperor insists they have the Denzee under control."

Harris shook his head. "The Barrier colony is under assault right now. We've managed to run some interference, including grabbing this ship, but that time is coming to an end. And the Earthers don't have anything that can stop the Denzee warships."

"Then why not ask for our help?"

"The emperor still has his mind set on conquering us all. If he can beat back the Denzee while building up his own fleet, he would be unstoppable should he come after us next."

"I see. Send me what you have and let the Denzee ship sit. I'll have a crew out there to move it."

Harris winced. "There is one thing. Your people will find about five hundred dead Denzee splattered all over the inside of the ship. We have the inside temp set at below freezing, but the mess is still there."

Bannis returned his own grimace. "We'll take care of it, Mr. Gruberg."

"Oh, and I'm sure the *Hailstorm* repairs are a significant cost. Let the colonel know we'll reimburse whatever that cost is. Along with the updates we're sending you."

"Will do."

The comm was closed, the data sent, and the *Gooch* returned to Midelon.

Chapter 26

Harris stood watching as Trish welded a hull plate from the Denzee ship onto the *Bangor*.

"I wish you wouldn't stand back there like that. Gives me the willies when someone's looking over my shoulder."

Harris chuckled. "I was just about to compliment you on your welds, but I guess that's lost now. Looks like you've already made good progress."

Trish nodded. "The nose is done. As long as we're aimed toward the enemy, we should be in good shape."

"Let's hope that's later rather than sooner. Would like to have the drive update in before we have to go out again."

"Will that make a difference? I mean, doesn't that only do any good for distance travel? We can already turn faster and accelerate faster in combat."

"True, but we can be outrun if they decide to leave, or we can be chased down if they decide to follow. And if we have to run, we need separation to open a wormhole."

Sharvie came over the comm. "The warships have returned to Barrier. They're in a fight with the Earthers, who have five cruisers and twenty-three destroyers. One cruiser has already been destroyed. And our hacks on the warships are no longer working. They've closed the holes we slipped in through."

Harris nodded. "Just do what you can. Even if it's just an annoyance."

Harris turned to Trish. "When will you be finished with that plate?"

"Five minutes. You aren't thinking of taking her out, are you?"

"We may have to. Just keep working while I talk this over with Tawn."

Harris walked into the supply hut. "The Denzee warships are back at Barrier."

Tawn shrugged. "Not much we can do about it. We don't have the firepower to do anything more than dent their hulls."

Harris let out a long sigh. "I feel like we can't just sit and watch."

"You have any suggestions?"

"Actually I do. Let's take a ride to Eden. See if Bax is there. She has the emperor's ear. Maybe she can talk some sense into him."

"When will Trish be done with the welds?"

"She's at a stopping point now, having covered the nose. Another day or two for the rest."

"So we taking the *Gooch*?"

"Unless you plan on flapping your arms with me riding on your back, yeah."

"Let's get this over with, then. And when are we gonna check out the next access level in that bunker? We've been finished with that for days now."

"Whenever we get Sharvie back down here. I just talked to her by the way. The Denzee are catching on and pushing them out of their systems. She says the Denzee are back in full control."

A jump was made to Eden space. Twenty minutes later a comm was relayed to Fireburg.

Baxter Rumford answered. "What is it? We're kind of busy here."

"We're watching the fight at Barrier. I'd say it isn't going well for your emperor."

"He's slowly coming to this realization. Just not fast enough. Barrier will be a huge loss. It's a ranching colony, and since its expansion, now produces 20 percent of New Earth's food. I think the Denzee picked that colony because of its fertile grasslands. They want to grow their population out here, and a planet with those resources fits their bill. I lobbied for sending a larger fleet, but His Highness was unwilling to commit.

"The fight out there has been cat and mouse the last few days. Will take two to three weeks to fall, but it will fall. And with it goes the huge food resource."

Tawn muted the comm. "I think we might have an opportunity here. Those billions of bogler on Farmingdale. I bet we could sell a million head a year and not make a dent in that herd."

Harris nodded as he flipped the mike back on. "Would the emperor be interested in purchasing bogler?"

"You have beef?"

"How many head does Barrier produce every year?"

"The data I saw said a million and a half as the annual production."

"Get us a price of what he'd be willing to pay per head. We think we could supply up to a million per annum."

"I'll check. That would certainly ease some of the pain they're gonna feel from this loss."

Tawn asked, "Have you managed to capture one of the Denzee ships?"

"I can't talk about that type of information without risking my head."

"We have one. And there's a lot of tech to be had from it."

Bax sat forward. "You have a Denzee ship?"

Tawn replied, "We did. Just turned it over to the DDI."

Bax winced. "Oh. Bad move. I could have gotten you probably half a billion credits for one. It's one of the emperor's priorities. And he wants some Denzee to go with it, for interrogation."

"We *had* a ship. The Denzee all fought to the death. It seems they're devoted to their queen. That's all they live for. Don't know if we could get you another one. We lost six good people getting it."

Bax scoffed. "Yeah, but you're slugs and stumps. That's what you do. You live for dying."

Tawn growled. "We love life just as much as you. Just because we're good at fighting wars doesn't mean we're eager to die."

Bax waved her hand. "Relax. Was just yanking your chain... or leash, or whatever it is they keep you on these days."

Tawn began to respond, and Harris stopped her. "What would your emperor be willing to pay to have the main guns damaged on those warships at Barrier?"

"You offering to take that suicide mission on?"

Harris shrugged. "Maybe. Find out what it would be worth to him."

"You got five or ten minutes?"

"We do."

"Hang on." The comm closed.

Tawn gave Harris a look of bewilderment. "You off your rocker? We can't take out those guns."

Harris chuckled. "Not yet. But I would like to know what he would offer if the day were to come."

A hail came in from Bax. "A hundred million credits each. You get rid of those ships at Barrier and that's what he'll pay."

Harris said, "That's to get rid of the main guns, not the ships themselves. A hundred million credits for each main gun."

Bax nodded. "Sorry for the mistranslation. He agreed to what you proposed. We can handle them without those ship killers they're using on us."

Tawn raised her chin. "You said us. That mean you're officially an Earther now?"

Bax scowled. "No. Just phrasing. So what do you say? We have a deal?"

Harris chuckled. "We don't have a deal. We have a bid. The emperor is offering a hundred million credits for each main gun. We have to go see if we can even attempt it first. And I'll add this: if we do even one and the emperor reneges, we will be drawing at least a hundred million in destruction from this colony and whatever ships of his we encounter. And if we feel that's insufficient, we'll do more."

"The emperor will keep his word."

Harris nodded. "I guess we're done here, then."

The comm closed on a scowling Baxter Rumford.

Tawn shook her head. "Glad you clarified that we would only be looking into it. Not worth risking my life for another hundred million credits. We already have plenty."

"Not true. For every one of those we kill, we can have another freighter built. And I want you to think about this... if the Retreat had five of those freighters, the colonel could declare independence from Domicile. Those five ships would be more than a match for the Domer fleet right now."

Tawn laughed. "Are you psycho? The Domer fleet could attack the Retreat and wipe everyone out. Five of those freighters might win in a straight up space battle, but if they attack the ground, Biomarines or not, even a couple cruisers making it in close could overwhelm their defenses."

"Again, not true. The domes are protected by the updated rail cannons. They can't get their ships close enough to do any real damage without killing themselves. Anyway, we won't solve this argument here. So let's get home."

A jump was made back to Midelon. Harris, Tawn, and Farker hopped from the shuttle and made their way over to the *Bangor*.

Harris said, "We had a short talk with Bax. She's still managing the titanium effort at Eden. According to her, she thinks Barrier will fall in a few weeks. And with it goes 20 percent of the Earthers' food supply. I had the idea that we might want to set up a ranching operation on Farmingdale where we round up bogler and sell them off to the Earthers."

Trish asked, "Can you do that?"

Tawn nodded. "All outer colony resources are considered public domain. You just have to file a claim with the local government and that claim has to be active. In other words, no filing claims just to camp on them. Those bogler are non-native. We can take as many as we want. Other than roundup labor and transport cost, they're free."

Harris said, "A live bogler on Domicile will fetch about five or six hundred credits at auction. The Earther market would be a million or more per year. Given the fact they are free for the taking, I can't imagine not making 50 percent profit."

Trish raised an eyebrow. "That is huge money. Way more than you were making from weapons sales."

Tawn chuckled. "And legit."

"We have another offer to discuss as well. The emperor is willing to pay a hundred million credits for each main weapon we can disable on those Denzee warships. Right now there are four doing their dirty business at Barrier. We take out those weapons and that's pure profit."

Trish shook her head. "Sorry, but the bogler sounds like a safer bet."

"Obviously you haven't been around any wild bogler," Harris quipped. "And that effort will take a full year, along with hiring a shipload of cowboys. Not sure Domicile has enough of them hanging around for us to hire."

Trish frowned. "You really want to go up against a Denzee warship with the *Bangor*?"

Harris laughed. "Yeah. I think we can take 'em. No. I'm thinking we have a shot with the *Bangor* and the *Hailstorm*. And if we can hold out another week after that, two more of those freighters. And if Barrier falls, we can always start up the bogler trade *and* try to knock out those Denzee weapons."

Trish groaned. "Well, aren't you the ambitious one."

"What I know is that if the Earthers can't turn back the Denzee at Barrier, we are looking at an overrun of all the Earther colonies within six months. And New Earth right after. Where do you think they would be coming next?"

"So this is more of a defensive move than for profit?"

Harris nodded. "It is, but I also think it's one that we could do well with. Every one of those guns we take out is a new freighter that we own. And those freighters are also ideal for hauling bogler."

Tawn said, "Sounds like you've already talked yourself into this."

Harris thought for a moment. "Hmm. Yeah. I guess I have. You in or out?"

Tawn scowled. "Well, I have to go where my partner goes. Can't let my investment in the business go bad."

Harris grinned as he began to walk away. "We are so going to do this and do it big."

"Where you going?"

"To talk to Alex. At the bunker. Where I can sit in a chair and pick his AI brain."

The holo-image of Alexander Gaerten came to life.

"Hello, Harris."

"Hello, Alex."

"What is it I can assist you with today?"

"You have all the recordings from our encounter with the Denzee warship, right?"

"I do."

"And can I suppose you've done some analysis on them?"

"You can."

"Good. What I want to know is your recommendations on how we might attack a Denzee warship and disable or destroy its main weapon. We hammered the hull plating to either side and disabled the one that attacked us. Would it be possible for us to do that again? This time using the *Bangor* and the *Hailstorm*?"

"Of course it would be possible, Harris. You have already proven such."

Harris leaned back in the chair, clasping his hands behind his head as he looked up at the ceiling. "I guess what I'm asking for is help in planning a raid to do it again. Now, given that you probably have the internal layout of that warship, harvested by Sharvie and her team, and you have the recordings of the damage we did using the *Bangor*'s rail cannon, can you map out a strategy for the lowest risk assault with the highest probability of success?"

"I can."

"Please do, then. How long do you need?"

"I have them. Would you like to see simulations?"

Harris sat forward. "Yes. Very much. Show me what you have."

An image of the warship, the *Bangor*, and the *Hailstorm*, floated above the table. "I would suggest the low risk approach would be where you draw the fire of the main weapon while at a distance, giving you time to react. It would appear the Denzee need time for the weapon to recharge. From the recordings, I would estimate a minimum of thirty seconds. From the data harvested by Sharvie and her friends, it would appear to be approximately fifty-four seconds."

Harris nodded. "Good. That should give us enough time to close and fire. Should even be able to hit that disc it fires from."

"I would recommend a round placed on either side as you did before."

"Well, you won't be driving, will you."

"Do you want my help, Harris?"

"I do. Am I being too much of a smartass?"

"You are."

Harris chuckled. "That's what I like about you, Alex. You're blunt. I like blunt. It's funny."

"I know. Now would you like to return to the simulation?"

"Sure. Show me what you've got."

The next hour was spent with a back and forth conversation. When Harris emerged from the bunker he walked straight to the supply hut where Tawn and the others were having a meal.

"What? Why didn't you comm me?"

"You're a big boy. Of everyone here, you certainly know when it's time to eat. What had you so wrapped up in there?"

"Alex was showing me a few simulations of how we might confront one of those warships. I like some of his ideas. He showed me simulations, and even threw in a few variables to make the decisions harder."

Gandy asked, "So how'd you do?"

"Nine out of ten tries we killed or disabled the weapon. Seven out of ten we survived."

Gandy frowned. "Sounds high risk."

"We're taking on a giant Denzee warship. Of course it's high risk. No pain no gain, you know."

Tawn said, "Seven out of ten against four warships? Doesn't sound all that bad."

"Oh, that was against one. Alex assumed we would be able to draw at least one ship away from the others."

Tawn scoffed. "I suddenly like this plan a lot less."

Harris opened a comm. "Sharvie, how many of those Denzee warships do they have total? I'm not talking about the rattle ships. Just the big ones?"

"Six. Two still at Rumanta and four at Barrier. And just so you know, we've been completely kicked from their networks. We have zero access. My teams are trying to get back in, but at the moment we have nothing."

Harris turned. "Gandy, when you finish, go up and bring her down. She needs the break."

Gandy stood and headed for the door. "I'm done."

Tawn chuckled. "I'd say the hard crush continues."

"And I think she's starting to soften," said Trish. "She likes the attention. Of course we are trapped out here, so her pickings are slim."

Tawn frowned. "That's your brother."

"Exactly," Trish replied. "I love him and all, but he can be a pest."

Harris took a bite from the mystery meat in an MRE. "When they get back we can check in with Alex and get started on the next level. Whatever that might be."

Chapter 27

The group discussed the options before them as Sharvie dug into her meal. When she had finished, they walked together to the bunker, through the several sets of doors, and into a new room.

A holo-image of Alex appeared. "Good, you're all here."

Harris asked, "So what's our next mission?"

"I believe you will like this level, as its requirements will be simple. To your left you will find a disc on the floor. Each of you will stand on the disc for a full body scan. When the scans are complete, you may go. In about two weeks you will receive further instruction as to what is required to move beyond this level."

Harris nodded as he walked toward the disc. "I can do that. And you're right, I like it."

"As was expected. Now, stand with your feet shoulder-width apart and your arms fully extended out to your sides."

"Like this?"

Tawn laughed. "You look like one of those scarecrows we saw on Farmingdale."

Harris replied. "Shush. I don't want to have to do this a second time."

Alex said, "Your scan is complete. Please move aside for the next person."

The other scans followed and the group returned to the supply hut.

Harris sat on a bench. "How's the plating on the *Bangor* coming?"

"Almost done," said Trish. "Two, maybe three more hours."

"Good. I want it ready if we decide to go after the Denzee ships."

Tawn shook her head. "You're really set on this path, aren't you?"

"I am. The Denzee need to be stopped. The Earthers may want to rule us all, but at least they want us to live. The fates of our friends on Jebwa tell us what the Denzee think of us."

Tawn sighed. "Fine. We do it your way. But I want right of first refusal before going in if I think a situation looks bad."

"Fair enough."

The following day, a comm was opened to Domicile.

"Mr. Morgan. I forgot to ask about the gamma-ray bomb the other day. Any progress? We could really use something like that against the Denzee."

"We still have several technical hurdles to overcome, Mr. Gruberg. I've beefed up the science teams working it and given them a near-unlimited budget. If it's possible, they will find a way to make it happen."

"How are the repairs to the *Hailstorm* coming?"

"She will be ready this afternoon—cosmetic damage aside."

Harris nodded. "Excellent, that's sooner than expected. Sounds like I need to talk to the colonel."

"You have something planned?"

"We're gonna find out. Either way, get us that weapon, Mr. Morgan. I think we're gonna need it."

Bannis was silent for several seconds. "You do realize that once this genie is out of the bottle there's no putting it back in? The gamma-ray bomb will be forever available for use or abuse."

"That's a risk we have to take if we want to survive. If you can contain that information on your end, we'll do the same on ours. Besides, if it *can* be researched and made to work, eventually it would be, whether by us or someone else."

Bannis nodded. "A point we've bandied about before."

The comm was closed and a new one opened to the Retreat. "Colonel, I know it's asking a lot, but I need a crew on the *Hailstorm*. I want to take her into a fight with another one of those Denzee warships."

"Has something changed?"

"Not really. What I need your ship and crew for is a distraction. If you can draw the fire of that main weapon, we'll go in and take it out."

The colonel frowned. "That weapon is a ship killer. You want us to be its target?"

"If you keep a proper distance you can dodge its fire. We've already done so. All we need is for them to take a single shot at you. That gives us fifty-four seconds to attack before they can fire it again. That's enough time for us to disable it. Once that's done, you come in and finish the job."

If we're successful against one ship, we'll do our best to lure away another. And, Colonel, if we can drive off those warships, the Earthers can handle the rest. And I might as well tell you now that part of our motivation for doing this is a bounty being offered by the emperor. A hundred million credits for each main weapon we take out. We could use that money to build more freighters."

"I can't say I like this plan, Mr. Gruberg. But if you're committed, we'll provide a crew. When would you want to do this?"

"Bannis said the *Hailstorm* should be ready for use this afternoon. The sooner the better on this, as the Earthers are taking a beating over there. And if you weren't aware, the Barrier colony is currently providing about 20 percent of their food."

The colonel sighed. "Sounds like a perfect opportunity to take the Earthers down a notch or two. Let Barrier fall, then we go in and stop the warships."

"That strategy has crossed my mind repeatedly. I just don't think we can risk waiting."

"Very well. I'll have a crew ready and waiting when the ship is released from the dock."

The comm closed. Harris sat back on the bench.

"That's it, then. We go this afternoon."

A short while later, Trish walked into the hut.

"Plating is finished. Our ship looks more like a shipping container than a ship now."

Harris nodded. "It can be the ugliest ship humanity has ever seen so long as it does the job."

Two hours passed before a comm was opened to the Retreat. Coordinates for a meeting point in Barrier space were given. Minutes later, the *Hailstorm* slipped through a wormhole, stopping beside the *Bangor*.

The colonel came over the comm. "What's our plan?"

Harris replied, "Wasn't expecting you on this venture, Colonel. Not that I don't appreciate your leadership, but I don't care to put you at risk out here. You're the heart of the Retreat and are needed there."

"I'm also a commander. And my worth is no more than any of the others on this crew."

Tawn stepped in. "OK, we're all here. We're all committed. Let's just get this done before the two of you either start fighting or hugging one another."

Harris chuckled. "The plan is we go in first and try to draw one of those warships out. If they fall for it, bring the *Hailstorm* in as a distraction while we take out the main gun. After that, we'll move on to the next ship while you either destroy or chase that one away. Simple."

Tawn nodded. "Simple plan for a simple man."

Harris turned. "It's a win-win for me. You'll either congratulate me and my simple plan if we're successful, or you'll be dead, in which case you won't say anything."

Tawn replied, "Whatever. Let's just get moving."

The *Bangor* swept in toward the Barrier colony. The four Denzee warships, along with twenty of the rattle ships, were squared off with twenty-eight New Earth destroyers and a dozen cruisers. The occasional plasma round was exchanged as the ships all remained in a cloud of slow-motion activity.

Harris said, "We're targeting this closest one."

Two of the rattle ships broke off from the others to engage the small incoming vessel. The ship vibrated and shook as dozens of plasma rounds began impacting the hull.

Tawn said, "That plating along with our shields is doing the trick. If this is the worst they can do, we could wipe out every one of the rattle ships by ourselves."

Harris nodded. "Let's see how they like tungsten. Let those rails rip when you're ready."

The first six pellets were sent to the ship approaching on the port side, with devastating results. Decks disintegrated and debris quickly filled the space surrounding the Denzee ship as it moved into a slow uncontrolled roll. A hard turn, another burst from the magnetic rail weapon, and the remains of a second defending vessel started into tumble.

Tawn smiled. "That was pretty sweet."

She opened a general comm to the Denzee and enabled a translation algorithm. "Send more ships."

Harris chuckled. "You trying to make them mad?"

"If that's what it takes to draw out one of those warships. Plus it was kinda fun."

Another three of the rattle ships came out in defense of the Denzee fleet. All three were dispatched with minimal effort. Harris slowed his speed as they neared the first of the warships, now turning their way.

Tawn shook her head. "They aren't taking the bait. That second warship is turning our way too. What's the new plan?"

Harris pushed the control stick full forward. "The plan is we take this right into them if they won't come out to play. See the red line on the display? That's our safety line. Beyond that we can dodge whatever that beam weapon is. We're going right up to it. And just for grins, why don't you put the guns on auto for one of those spiral shots? That will force them to move."

The *Bangor* approached the distance Harris had designated as safe. Tawn fired off several rounds of tungsten pellets. The warship's movements were only side to side.

A hail came in from an Earther ship. "We were told you might show. How can we help?"

Harris said, "We need that ship to fire its main weapon. That will give us the time we need to go in and disable it."

"Consider it done."

The comm closed as an Earther destroyer charged forward toward the nearest Denzee warship. The massive ship turned to face its new attacker. The lights on the exterior of the claw-hammer went dark. Seconds later the disc on her front glowed bright blue. The Earther destroyer turned, but the back third of the vessel failed to escape the beam. Explosions followed as the aft of the ship disintegrated, sending the remains into a slow spin.

Harris pushed the throttle full. Fifty-two seconds later, Tawn Freely opened up with the rail cannons set to auto-feed. Five rounds struck the plating surrounding the Denzee weapon. The ship's lights failed to extinguish and the weapon didn't fire.

An endless stream of plasma rounds sprang from the other guns that made up the arsenal of the warship. The *Bangor* jerked, rattled, and shook, but without taking noticeable damage.

Turning, they took a second run at the weapon. Dozens of tungsten pellets impacted the disc and the area surrounding it. Massive depressions formed in the thick hull, but with no evidence of a breach. The *Hailstorm* quickly moved in as the behemoth turned and began to move back toward the others. A fleet of short range missiles were launched at the *Bangor*. All were easily avoided.

Harris winced at the tremendous beating the port-side hull of the warship was taking from the hypervelocity tungsten rounds.

Tawn opened a comm to the *Hailstorm*. "Break off, we're done with that one. Hang back as we try to draw another one out."

A second and then a third claw-hammer ship saw their main weapon disabled. Two more Earther destroyers and their crews sacrificed themselves for the effort. The final warship turned away, jumping back to Rumanta. The other Denzee ships followed.

Harris turned the *Bangor* to follow. "*Hailstorm*, New Earthers, we're going after them. If we can manage to take out the other three warships, you Earthers can wipe out the rest."

An Earther admiral replied, "Lead the way. We will follow."

A jump to the Rumanta System was met with a dozen of the smaller rattle ships racing out to meet the incoming attackers. The *Bangor* ran between them, firing as it went, its hull largely immune to the plasma cannons fired by the Dulons.

A fierce battle ensued. New Earth ships powered in to take on the remaining active claw-hammers, taking heavy damage but inflicting some of their own. The *Bangor* swooped in, diving in and about the Denzee ships, moving with impunity and timing her attacks on the behemoth warships. A fourth and then a fifth main gun were taken out.

A general hail came over the comm from the Denzee. "This is Queen Nuerba. You have proven a worthy opponent. Permit us a short time of peace and we will leave your system."

The Earther admiral was first to reply. "We will crush you here and now!"

Harris cut in. "Admiral, let them go. If they leave in peace we don't lose any more people or ships. And you will have regained all of your territory. Should you choose to continue, you will do so without our assistance."

The admiral was silent for several seconds. "Very well, Denzee. You have your peace. Make haste. Be gone from our space."

Tawn turned with a smile. "If this is true, it's fantastic."

Harris shook his head. "Except for the fact that we probably just unleashed the Earthers to come after us. The politicians on Domicile still have their heads stuck in the sand."

"True, but we now have the *Bangor*, the *Hailstorm*, and two other ships that are capable of taking them on. Add in the updates Mr. Morgan will possibly be making to our fleets and we should be able to maintain our advantage for some time. That at least gives us some wiggle room to work with."

Harris tilted his head back in thought. "I guess... And I suppose we could always attack and shut down the production at Eden with these ships."

Tawn nodded. "Now you're talking."

Over the ten hours that followed, the Denzee emptied their hives. With loaded ships, they departed toward their original colonies, at first through a wormhole to the edge of the boson field, and then at sub-light speed beyond.

The Earther fleet remained at Rumanta. The *Hailstorm* returned to the Retreat. The *Bangor* jumped to Eden. A comm was opened and Baxter Rumford hailed.

"What?"

Tawn said, "We just crushed the Denzee. They're packing up and leaving our space. And the way I see it, you, or the emperor, whichever, owe us for shutting down five of those warship main guns."

Bax was silent for several seconds. "How were you able to pull that off?"

"We're just that good, that's all. Now, where are our credits?"

"It may take time to get those released."

Tawn shook her head. "Those are electronic. The only release they need is for your emperor to give them up. Make the comm and tell him we'd like to be paid for our services."

Bax sighed. "You'll have to give me some time. The emperor has to be willing to accept my comm."

"Just do it. Stalling doesn't make a difference other than to make people unhappy. And unhappy people can be prone to retribution. Your emperor knows what we just did to the Denzee. Unless he wants to see that happen here at Eden, he needs to pony-up on what he promised."

Bax was again quiet for several seconds. "As I said, I need time. Give me ten minutes and I hope to have an answer for you as to when you can expect it."

The comm closed.

Tawn crossed her arms as she sat back in the chair. "They try to cheat us and there won't be a building or piece of machinery left down there that's usable."

Harris replied, "She knows that. This is all on the emperor and how he wants this to go. He'd be a fool to not pay. Not only could we shut down those mines down there, we could shut down his ship factories. Nothing stopping us from going into New Earth space—with these ships, that is—when the updates are finished."

"So you'd declare war on the Earthers?"

"Haven't we already done that a dozen times over?"

Tawn chuckled. "Yeah, I guess we have."

Bax came back over a comm. "Hold up your credit store."

Tawn complied.

"Five hundred million credits. Quite the haul given you didn't lose anyone."

Tawn said, "We lost eight destroyers full of Earther crews. I would hardly call that a picnic."

"They were defending their empire. Another week or two at Barrier and they would have all been dead. Anyway, the emperor sends his regards. And he says if you ever want it you always have a place in his royal house. He has fifteen daughters or nieces and eighteen sons or nephews who are yet to wed. He says you could have your pick. As members of the royal family, you would live the rest of your lives in luxury and ease."

Tawn smirked. "We just earned a half billion credits. The way I see it, we can choose that life right now, without having to be in the royal family."

"He offered. And I think you know why. At least I imagine you will know why within a years' time. All this titanium will be put to use."

"You're on the wrong side of this fight, Rumford," said Harris. "One day you'll regret it."

"We all have regrets, Goober. It goes with living."

The comm closed.

Tawn looked at the display on her credit store. "Wow. That's a big number."

Harris nodded. "Yeah, too bad it has to be spent on more of those freighters. And I'd like to get the drive here on the *Bangor* updated with that new housing. Maybe some more padding for the pilot's chair. Gets kind of rough on the bum with all the jerking around from those plasma cannons."

Tawn chuckled as she glanced down at Harris' back. "I'd think you've got more than enough padding back there to compensate."

"Hey, it's not as big as yours."

"I'm not the one complaining."

A jump and a short run had the *Bangor* landing at Midelon. A short victory lunch was had by all. Afterward, Trish and Gandy began an inspection of the plating and how it had held up in the fights. Their report came back with no issues found.

Harris opened a comm to Bannis Morgan. "I'm sure you've heard about the Denzee threat being removed."

"Just heard a few minutes ago. Great news."

Harris nodded. "Yes and no. The Denzee are gone, but now we have the Earthers to contend with. That invasion probably cost them fifty ships, along with their trained crews. That's a big hit. But with that mine running full-bore, they are likely to make up any shortfall in a hurry. Which is why I commed you."

"The freighters should be finished in the coming days. I just talked to the colonel about the *Hailstorm*. I told him this go-round we might need at least two weeks for repairs."

Harris replied, "Expected as much. What I want to ask you though is what you would need to build another five of those freighters? Including the latest updates we sent over."

"Are we talking cost or time?"

"Both."

"Just throwing out a few ballpark numbers here. Since we have the facilities up and running, with the personnel who are now trained... I believe we could manage about seventy-five million credits each. And two to three months of schedule."

Harris nodded. "Excellent. We'll take five. That will leave us a contingency fund for maintenance and repairs."

Tawn whispered, "We still have the money from Sharvie's friends. Close to nine hundred million."

"And we'll need every bit of that should we have to take on the Earthers."

Tawn chuckled. "You mean, *when* we take on the Earthers."

A credit transfer was made before the comm was closed. A second comm was opened to the colonel.

"Gruberg, just got word back from my DDI contacts. They are quite pleased with the departure of the Denzee. So much so that they've managed to retract all the warrants they have out for you and your team. You are now free to travel back to Domicile or out to the colonies, including here to the Retreat."

Tawn asked, "Any guarantees that we won't be grabbed or harassed by the DDI or any other government officials or agents thereof?"

The colonel nodded. "I knew you would ask, and I have been given assurances that you will not be bothered. That order comes straight from the President."

The conversation went on for another ten minutes before the comm closed.

Harris stood in front of his team. "We have new freighters coming. And we have updates to be made to the *Bangor*. And if you were paying attention just then, we are supposedly free to go back to Domicile or wherever we want. Personally, I plan on dropping the *Bangor* at the shipyard for a drive update, followed by a week of rest and recuperation at a hotel on Chicago Port Station. There are a number of buffets that have been calling my name."

Tawn sighed. "I guess that's where I'll be too. Can't let my partner run around unchecked. He'd just get himself in trouble. And the rest of you are welcome to join us."

Sharvie said, "A week of luxury and gluttony? I'm game."

"I guess that means we'll be keeping an eye on her too," said Gandy. "What about visiting home?"

Trish replied, "We'll have to do at least a day at home. Parents probably won't even have missed us, but I'd like to visit just the same."

Harris smiled. "Pack your bags then and we'll be off."

~~~~~
~~~~~

What's Next?

(Preview)

ARMS

(Vol. 4)

Eden Lost

This Human is asking for your help! In return for that help I have a free science fiction eBook short story, titled "THE SQUAD", waiting for anyone who joins my email list. Also, find out when the next exciting release is available by joining the email list at comments@arsenex.com. If you enjoyed this book, please leave a review on the site where it was purchased. Visit the author's website at www.arsenex.com for links to this series and other works.

The following preview is the first chapter of the next book in the series and is provided for your reading pleasure.

Stephen

Chapter 4.1

Tawn took a deep breath after dumping a drunken Harris Gruberg on his bed.

"You people are too dense," said Gandy. "He weighs a ton."

"I think he's added at least ten kilos this week alone. I mean, I can eat, but he was ravenous. The Emporium people were mad until the spectacle started drawing in customers. Even with what he was eating they were making money off him."

Gandy chuckled. "You weren't any slouch in there."

Tawn rubbed her belly. "Yeah, I'm guessing I added a couple kilos myself."

Gandy sighed. "I'm almost sad it's over tomorrow."

"Yep. We have a lot of work to do if we're gonna shut down those mines."

"I can't believe Mr. Gruberg was even talking about going to New Earth to visit the emperor. That just seems crazy."

"We were invited. Not often people get offered the opportunity to be a part of the royal family. Not that we would ever accept such a deal. I think he just wants to see the emperor face to face."

Gandy frowned. "Seems kind of dangerous to me. For the same reason we don't want to talk to the DDI... Midelon."

"I think it's more talk than reason at this point. I know he was going on and on about it tonight, but I don't think that will be the case once he's sober."

The week of festivities had come to an end. Several extra days were taken for Trish, Gandy, and Sharvie to take care of business on Domicile while Tawn and Harris jumped to the shipyard orbiting above the Retreat.

Bannis Morgan was visiting. "My engineers have finalized the updates we'll be making to the freighters. I have three proposals in with the DDF for ship modernization. So far, regardless of the pleas by every single admiral in the force, the politicians are not loosening the purse strings. Furthermore, I'm a bit nervous at the lack of security effort being put forth by our government officials."

Harris asked, "You worried about the updated designs getting into the hands of Earther spies?"

"Those designs have yet to leave my facilities, but yes, it's as if people have forgotten we were at war with these people for nearly two thousand years. They haven't just up and changed overnight. I tell you, these pacifists are going to be the death of us all. You even mention military spending and they cover their ears. I'm starting to believe half of them are double agents. And the other half are just fools."

"I walked by the dock where they had the *Bangor*. Thought those updates would be done by now."

Bannis half frowned. "We've had some difficultly with the removal and refit of that drive. The old unit was made up of more than a dozen sections. They were all welded together in-place. It's out. But we ran into a second issue. That unit was hardened. It could take a substantial beating, which is probably why you kept flying while being nearly shaken to death. We're having to harden the new unit before installing it.

"So we'll be able to hit just over 50 percent light-speed with this mod?"

"I'd say so. My designers have a few tweaks to add they believe will get you close to the top end speed of the Denzee ships, only you'll get there faster."

Harris nodded. "I like the sound of that. We already had an advantage when down at fighting speed, so this can only help. Your people had a chance to dig into that rattle ship?"

"They have. And we believe there are more discoveries to come. For instance, their method of creating an inertial dampener field is very different from ours. My team thinks they may be able to combine the best points of both designs and come up with an improved field that will allow even tighter turns when fighting."

Harris smiled. "Better turning and more speed would both add to our ability to dodge incoming rounds. Any idea when they might have something like that up and running?"

"All just theory at the moment. And the same can be said for their plasma weapons. And as you know, their exterior plating."

Harris rolled his eyes. "Those warship hulls were impossible to breach. We put a heckuva beating on several of those ships and there was no indication of atmospheric leaks. I'm sure it was a violent end for anyone near those hits, but the ship's vital systems went undamaged."

Bannis said, "One more thing. We've managed to pull the recordings of their fights with the Earthers. We're doing a full analysis on what worked in those fights and what was unsuccessful."

Harris nodded. "Good. Useful info. I'm sure we'll be needing it before long."

"You have plans forming up for an attack?"

Harris shook his head. "Not yet. Would like to get our own force up and running, and get some training behind a few crews. When we do hit Eden, we'll want to hit it hard."

"You do realize the moment that happens the emperor will complain and those warrants for you will be reissued, right?"

Harris sighed. "I'm expecting as much. Which is why between now and then I'll be pushing for Trish, Gandy, and Sharvie to spend as much time here on Domicile as they can. Once we stop the Earthers' operations on Eden, we'll be in exile again."

Bannis stood. "Have you had a look at the new construction bays?"

"Didn't know there was such a thing. Are they different than where the *Bangor* is parked?"

Bannis nodded. "Very. That's a repair bay for smaller ships. We have two of the three full bays completely enclosed. I'm surprised you didn't notice as you were coming in."

Tawn chuckled. "We had the autopilot set and were both taking naps. Has been a tough week at the buffets. We needed some rest."

Bannis furled his brows. "I see. Anyway... two of the full bays are now enclosed. Work can be performed without wearing suits. It speeds and eases almost every aspect of ship assembly. As a consequence. I can cut as much as fifteen million credits from the cost of each of those freighters. When we're done, if you like I'll have those credits ready to refund."

Harris smiled. "Sounds like you just got a contract for a sixth additional freighter."

Bannis nodded. "Was hoping you'd say that. Here, bay one is just down this hall."

Tawn said, "I find it hard to believe you can produce that ship for such a low cost. I can spend seven million on a high-end shuttle. The freighter is huge in comparison."

"You're still buying a freighter, Miss Freely. Highly modified, but a freighter. If I were to turn that into a warship that I was producing for profit, the cost would likely triple. It would of course be more rugged and capable, but expensive. And as I said, it would be for profit."

"You aren't making anything off these?"

"On the contrary, the shipyard and its enhancements are paid for. That is a huge capital outlay my company doesn't have to make. The NRE, the non-recoverable engineering, and other expenses such as operational costs are all covered by you. Once we have that third bay enclosed and have the opportunity to really have a hard look at our costs, we may be able to lop another ten million credits off each of those freighters. I'm talking future units of course."

Harris asked, "What if we took everything there that is freighter out and just made it a hardened warship."

"Hmm. Would be far smaller of course, but again less expensive. Are you talking warship for you or warship to sell to the DDF?"

"For us."

"I would put a ballpark of thirty million for such a ship. Only I wouldn't be able to produce it here. The Domicile government wouldn't allow it. The only reason they've allowed the construction of these freighters is because the rail cannons are being installed out in free space. We managed a modular unit that replaces a very weak cannon. The phony unit can be removed from outside and the complete rail cannon package inserted in its place in about twenty minutes."

Tawn shook her head. "Your people have really engineered the crap out of this stuff, Mr. Morgan. I'm still stunned at the turnaround times you've managed."

"I've been doing this for eighty years, Miss Freely. If you also take into account the lack of government red tape and paperwork, it becomes a much easier proposition."

"Still... impressive."

The tour of the construction bay took several hours. After one last stop to see the *Bangor*, the pair made a run down to the surface for a visit to the Retreat.

The colonel greeted them as they stepped off the *Gooch*. "Welcome back as free citizens."

Harris nodded. "Still looking over our shoulders for the men in black. So far they've remained inconspicuous if they've been there. Domes look good. I like the landscaping around the base."

"When the work finished we opted to spruce things up a bit. Was more of a busywork program than anything. Two thirds of our citizens are up there at the ship factory working now."

Tawn nodded. "I noticed a lot of them walking around."

"You two have somewhat of a celebrity status around here now. Your efforts built this place, provided food and housing, and now with that factory up there, jobs. I've seen thousands come in here with crushed spirits after struggling to work and fit in on Domicile. They're all smiles now."

"I can see them being thankful," said Harris. "I would be. But celebrity status? Where would they draw that from?"

We have our own daily news broadcasts. The exploits and accomplishments by you and your team are always a favorite. Especially your recent eating frenzy on Chicago Port. That has been popular all week."

Tawn said, "You're the only one we talk to here, Colonel. This your doing? You had someone filming us?"

"Guilty as charged. I decided it might be good to use you as a unifying force for all slugs and stumps. Something to be proud of besides our prior accomplishments. It keeps them enthused with what we're trying to do, and also means I have no shortage of volunteers. You're easily the best marketing tool I have when it comes to meeting our needs."

Harris nodded. "I heard you've started a memorial cemetery for the fallen. I'd like to visit and pay tribute if I could."

"That goes for me too, Colonel," Tawn added.

"Was the least we could do to honor their sacrifices."

Harris asked, "Any thoughts of bringing our fallen brethren out here from Domicile? We could sponsor that move."

"The possibility had crossed my mind, but I thought better of it. Those men and women made their sacrifice for Domicile. It was their home. And I think they serve the large population as a reminder of our commitment to keeping them free and safe. And just so you know, there have been a number of positive news stories about you on Domicile as well. Surprised you weren't noticed and mobbed by fans."

Tawn chuckled. "He was mobbed by fans watching him eat. Wasn't out of admiration though, was definitely for entertainment. There was a line of people trying to get in the Emporium within ten minutes after our arrival. Would never have imagined we'd be popular for our eating habits. The world is getting strange, Colonel."

"We're in a period of peace. We have no experience with it, none of us. While unemployment may be high, the stresses and worries of war have gone away. Partly why the pacifists have been popular of late."

Harris frowned. "That false notion of security would be shattered if they knew and understood what the Earthers were doing right now. There's no amount of negotiation short of full surrender they would accept. Within a year, I think that reality will be settling in and the pacifists will be getting clobbered in elections."

The colonel nodded as they were escorted into the dome. "Let's hope you're right, about the elections that is."

The colonel stopped. "Major Wilhoite, I'd like you to take Miss Freely and Mr. Gruberg over to the memorial garden. When you're done, bring them into the cafeteria."

"Yes, sir."

With the major they toured the grave sites of the recently departed heroes of the Biomarines. Broad white marble arches marked the entrance to a field that would one day house most of the remaining genetically enhanced fighters for freedom. Harris and Tawn each said a few words over the graves of the most recently fallen, the group of volunteers who had assisted with the capture of the Denzee ship. Upon return to the dome, they were escorted to the cafeteria. A large crowd was waiting, and cheers erupted.

The colonel grinned. "Thought you could use a pick-me-up."

Tawn shook her head. "You're gonna give him an ego complex, Colonel. That fat head of his is likely to explode."

Harris stepped up onto a tabletop, waving to the crowd of slugs and stumps with a broad smile on his face.

Tawn chuckled. "You may have created a monster."

The colonel gestured toward the table. "Climb up there with him. As I told you, you two are a recruiting tool for me when I need volunteers. You've made them once again proud to be Biomarines. Get up there and take your bow."

Tawn sighed as she stepped up on a bench, and then up onto the table. Smiles, nods of thanks, and waves were sent out to the crowd before them. After several minutes on display, the partners hopped back to the floor.

Tawn said, "I saw a lot of regulars out there. Wasn't expecting that."

The colonel nodded. "They come down from the ship factory. With near normal gravity they have no problem spending time here in the dome. And we benefit by them spending their credits. In fact, we have about a thousand hotel beds between here and dome two that are always booked. With your exploits, all slugs and stumps have gained a bit of celebrity. And acceptance. Something we didn't have before."

Harris smiled. "Now my head *is* getting bigger. I can feel it."

Three days were spent at the Retreat while the *Bangor* was receiving its renewed drive. Once back at the factory for the pick-up, Tawn insisted on piloting the refurbed craft. A jump to Domicile to collect the Bolemans and Sharvie was followed by a return to Midelon.

After Tawn took the ship for a run around Midelon, Harris was waiting in the supply hut when they landed.

Tawn walked in. "Wow, just wow. Acceleration is improved, turns have improved by at least 10 percent. And we have a new top speed of 63 percent light-speed. That is just incredible."

Gandy said, "Several more surprises too. A new set of ion inhibitor boxes have been fastened to the new hull plating, making it even less vulnerable to plasma fire. And Mr. Morgan's team made a fix to the rail cannons where we don't have to dial down the power when using the autofeeder. We're now capable of four rounds per second when counting both barrels."

Trish grinned. "And best of all, you got your new butt-pad for your chair. It now has Tawn's imprints, but I'm sure you can work them out."

Harris nodded. "Outstanding."

Tawn gestured. "I think you'll be happy with the new *Bangor*."

"She tell you about our trip to the Retreat?" asked Harris.

Gandy replied, "About our popularity? We got some of that the last couple days at home. Our old neighbors threw a big barbecue for us. The whole street was full of people. Thought my hand was gonna fall off after so much shaking and waving. The news channels were broadcasting clips from your fight with the Denzee."

Harris winced. "Where'd they get those? The colonel wouldn't have released that."

Gandy shook his head. "Came from the Earthers. Video streams were from their ships. Was even a clip of the emperor thanking you and Tawn personally with a message. I'd say we scored big with the pacifist crowd seeing as how our own military wasn't involved. Of course, they're using that to further justify their budget cuts."

Tawn scowled. "And they're playing right into the Earthers' hands. And here's the bad news for the three of you as well as us: when we hit Eden, which we plan on doing, that celebrity status will turn to loathing and hatred, as you'll be viewed as trying to provoke a war. We know different, but that won't be the message the public gets."

"Well," said Gandy. "I guess it was fun while it lasted."

Harris rubbed the back of his neck. "I don't see an immediate attack on Eden coming. Maybe we can get you back home a few more times between now and then."

Sharvie said, "I was able to talk with several of my friends. They were happy to contribute while staying out of the spotlight."

"I've been meaning to ask you about them," said Harris. "They got us that huge horde of credits. I don't think we offered them anything for their help. We could easily give them all comfortable lives."

Sharvie waved. "Pfft. You don't have to worry about them. They skimmed 5 percent from all those accounts. None of them will ever have to work again. Not that they worked anyway, but you know what I mean. They're sitting on their own fat mountain of credits. And just so you know, they're continuing their crusade against the Earther spy networks. I think they've located a new stream of accounts. You may have even more funds coming."

Harris chuckled. "That has to be driving the Earthers nuts."

Trish said, "I know I don't have to say this, but anyone else hungry?"

Harris grinned. "Best first mate I ever had."

"Only first mate you ever had."

The group broke out the MREs, taking a moment to reflect as they came across the last of the meals supplied by the pacifists from Jebwa. Runs to Domicile would have to be made to replenish their stockpile. Trish, Gandy, and Sharvie were more than happy to volunteer.

Harris took a large bite from a bogler rib. "Farker? Does Alex have anything new for us?"

Three farks were returned.

"Open a comm."

An image of Alex floated in the air. "Hello, Harris, Tawn, others. I have good news."

"You finished working on whatever you took those scans for?"

"I did. If you would kindly come into the complex, you can each meet with your new assistants."

Harris looked up from a chew. "Assistants?"

~~~~~

Once again, this Human is asking for your help! If you enjoyed the book, please leave a review on the site where it was purchased. And by all means, please tell your friends! Any help with spreading the word is highly appreciated!

Also, I have a free science fiction eBook short story, titled "THE SQUAD", waiting for anyone who joins my email list! By joining, also find out when the next exciting release is available. Join at comments@arsenex.com. Visit the author's website at www.arsenex.com for links to this series and other works!

Take care and have a great day!

Stephen
~~~~~

24831931R00167

Printed in Great Britain
by Amazon